Demon Squad: At The Gates

By Tim Marquitz

Damnation Books, LLC.
P.O. Box 3931
Santa Rosa, CA 95402-9998
www.damnationbooks.com

Demon Squad: At The Gates
by Tim Marquitz

Digital ISBN: 978-1-61572-554-0
Print ISBN: 978-1-61572-555-7

Cover art by: Jessica Lucero
Edited by: Isaac Milner
Copyedited by: Kim Richards

Printed in the United States of America
Worldwide Electronic & Digital Rights
1st North American, Australian and UK Print Rights

To my family, friends, readers, reviewers, and everyone else who has made this journey such a pleasure. Thank you all.

Chapter One

It had only been two weeks since I helped to raise the Anti-Christ, so when my cousin Scarlett showed up, beaten to within an inch of her life, telling me Heaven had fallen, I can't say I was happy to see her.

The words out in a breathless rush, she fell into my arms, a rag doll of crusty blood and blackened scabs. Chunks of her golden hair were missing, ripped out from the roots. Streaks of reddened ooze stained her scalp and sporadic burns covered her skull, the flesh bubbled and peeling. The acrid scent of seared meat invaded my nose, settling thick on my tongue. My stomach roiled.

Her eyes lolled back in their sockets as she tried to focus through lids encircled by sunken black rings. She clutched to me with piercing fingers, one of her hands obviously disfigured. Her desperation lent her strength, despite it all.

As I bent to scoop her legs up, I saw a close trio of deep gouges that ran the length of her neck and came to a jagged stop at her chest. The tar-like seep of a supernatural wound filled their depths. I could see bone.

Though horrific, her injuries didn't stop there.

I saw evidence of a losing battle everywhere I looked. Bruises tattooed her skin in swaths. Burns and ragged cuts covered her like gory paint upon a canvas. Her clothes were shredded. Muted yellows and bluish-blacks peeked out from beneath the torn leather.

The hilt of her sword, Everto Trucido—loosely translated as Demon Slayer—was crusted in dry, flaky blood, so much so the design was lost in the thickness of it. The lower half of its sheath was cracked and there was a piece missing, the stained point visible through the hole.

Though Scarlett and I had our moments when it came to getting along, often butting heads over the stupidest of things while I snidely wished her bad luck, it sickened me to see her like that. My face flushed as I carried her to the couch. A boiling knot of fury welled up in my guts to replace the sickness. Since Lucifer moved on, whatever our differences, she was the only family I had left...

...and *no one* fucks with my family.

In a crimson haze, I left her on the couch and hurried to retrieve a vial of my departed uncle's blood. Just a couple of drops would heal Scarlett in minutes, but before I got two feet from the couch, a wave of cold insistence peppered my senses and raised the hackles on my neck. My eyes went to the open door.

Out in the street stood three figures, little more than darker shadows against the backdrop of night. Whoever they were, they must have followed Scarlett. If they were the ones who'd hurt her, things were about to get interesting...for them.

No time to batten down the hatches and get my cousin into the mystical bomb shelter of the basement, I decided it best to go out to meet our uninvited guests. Exhausted as I was from trying to whip my newfound magic into shape, my anger provided me with a nice pick-me-up, energizing me with adrenaline and fury. Who needs caffeine when you've got rage?

"Call for backup, CB," I shouted over my shoulder to Chatterbox, my zombie-head roommate. As I ran outside, I snatched my pistol off the end table.

"Roggggggggerrrrrrrr, Doddddddddggggggerrrrrrrr."

I'd taught him a few basic codes so he could relay emergency messages to DRAC, and even set up the speed dial on the phone to make it easy for him, seeing how he only had his tongue to work with. Given my track record, I'd probably need all the help I could get. If nothing else, I'd need a cleanup crew.

The only downside to letting him use the phone was the rancid trail of spit he'd leave across the number pad. It was a good thing I didn't make many calls.

Once outside, the door slammed shut of its own volition and I felt the protective wards go up, sealing the house off. They were good in a pinch, but they wouldn't hold against a determined assault; they were more of a speed bump. Though in the mood I was in, they wouldn't have to do much.

"Who's first?"

The trio spread out a little, making it harder to hit them all at once. They knew what they were doing. That fact sobered me, and I was glad I'd thought to get a call into DRAC. My anger dropped off a few degrees as I looked them over, my senses drifting out to take their measure.

The one in the center was a woman—or something vaguely resembling one. Easily six foot and a handful of change, she was built like a professional wrestler; powerful. Her broad shoulders and huge arms were barely contained by the skin-tight workout shirt she wore. The muscles of her stomach were defined in granite underneath. Her sandy blond hair was cropped short, helping to emphasize the more masculine traits of her face; the squared jaw and slightly protruding set of her forehead. Her linebacker thighs were encased in Spandex and the narrowness of her waist would have made Charles Atlas proud. If it hadn't been for the pair of double-D's strapped tight to her chest, I would have thought she was a man had we passed on the street.

Her gray eyes met mine, her stare icy. On each of her hands she wore what looked like modified brass knuckles with three sharp, jagged spikes protruding from them. They looked like a perfect match for the wounds on Scarlett's chest. That got my blood boiling again.

Though she didn't appear afraid, she did seem hesitant. She set her feet without advancing. I'd apparently screwed up whatever they had in mind. I'm good at that.

The guy to her right was the polar opposite. Rail thin and pale as milk, he stood five feet tall, if he was lucky. His face was narrow, with sharp cheekbones and a hooked nose. I could have opened a can on his face. Weasel eyes stared out at me from under a mane of long black hair.

He wore a Nine Inch Nails T-shirt, which hung off him like a bed sheet, and a pair of way too tight black jeans, which only emphasized his genetic failings. He carried twin, twelve-inch daggers to compensate.

The last of the motley crew was a public service announcement for the wrongs of a fast food diet. Tipping the scale somewhere close to six hundred pounds, he was a behemoth with stubby limbs. His massive head was shaved bald and I saw the rolls of his neck peeking out from behind his ears. Round, and far from what anyone with eyes would call attractive, his face bore a close resemblance to a Bassett hound. Mottled jowls hung loose and sagged into his wattle. Even his eyelids looked fat. I'd bet money blinking was an aerobic exercise for the guy.

His clenched fists were empty, but seeing how they were the size of canned hams, he probably didn't need a weapon. He didn't look like the kind of guy you wanted to cut in front of at the buffet. You'd probably lose a finger or two.

After a few moments of tense silence, the woman spoke, her voice a profound basso. "Our feud is not with you. Give us the angel."

"Sorry, sweet cheeks. You want her, you're gonna have to try a little harder than that."

While I would normally be more cautious when facing down an unknown enemy, my senses weren't registering these guys as world-beaters. They had some power between them, no doubt about that, but after all I'd been through in the last few months, it felt like I was swimming in the kiddy pool.

That told me one thing. There was no way these three were responsible for taking down Scarlett. They could finish her off, weak as she was, but it hadn't been them who laid the real beating on her. They'd picked at the scraps though, and that was enough for me.

Big boy looked to the woman, apparently waiting for her to decide their next move. The gesture told me who to hit first when things went south. Chivalry be damned.

"Let's just kill him, Venai," the pale one demanded, his words like razors. Though he spoke brave, he stayed in place, waiting for orders.

"Be quiet, Zellick." Venai squared her stance to reinforce her command, the other two seeming more than happy to follow her lead. "This is your last warning, demon. Turn over the angel or face the consequences. We will not be denied."

I couldn't help but laugh. So I did. A lot.

The little guy must have had esteem issues because he leapt at me without waiting for the go ahead. Bared teeth and silver blades led the charge, his hair whipping out behind him. Combat reflexes taking over, I circled from his path and got out of his way, keeping him between me and his buddies.

It seemed as though he moved a few notches below normal speed, which was weird. Used to being the slow one, it felt good to have the advantage for once.

He landed with a huff, his posture turning defensive the instant his feet hit the ground. His face was screwed up in a mishmash of fear and worry, realizing I hadn't even raised my gun. He moved away to cower behind the woman. It was clear who had more testosterone out of the three, not to mention the bigger dick.

I waggled my finger at him. "Try that again, Twigs, and I'll blow the Emo out of you."

The lines of Venai's face etched deep, starring the corners of her eyes, I knew she had made up her mind. She hunched and lumbered forward. Swinging my .45 up to meet her, I spotted big boy raising his arms. My brain clicked on just as he swung his ham hock fists. They crashed into the ground with a boom that rang my ears like church bells, the sidewalk jumping beneath me.

Jell-O under my feet, my legs buckled and I fell on my ass. Venai waited just long enough for the ground to stop moving, then came at me fast. My body shook like I'd been caught up in turbulence, and she got to me before I could put my gun to use.

Her spiked fist crashed into my left side and I screamed as she dug in. The sound drowned out the snapping of my ribs. A lightning bolt of pain followed as she yanked her fist away, the jagged spikes ripping clear of my flesh. Blood and black ooze was flung away in a messy arc that stained my vision. My eyes teared up, blurring the look of Venai's satisfaction as she pulled her hand back, ready to hit me again.

Out of instinct, my finger hit the trigger and I heard my gun's report off to my side. Though I hadn't aimed the shot—my conscious mind not registering I was still holding the gun—the bullet hit her in the shin. She shrieked, her voice octaves above her normal basso growl, and stumbled backward into Zellick who'd come up behind her. The two went down in a heap, pale boy on the bottom. He was probably used to it.

"Jorn!" he called out, breathless from beneath Venai's solid bulk.

Presuming he meant big boy, I looked up to see the mountain of Manwich shambling toward me. Not feeling too confident a bullet would suffice to bring him down, I extended my left hand, whimpering the whole time as my ribs screamed at the movement. Though I had a hard time concentrating, my side feeling as though it had been gored by a bull and then rolled in salt, I gratefully felt my magic well up.

Still new to having power, I'd practiced for the last two weeks, struggling to gain some measure of control over how much energy I released and what form it took. It hadn't been much of a success.

The bomb shelter of my basement had taken a beating as I worked on different combinations of force. Seared black walls and a few scorched pieces of furniture were a testament to the competence of my incompetence.

Out here, with big boy closing, I didn't have to be precise. Without having to second guess my ability or worry about burning my house down, I smiled and let loose. A burst of fire erupted from my palm and sprayed out like a flame thrower, heading straight toward Jorn.

His eyes flew open wide and he covered his head with his arms just before the flame engulfed him. An ear-piercing shriek cut through the night as he tumbled back. Fiery tongues of red and orange licked at every inch of his massive frame.

His burning body lighting the night, I closed my hand to cut off the gout and smelled burning flesh. Black smoke wafted from between my fingers. Jorn fell to his back with a thunderous boom and tried to roll, but his size prevented it. His monstrous torso held him in place, and his screams continued.

I hauled myself to my feet with a groan. A wave of light-headedness washed over me, spurred on by the pain from my side and the manifestation of my magic. Through tunneled vision, I saw Venai had gotten up as well. She dragged her wounded leg behind her as she raced as fast as she could to assist her burning companion. Zellick was nowhere to be seen, though I realized where he was the second I heard a boot scrape the porch behind me.

My speed advantage taken away by surprise and injury, I just started to react when he buried his dagger in my back. The blade cleaved through the flesh and muscle and slid between the ribs on my previously unwounded side. The tip settled inside my lung.

Though I'm sure I intended to scream, what came out was closer to a barked gurgle. Blood spewed from my punctured lung and ran up my throat. It gushed from my mouth, deep black and ugly. I tasted the bitter sickness as my body reacted to the magical blade. Its pungent nastiness filled my lungs with blood and gooey pus instead of air. Given enough time, I would drown in my own fluids.

Spurred on by that pleasant thought, I dove forward. The momentum of my panicked retreat spun me away from Zellick and the gloating smile carved across his thin lips. I didn't get far, the ground rushing up to meet me. The fall drove the blade in even deeper. Another cry burst from my mouth, this time in crimson, not words. I managed to roll onto my stomach to relieve the pressure.

Pale boy out of sight behind me, my gun uncomfortably grinding into my gut underneath, I expected the next thing I felt would be the last thing I *ever* felt; him finishing the job. It would serve me right. I'd been too confident.

"Zellick!" Venai's voice shook the air. "Help me!"

The knife wielder growled above me, but rushed to her side without hesitation, leaving me to bleed out.

My sight still fubar'd, I watched as a blurry Venai slid her arms under Jorn's bulk, ignoring the flames that gnawed at them, and heaved. She lifted him several inches, then a foot, the veins on her monstrous biceps bulging.

The wound in her leg was a seeping mess, blood pooling at her feet, making it hard for her to gain leverage. Her back strained Herculean under the tight shirt, the fabric stretched to its limit. She faltered just as Zellick reached her, his own pale arms joining hers, using the momentum of his run to counter gravity. It was just enough.

Jorn tumbled over with a ground-rumbling thud, the flames smothered in a whoosh of air and blubbery mass. His scream drifted off and was replaced by a low, wrenching moan that seeped from his mouth. Venai fell to her knees at his side, burying her face in the flab near his ear.

Zellick, on the other hand, turned his attention back to me. A wicked gleam in his eyes, he waved his remaining dagger in the air and stalked forward.

"You are so going to pay for that."

Marilyn Manson would be so proud.

Unable to catch my breath, more blood than air filling my lungs, I forced my hand beneath me and dug for my gun. Doing everything I could to ignore the agony chewing at my every nerve, I felt the cold solidness of my pistol grip and latched on. Shredding my knuckles on the concrete, I hauled the gun out and pointed it in the general direction of Zellick.

He squeaked as I pulled the trigger. Unable to hold the heavy pistol steady, my arm strafed right. The first two shots went wide, though their whistling threat stopped him in his tracks. The third, all credit to luck, clipped his shoulder. He cried out and skittered back, fear and agony painted across his face in equal measure. He ran to his companions' sides, clutching at his wound, his eyes on me the entire time.

Before I could realign my arm and get off another shot, Venai drew a glowing symbol in the air and opened a portal between us. She dragged its shimmering blue shape over them like a blanket, its mystical depths swallowing them whole. They disappeared in a flash. By the time my eyes adjusted, the night was empty, though several of my neighbor's lights were on. Worse still, I thought I saw movement behind one of the windows across the street.

I sighed. There was nothing I could do about it now. Michael Li and his cleanup crew would have to take care of it...if they ever showed up. DRAC had yet to recover from Asmoday's treachery, not to mention the latest Anti-Christ fiasco. They were stretched so thin as to be see-through.

I got up and made my way to the house. Blood and oozing

blackness ran down my chin as though I were a horror movie extra. The door was a blur. It was as though I peered at it through binoculars, my vision little more than hazy pinpricks. Every step was a trial.

Who'd have thought walking thirty feet could be so hard?

The door popped open by itself and I stumbled inside. I heard it close behind me as I staggered down the hall to my bedroom. A trail of red stained the carpet, blood squishing beneath my feet at every step. No energy to go around the bed, I tossed my gun away and plopped down on the mattress with a barely repressed scream, and slid across to the other side. With one arm, I reached down over the edge of the bed and knocked the small nightstand out of the way. Catching the corner of the carpet, I pulled it back, stuffed it under the frame, and tapped up the corner tile beneath it.

From within the cubby hole, I pulled out one of the last few vials I had of my uncle's blood, and slid off the bed the way I came. Using the spring of the soiled mattress to help me to my feet, my teeth grinding to shards as the dagger wiggled in my lung, I drifted back toward the living room.

Stopper off, I swallowed two tiny sips and dropped two more into Scarlett's unconscious, open mouth as I passed. With a dripping sigh, I sealed the vial to keep it from spilling and crumpled to the floor, a pool of warm blood forming under my head. All that was left to do was wait...

...and suffer.

It didn't take long, though it sure felt like it had. After just a moment, a sensuous flush of energy trickled down my body, heating my cold skin. Goose bumps tickled as the overwhelming pain started to become manageable under the orgasmic rush of Lucifer's claret. My eyes closed of their own accord and I lay there trembling as though I were spooning Keira Knightley.

More a stiff pressure than pain, I felt the dagger slip from my back, hearing it thud to the ground beside me, pushed out by the healing process. Then, with a last cough to rid my mouth of blood, I sat up and leaned against my armchair to look over at Scarlett.

She was still out. Her injures far worse than mine, she shuddered and twitched. Low moans echoed deep in her throat as the blood performed its miracle. Her leathered knees squeezed together and her hands, the disfigured one already on the mend, clutched at her ample chest in a way that was impossible to ignore. Trust me, I did my best.

Well...not really my best.

Chatterbox whistled low and winked at me. He was enjoying the show.

A moment later, Scarlett sat up with a start, her frantic eyes searching the room. Her now healed hand was on the hilt of her sword, white knuckles shining through the grime and blood. She saw me and exhaled hard, realizing where she was. She slipped back into the cushions of the couch, swiveling the sheath to lay the sword across her lap.

"How long?"

"It's a good six or seven inches, depending on how I hold the ruler."

If looks could kill.

I raised my hands in surrender. "You've been here about ten minutes, maybe less."

She hopped to her feet in a flurry of movement. "Then there's still time."

"Time for what?"

"To save Heaven."

Chapter Two

"Sillylittlewingedcousinsaywhat?" I really needed to stop watching Hannah Montana.

She glowered at me. "We must save Heaven." She had apparently forgotten whose nephew I was, because she went on as though I was expected to care. "Michael freed Gabriel from his imprisonment and they have laid siege to the Garden of Eden."

That couldn't be good. After Asmoday's attempt at bringing about Armageddon fell apart, my old mentor and demon lieutenant, Duke Forcalor, had dragged Gabriel back to Heaven to face judgment. Though I hadn't heard what they'd done to the archangel, he hadn't been seen since. The fact he was now free to seek revenge meant things were gonna get real bad in record time.

"Why Eden?"

Scarlett growled as though I'd missed something. "Eden is all that's left of the Heaven I knew." Apparently I had. "Gabriel and Michael rallied a secret army from amongst the Angelic Choir, those angered that Forcalor was allowed back in. Gabriel's forces ready to strike, they shut down the portals to Heaven so no one could escape.

"As dawn broke, they set upon those who had not spoken out against the duke's return to the Kingdom." Tears ran silver down her cheeks. "Too many of my brothers and sisters died before we even knew we'd been betrayed. The rest of us made for the protection of Eden, the only piece of Heaven Gabriel didn't yet control. Uriel barred the gates. He and Forcalor held off the advance until we could regroup. There was no mercy on that field."

Tremors rattled her body as she continued. "Uriel feared Gabriel might use the Earth-side gate to assault us from the rear, so he ordered it sealed. He sent me out to seek help just before Eden was locked down."

"That's where your groupies come in?" I gestured to the street.

She nodded. "A number of the Nephilim were camped out on the Earth-side of Eden. They attacked me as I came through. Wounded as I was by Gabriel's onslaught, I barely made it past them." Her voice cracked on the last, as if unable to believe she'd nearly been killed.

I shuddered, thinking about all the possible reasons for them being there. The Nephilim were the bastard sons and daughters of angels and humans; the mutts of the supernatural world. Kind of like me, only a little further down in the pecking order, if you can believe that.

Barred entrance to Heaven due to their impure bloodlines and dubious conceptions, they were often spiteful. They sided with demons to cause trouble for the Angelic Choir whenever they had the chance. If you saw one, you could be assured havoc would follow.

They trended toward the lower ranges of power, inheriting only a miniscule portion of their angelic parents' magical abilities. They were far tougher than humans, though much less so than most angels and demons. What they lacked in brute power, they made up for in numbers. There had to be tens of thousands of them roaming the planet, perhaps even more now that God wasn't around to curb their reproduction.

"How many were there?"

"I didn't have time to count, but I'd guess a hundred or so, maybe more."

A chill ran down my spine. We'd gotten lucky only the three had followed her.

Right then, I heard a noise in the rear of my house. Cursing, my gun somewhere in my bedroom, I readied my magic as Scarlett drew her sword. Before we had a chance to do anything else, the door to the spare room burst open.

Katon, DRAC's resident enforcer and all around badass, leapt into the hall, his sword shimmering in the lead. On his heels rushed Michael Li, the organization's mentalist and psychic PR guy with a 9mm in his hand. My heart rate thudded back to normal at seeing them, and I let my energy dissipate.

Behind them, I saw the glimmer of fading lights from the spare room and realized they'd come through the dimensional gate my uncle and I'd built. Though I vaguely remember giving them access to it, they'd never used it before. It gave a whole new meaning to the term *home invasion*. Ice-T could only wish he'd had it so easy.

"Good thing you're not the pizza guy or we'd be getting it for free."

Katon grinned, the sharpened points of his eyeteeth visible. "I see you're still alive, Frank. Scarlett must have arrived just in time to save your ass." He sheathed his replacement sword with a clack, his dark face creased with relieved amusement.

While he looked like a backup singer for the legendary heavy metal band Judas Priest, dressed from head to toe in black leather adorned with silver spikes, Katon was Hell on wheels. We'd gotten closer over the course of our mutual death-defying adventures in DRAC, but he wasn't a guy you pushed too far, no matter how good of friends you were.

Though he'd lost his prized sword in our most recent adventure, made from the Spear of Longinus, he'd acquired another magical blade imbued with a powerful, fast-acting paralytic. It wasn't quite in the same league, but it didn't make him any less dangerous. His being a vampire only emphasized his threat.

"For once," Scarlett said, striding to embrace Katon, a sad smile on her full lips, "it was the other way around."

He returned the hug, and then pulled away to look her over before his gaze drifted up to her eyes. At last he sighed, his down-to-business face firmly in place. "What happened?"

We went over what they'd missed. Once we were done, Michael headed out to *speak* to the neighbors.

His mental powers an impressive mix of mind reading, telepathy, and thought control, Michael was the head of DRAC's cleanup crew. He went behind us and made sure every trace of our presence was wiped from the minds of those unfortunate enough to witness us in action. It was his job to keep humanity ignorant of the growing unrest in the supernatural world brought on by God's disappearance. Like tonight, a little psychic reorientation would help keep our little scuffle out of the legitimate news.

Once Michael was gone, Katon turned to Scarlett. "So, Uriel needs help to defend Eden?"

If I'd had an extra cape, I'd have given it to him; Captain Obvious in the house. "Given what DRAC has been through recently, I don't think we're in any shape *to* help," I said.

Katon sighed, nodding in solemn agreement. "We'll do everything we can, Scarlett, but Frank is right. Asmoday's dread fiends decimated our ranks and we've yet to replenish them. Worse still, Rahim is but a shadow of his former self. Though he insists on working, Abraham has restricted him to light duty to ensure he recuperates fully." Sadness washed over his face for an instant as he spoke of his friend, before his stoic mask reasserted itself. "We'll be hard pressed to raise an army, let alone one that stands any hope of going to war with angels."

Scarlett's shoulders drooped, her tears returning. "Though I knew that in my heart, I prayed a miracle might avail itself." She let out a quiet laugh, the sound harsh and bitter. "It seems fortune has abandoned us, as well as God."

Caught off guard by the rancor in her voice, I just stared. God's reconciliation with Lucifer and his departure from existence had hit the angels hard, Scarlett more so than many. Despite that, she stayed dedicated to His path, defending the vision of Heaven she had always known. Lately, that vision had let her down, and let her down hard.

Captured by Gabriel, and handed over to the demon lieutenant Asmoday, had been a betrayal that nearly broke her spirit, its wound piled atop that of God's abandonment. Heaven was no longer the sanctuary she believed it to be; the one she needed. To see the archangels slaughtering her people, the family she loved, had apparently been the final straw. Her faith was failing.

"We *will* fight, Scarlett," Katon assured her, his dark hand squeezing hers. "I'm just not sure it will be anything more than a glorious attempt at failure."

She tightened her grip on his hand, defeat etched across her expression. "Thank you. I can ask for nothing more."

"We need to speak with Abraham and see what he says." My expectations of success weren't any higher than Katon's, though I'd learned not to discount Abraham's ability to triumph in the face of adversity. He was a wily old coot.

The founder of DRAC, and a king among psychics, Abraham foresaw the disappearance of God and the troubles to follow. His keen wit, sharpened by the adversity of having to outwit immortal beings, and tempered by the fires of experience, he had an understanding of the world unlike anyone else. If he didn't know what we needed to do, he'd figure it out.

With a loud crash, the front door flew open. "You guys need to get out here," Michael shouted from the porch. His voice was raw, his tone piercing.

His panic was contagious. We flew outside, filing down the sidewalk to the street behind the mentalist. He pointed and we looked.

Off in the distance, not more than a couple of blocks away, the sky was awash in brilliant light. Strange, localized white clouds stood out against the night's darkness. They roiled with purplish lightning that crackled through their interior in sudden bursts. The clouds sat low in the sky, unnaturally so, not more than a hundred yards above the trees.

The whistling howl of wind drifted to my ears, a stiff breeze buffeting us in waves, the gusts coming off the clouds. Then suddenly the wind stopped cold. The cloying scent of ash and decay settled in the air, its taste sour. Muffled thunder rumbled in time with the colorful lightning, and a fine mist of ashen snow began to fall from the clouds. It floated lazily, settling over everything underneath it.

Scarlett let loose a whimper and stumbled. Katon caught hold of her to keep her steady. I didn't even have time to ask what was wrong before Michael cried out and fell to his knees, his hands clutching to his head. His teeth were clenched, agony scarring his features.

"It's death," Michael groaned as a streamer of blood ran from his nose and down his chin.

Heedless of the obvious warning, I raced down the street to get a closer look. Though it covered a good three to four block radius, the storm was static. The clouds hovered in place with no forward motion, which made it easy to reach.

That weirdness alone should have been enough of a hint to stay away.

The rancid smell grew thicker as I approached, the scent of an old tomb unearthed. My ribs tightened, the air thick in my lungs, biting as though a mound of fire ants had taken up residence in my chest. As I reached the edge of the fall, my senses kicked in and warned me off, a banshee's scream inside my head. I could only imagine what Scarlett and Michael felt. Eyes watering, coughing up cinders, I looked to the drift and froze.

Wisps of gray smoke rose from everywhere the ashen snow touched. The ground beneath was charred black. Grass and trees died in its wake and withered before my eyes. Nothing seemed immune. The asphalt of the road bubbled and melted, turning to gravel, then dust. The metal fences and rock walls sagged and crumbled. Even the vehicles were being eaten away, obsidian circles of rot appearing on their surfaces, the blackness spreading as destruction took hold.

In a nearby yard, a dog lay twitching on the ground. Any whimpers it might have made had been cut short by the merciless fall, its snout devoured whole. What was left of its tongue was little more than dripping red strands, which lolled from under its panicked eyes. It stared at me, black dots screaming in silence for pity. Its hindquarters were gone, intestines splayed out behind it only to meet the same grisly fate beneath the ashen snow.

My stomach clenched. Churning sickness begged for release

as it scaled the back of my throat. I summoned my energy to end the creature's suffering, but the storm finished it first. The dog twitched one last spasm, and then its head collapsed. Its fight was over.

A sudden thought hit me, my eyes jerking to the houses. The nearest one, a nice two-story similar to my own, was missing most of its roof. The virulent snow ate away at its remains, billows of smoke whooshing up from inside. There were no sounds from within, no panicked screams or cries for help. It was likely no one was home.

The sick in my stomach hardened, knowing full well that one instance of mercy was all I could hope for. As I surveyed the neighborhood, it was awash in deadly white. Faster than I could have imagined, homes had been undone, as had anyone inside them: children, wives, mothers and fathers, grandparents, all consumed, leaving naught but ash. Nothing could survive the storm. In just minutes, that's all there would be: nothing.

I reached out, extending my hand into the fall. Flakes struck my arm in several places, their touch a fiery brand at every impact. Clenching my teeth to restrain my scream, I yanked my arm back, staring at the blackened dots that ate at my flesh like ravenous piranha. They warred with my immune system, the devil in me slowly gaining the upper hand, but they fought hard. Searing agony accompanied the entirety of the battle as I realized the storm was somehow natural in origin, not magical.

Katon, at my side in huff, pulled me further from the fall, a sharpened snarl on his lips. He didn't say anything, but he didn't need to. I knew what he was thinking, but there weren't any suicidal tendencies in me, nor was I going crazier than normal.

There was just a part of me, a piece of my mother buried deep inside—her compassion, her selfless dedication to life—that felt the need to suffer with those I couldn't save. It wanted to feel what they felt, to understand the horror that befell them. It needed me to know what they went through, so I would never forget. I needed to hurt to find the strength to prevent it from happening again.

Either *that* or I'm just a masochist hiding behind the memories of my murdered mother. Either is possible.

Scarlett and Michael came up behind, their breath rasping in rhythm as they viewed the atrocity splayed out before us. They'd both felt it far stronger than I had, their senses far more refined. They, too, were suffering, but I couldn't bring myself to face them. That would be too much.

Once more I looked up at the clouds, only to see them shudder as though having a seizure. Their motion slowed and collapsed inward, the slow whirl of a cosmic drain. The dancing lightning inside their depths flashed a few more times, streaks of purple staining the all-encompassing white, and then ceased. The thunderous rumble ended with it. Then, as though it had never been, the storm darkened and faded away into the blackness of night, its cancerous snow disappearing with it.

What it left behind was a ruin far worse than any war could have ever aspired to. Though the damage was confined to an area less than four city blocks, it had been absolute. Save for a few scattered walls, their angle such as to avoid direct contact with the fall, there was nothing left. A blackened crater, more than a foot deep, marked the boundaries of the storm.

No blood or gore, no hair or bone, was left to mar the perfect abyss of emptiness. Even the smell disappeared. There was simply nothing left but the hard black earth, cleansed of all life. Everything that once towered above existed now only in memory, or perhaps a photograph or two. The space had become a void.

My chest ached and I, at last, turned around. Scarlett's normally green eyes were assailed by red, her nose and cheeks flushed. Michael didn't look much better. The pair hung onto each other in mutual discomfort. At a loss for words, I tried to say something to ease the moment, but a movement in the shadows just beyond the dead zone caught my eye, stilling any trite commiseration I might have come up with. Someone was watching us.

As though the figure realized I'd seen it, it slipped into the deeper shadows of the distant houses. Like a bat out of Hell, I ran after it. My heart pounded in my chest, a galloping blast beat that drove me forward with frantic insistence.

The horrific images of what I'd witnessed forever seared upon my memory, there was only room for one more thought inside my head. Murder.

Chapter Three

My breath huffed like a freight train as I rounded the corner where the figure had disappeared. There was nothing but open space. I let my senses loose and pushed them to their limit, a billion-legged octopus freed to wiggle its receptive tentacles into every nook and cranny, seeking the shadowy figure. Again, they could find no one. Whoever had been watching us was gone.

Frustration boiled over into a scream, my throat ripped raw with its intensity, an acid bath of emotion. My chest tightened as my lungs cried out for air. A cyclone of ugly thoughts whirled inside my head, begging to be unleashed on whoever had masterminded the storm, and on the voyeur whose cheap thrill came at the expense of innocent lives.

Katon and Scarlett dashed around the corner and stopped cold when they saw me. Michael brought up the rear, coughing as he struggled to breathe. I could see the worry on their faces and could only imagine what I looked like to them. It didn't really matter right then.

Finally, when I could scream no more, I let my voice trail off. I took a minute to regain my composure before joining them.

"We're in way over our heads. Let's go talk to Abe."

His expression wary, but agreeable, Katon nodded.

* * * *

Through the gate at my house, we arrived at DRAC after just a few minutes. We appeared in the secure entry room where every portal into the main DRAC headquarters is funneled. A silver pentagram was inscribed on the floor, its points surrounded by the summoning circle we'd use to port in. Carved into the walls was a massive array of defensive wards designed to take out most any supernatural threat. I'd never known their specific use, and would happily live my life without seeing the business end of them.

Hidden alongside the wards were a number of jets that could fill the room with poisonous gas in seconds. To top it all off, the ceiling was a thirty ton weight, powered by a massive system of hydraulics, designed to be dropped on unsuspecting enemies, turning them into jelly. That one always made me nervous.

My focus was on the roof until the security scans finished, and the door, set flush with the walls, swung open with a whoosh to let us into DRAC proper. Chivalry and consideration saved for when I wasn't at risk of being *smooshed*, I hightailed it out of the chamber as fast as I could, nudging past the security officer standing outside.

"I'm with him." I pointed to Katon and kept walking. The officer sighed and stepped aside, not bothering to argue. He knew me.

Through the labyrinthine halls, we made our way to Abraham's office, sans Michael. He'd gone off to rally his men. Given the widespread nature of the strange storm, he was gonna have his hands full trying to keep this one under wraps.

Having spent a while sleeping on the couch in Abraham's office while my house was rebuilt, it felt almost like coming home. I barged in without knocking. The decadent scent of old knowledge wafted out to greet me. Rows upon rows of old books stood neatly arranged on a handful of shelves along the back wall. They ran the gamut from magical tomes to historical texts, encyclopedias to archaic religious works. Many of them were so rare as to exist only here, in this room. They were Abraham's pride and joy.

Unlike his desk, which looked like an orphan from Clutterville, dozens of stacks of manila folders and papers littered its face. His computer was covered in a colorful assortment of sticky notes. Tiny black slivers of his monitor showed through between them, here and there.

Abraham peeked out from behind the piles and gave us a grim nod, mustering a weak smile for Scarlett. His glasses amplified the green of his eyes and he stared at us with subtle apprehension twitching across his face.

He'd taken to shaving his head. Most of his white hair having gone to pasture already, it made him look younger, more vital. The consummation of his relationship with Rachelle Knight, the third member of DRAC's triumvirate of power, a powerful mystic in her own right, had helped, no doubt.

"Judging by the looks on your faces, this isn't a social call."

With a huff, I dropped into one of the large chairs out in front of his desk as Scarlett sat in the other. Katon stood behind her, his posture uncharacteristically protective. While a bit surprised by Katon's show of propriety, I put it out of my head. There were more important things to worry about.

"Is it ever?" I answered.

Abraham shook his head, forced to agree. We caught him up on everything, starting with Scarlett showing up at my door and ending with the storm. When we were done, he slid his glasses off, dropping them on the desk, and sat back in the chair with one hand rubbing at his temple.

"This isn't good."

That, ladies and gentlemen, is why he's in charge.

"Ever hear of anything like that?"

"No. It's an anomaly we've yet to encounter." He motioned beyond the door. "Rachelle sensed a mysterious building of energy minutes before you say the storm struck, though she had no idea what created the flux. Your information might help us determine its cause and at least now, we'll know when one is building."

"For all the good it'll do us. That thing took out four city blocks in the time it took me to scratch my ass, Abe. A minute or two isn't gonna give us time to evacuate anyone, let alone defend against it."

"Some warning is better than none, Frank. We'll take what we can get." He waved me to silence, turning to look at Scarlett. "Could this have something to do with Gabriel's assault upon Eden?"

She sat silent for a moment, and then shrugged. "It's possible, though I'm not sure how. He and Michael are on the front lines, and have been since the attack began. Uriel and Forcalor would crush their forces should either of the archangels withdraw from the field."

Abraham exhaled slow as he clearly pondered everything he'd learned. "I'll gather what forces we have available, but they will hardly be adequate for Uriel's purpose. I'm sorry. I wish I could tell you otherwise."

"I understand," Scarlett replied with a fractured smile, her voice little more than a whisper. Katon gave her shoulder a gentle squeeze, smiling down at her.

"What about Baalth?" Abraham asked me.

"He's got the power for sure, it's just whether there's something in it for him. He's not gonna jump to save Heaven unless it advances his interests, especially considering the history there. I don't see him being excited enough to pitch in on this one."

"It can't hurt to ask."

I chuckled, thinking about just how much it *could* hurt to ask. "I'll see what he says." Or throws, or kicks, or burns. Just recently free of all my obligations to Baalth, I wasn't looking forward to mortgaging my ass to him again.

"Find out what you can about the Nephilim," Abraham said, turning to Katon. "Their gathering near Eden cannot be a coincidence. Perhaps they know something that will aid us."

Katon slowly reclaimed his hand, nodding to Scarlett who returned a wan smile. He looked reluctant to leave. After a moment of tense silence he did, closing the door loudly behind him.

Abraham raised an eyebrow Spock-like, but said nothing. He didn't have to. He was king when it came to speaking without words.

"This can't all be a coincidence, can it?"

Abraham shook his head. "I don't believe so, but without more information, there's no way to be sure. I'll start gathering our people. Perhaps by the time we're ready, we'll know more."

Frustrated that we were just as much in the dark as we were when we'd arrived, I said goodbye to Abraham, intent upon scampering off to Old Town. Scarlett tagged along looking like a lost puppy dog.

After we'd scrounged her up some clothes to wear, I stopped off at the armory and re-equipped myself, swiping a pair of guns and plenty of ammunition—the DA slayers—and made for the portal room.

It was never a bad idea to have an arsenal when going to visit Baalth.

Chapter Four

After gating through the closest portal to Baalth's territory, we emerged from an alley onto the dusty streets of downtown El Paseo. A short walk later, we slipped across the invisible boundary into Old Town a few hours before dawn.

Most of the late night revelers were already done, gone home or passed out in some darkened alley. The morning crews had yet to get out of bed.

We skirted what was left of Fiesta Street, the major party area of Old Town, and were surprised to find the street quiet; eerily so.

Though, in retrospect, considering Baalth had set off the magical equivalent of a nuke smack dab in the center of Old Town just a couple weeks back, I guess I shouldn't be surprised.

Nothing says *go the fuck home* like an uncontrolled detonation of magical energy.

In a moment of weakness, his men assaulted and kidnapped in the heart of his territory, Baalth had lost it. He left behind a smoking crater several blocks in radius as a reminder of his power. He'd paid to rebuild it, though the work had only just begun. While he could pay to keep the citizens silent, trust was a lot harder to buy. It'd be a while before Fiesta Street lived up to its name again. Damn shame, I tell ya.

A bunch of the buildings at the edge of ground zero were nothing more than burnt out husks, and that was being charitable. Those that had stood closer to the epicenter stood no longer. Rubble and gathered detritus clogged the open spaces, much of it pushed into teetering piles that rose up ten feet high in places. The asphalt of the roads had been melted during the conflagration, and now that they'd cooled, they were marred by wavy rivulets like those at the bottom of a creek. The sidewalks had buckled, pitched up as though they were a tiny mountain range.

We made our way around the rubble and ruin, skirting piles of trash as we made our way further into Old Town. As we reached the evacuated section just beyond the ring of destruction, it felt as though we were traveling through a third world country. Most of the windows were shattered and there were scorch marks seared black onto the brick faces of the buildings. The only thing missing was the whistle of incoming artillery and the propaganda leaflets.

None of the streetlights worked, and though I could see well enough, the gloom weighed on me. There was a palpable sense of death in the air, my skin prickling under the pressure. It was like walking into a graveyard during a full moon. You never quite saw what lurked in the shadows, but you sure as Hell knew something was there.

Beside me, Scarlett drew a quick breath and her hand went to her sword. That's when I realized I hadn't just imagined the feeling. The feral growl that rumbled through the darkness confirmed it.

Gun in hand, Scarlett at my side, we turned to face the sound. From a nearby alley, the harsh scrape of something sharp dragged across the asphalt was preceded by a looming bulk that strode from its depths.

Scarlett gasped and took a step back as I craned my neck to see all of the behemoth who trundled into the street. I did a double-take as my mind struggled to register what my eyes were seeing. Not remembering having had a drink recently, what I saw didn't make sense.

It was a bear, but not like any I'd ever seen before. It was a werebear. Smokey had nothing on him. Right around then, the only thing I wanted to help prevent was me shitting my pants.

Almost ten feet tall, and easily as wide as the alley, it was a mountain of muscle under a thick coat of glistening brown fur. Its deep-set eyes simmered with reddish light as it hunched to look down at us, its stubby snout screwed up in a wicked smile. Its shoulder rippled as it raised a massive paw in our direction. Dagger-like claws gleamed in the oppressive dimness as it rumbled a gravelly challenge.

Unable to tear my eyes from the furry hulk, I almost missed the shades that slithered from the alley behind him. My senses rattling my brain like a scorned wife with a frying pan, I dared a quick glance their direction, realizing they were what I had felt.

The sorry remnants of my courage made a mad dash for my ass.

Their sharpened eyeteeth a dead giveaway, the three vampires eased alongside the bear. Used to the suave darkness of Katon, it was as though they were a completely different breed. Their sallow faces were long, with severe features that jutted from their skulls at sharp angles; a building block set with too many triangles. Yellow eyes seethed in narrow sockets as brittle smiles fractured their lips. Their lithe limbs swayed in time to music I couldn't hear, kinda like a crack-head in need of a fix.

A gravel-throated voice yanked my eyes back to the furred monstrosity.

"Someone's been pissing in my Cheerios, and he's right here." The words roared from the werebear's mouth, guttural and fierce. The withering heat of his gaze fell on me.

Scarlett groaned and nudged my ribs, as if she'd suspected it was my fault all along. Taken aback, I could only shrug as my mind flitted through my memories to see if there was a bear in any of them.

"If this is about that one time with the rug, I'm sorry. I didn't know you were related."

The big guy chuckled; at least I think that's what it was. He could have been swallowing a squirrel.

"You have no clue, do you?"

"Not usually," Scarlett answered for me over my shoulder.

I just shook my head. Life was so much easier when the bad guys told me why they wanted to kill me rather than expecting me to guess. The onus of the monologue was on the bad guy. Doesn't anyone read the damn handbook anymore?

"You should have let the half-breeds take the little dove there." He snorted toward Scarlett.

One eyebrow raised, I cast a quick glance her way. "See? It's not *always* me." Curious as to why the Nephilim, the undead, *and* a lycanthrope wanted a piece of my cousin—all sexual innuendo aside—I chose the direct route. Though I have to admit, it was mostly because I couldn't think of something witty to say. "Who are you and what do you want?" I really need to work on my social banter.

The vampires hissed in slithery tandem, their rhythmic gyrations becoming agitated, though they stayed put. It was weird seeing them following the lead of a were-critter, as the two factions rarely mingled, let alone got along.

As usual, something was going down and it wasn't on me.

The bear rose to his full height and widened his grin. "You're a brave mutt; I'll give you that. The name's Grawwl." He ran the meaty slab of his tongue over his razored teeth and leered down at Scarlett. "All I want is the angel. You can run along home, little man."

My ass weighed the cost of turning Scarlett over, but the negotiations stalled somewhere between my heart and my mouth.

It wouldn't be the first butt kicking I'd taken for her. I could only hope it wouldn't be the last. "All I want is five minutes alone with Jessica Biel's panties." Cursed with a vivid imagination, it took a second to get back on track. "Much as I could use the peace and quiet, that's not gonna happen."

"That's okay." He clapped his huge paws together. "I don't mind doing this the hard way." He lifted his chin and loosed a throaty roar, which set my ears to ringing.

Minus the verbal theatrics, the vampires leapt to the attack, clearing the intervening twenty feet in an instant. Out of instinct, more than anything resembling rational thought, I darted off and put my gun to use.

Three bullets slammed into the chest of the lead vamp, blowing jagged black holes through him. Wisps of smoke steamed from his back while he shrieked and twitched, clawing at the wounds. The other two ducked past and went for Scarlett as she circled away.

Before I could fire on them, the shadows overhead thickened and I heard a *whoof* of breath to my side. That's when Grumpy Bear plowed into me. While I'd expected him to take a shot at me as soon as I was distracted, I hadn't factored in his speed.

A bright light flashed before my eyes and when I opened them, the world spun in a streaked blur around my head. There was a vague sense of weightlessness and motion, which came to a sudden end as the ground rushed up to meet me.

The bone-jarring impact snapped me back to my senses as tremors traveled the length of my extremities, my fingers and toes tingling. I rolled to get my bearings and was suddenly aware of the searing lines arcing across my upper back. Pain flooded over me, a whitewash of sensory overload. Had it not been for the lingering jelly-brain from my crash landing, I'd have probably passed out. As it was, it was hard to focus, though things could have been worse; he could have bitten me.

I'd seen a demon contract lycanthropy once. It's something I'll never forget.

His natural regeneration fought against the infection for days, the two waging a virulent war at the genetic level. There's nothing like watching a body rot from the inside, pustulant boils erupting with rancid, tar-like blood and gooey red pus. To a symphony of gargled screams, the demon's eyes had boiled from their sockets as his face blistered, then ruptured, oozing away from his skull. His cries lasted only a few moments after that. I still hear them in my sleep sometimes.

Not wanting to be *that* guy, I got to my feet, my knees quavering. My eyes refused to look the same direction. Through my right, I saw Scarlett flitting between the vampires, obsidian blurs trailing in the wake of her sword. She was holding her own. Lucky her.

Out of my left, I saw Grawwl, a toothy smirk on his muzzle as he wiggled his claws, stained in my blood. A few feet in front of him, silhouetted by the bear's dark bulk, was the furious face of the vampire I'd shot.

Fangs came at me howling as I closed my right eye and raised my gun to meet him.

Or I would have, had it still been in my hand.

Undeterred by my imaginary show of force, the vamp barreled into me, sinking his sharpened fingers into the deep gouges of my back. Bright dots welled up in front of me as I dropped straight down to avoid him nuzzling my neck. I whipped my legs up underneath him. Caught off guard, my foot up his ass, he was flung past me, his momentum turned against him. There was a pissed off hiss as he rebounded off the concrete and skittered into the mounds of debris, but he was the least of my worries.

I got to my feet just as Grawwl dropped to all fours and rumbled forward, the knot of muscles at his back coiled. With nowhere to go to escape the charge, I summoned my energies and squared my shoulders. Grumpy just laughed, frothy white spittle emphasizing his apparent disdain for my magic. What little hope I had took a dump and trickled warm down my leg alongside my confidence.

It was times like this when I wished I'd taken my uncle up on his offer to become the Anti-Christ, but no, I had to be all self-righteous and give up my inheritance and the power that came with it. At least I'd get a good epitaph for my supposed integrity.

I looked to Scarlett and saw she'd taken out one of the vamps, but was still busy with the other one. Things didn't look good; for me.

Right then, I caught a flash of movement out the corner of my eye. Grawwl hesitated as his gaze shifted toward the motion. His smirk morphed into a sneer.

Out of the shadows, between the buildings, stepped an old man. Wild gray hair flowed over the bronzed plates of his battered armor. He wielded a gilded broadsword with intricate rune work etched down the length of the blade and woven into the hilt and pommel. His face was like a worn leather hide, deep wrinkles streaked throughout, etched by time. Two fierce blue eyes glimmered from lined and sunken sockets, crow's feet gone pterodactyl at the corners.

He faced Grawwl, his blade set before him. "You might want to watch your back," he said over his shoulder, his voice thready.

Remembering the vamp, I drew my backup pistol and spun to see my dance partner sprinting toward me. I decided to lead this time and unloaded what was left in the clip into his sour puss. He screeched and howled as he dropped. His hands went to his face in a frantic attempt to tear the bullets out.

Not interested in him getting up again, I reloaded and held the barrel over his throat. In a sweeping motion from right to left, I fired fast, each bullet shredding a section of his neck. His screams turned to gurgles as the bullets tore through his vocal cords. Bubbling blackness squirted from the wounds as though I'd struck oil. His face went rigid as spasms shuddered across his body.

With little more than tattered remnants of meat holding him in one piece, I pulled back my foot and soccer-kicked his head from his shoulders. It gave way with a wet ripping sound and flew up into the air, splattering my boot and the street with a warm, dark rain. I fought the urge to yell, "*Goooooooooooooooaaaaaaa alllllll*," as his head split the frame of a nearby doorway.

I turned back around just in time to see Scarlett drift toward me. The last vampire twitched on the asphalt behind her, his body diced neatly into a couple dozen dripping parts even Dali would have found disturbing.

Much to my surprise, all I saw of Grawwl was his furry ass as he hightailed it out of sight. I added a bullet to speed him along. Can't say I was sorry to see him go.

Grateful for the rescue, I looked to the old man. "You got a name?"

He shook his head and gestured the way the werebear went. "No time. The vampires and shifters know what's going on in the Kingdom."

Scarlett gasped, her eyes going wide. "But—"

The old man waved a grizzled hand to cut her off. "They and the Nephilim seek a key to turn the tide against Heaven. It must not be them who find it." He gave a curt nod and raced off after Grawwl.

After he was gone, I looked to Scarlett. I imagine I had the same dumbfounded look on my face.

"Today just keeps getting better and better." My adrenaline

fading, the gashes in my back started to throb. A sudden chill prickled my skin as the pain settled in.

"Should we follow?" Scarlett asked.

"No." I waggled my finger. "Let grandpa deal with Grawwl. If the lycanthropes and vampires have set aside their differences to go against Heaven, we're neck deep in some serious shit. We're gonna need all the help we can get."

Scarlett's green eyes met mine, a glimmer of resignation welling up. "Baalth?"

"Baalth."

Chapter Five

"You have got to be fucking kidding me!"

"I'm sorry, Mister Trigg," Poe answered, his voice like silk. "Baalth is unavailable."

"What do you mean, unavailable?"

"That would be the opposite of available."

I just stared at him, imagining choking some color into his expressionless face.

A mentalist of impressive power, Alexander Poe was Baalth's right-hand man and confidante. I'd grown to respect the man's integrity and courage, and could even say I liked him on occasion, depending on how many drinks I had in me, but the dark stare and rigid detachment grated on my nerves. He was one cold fish, but his loyalty to Baalth was unquestionable. If the big guy told him to stonewall me, I wasn't gonna get a damn thing out of him.

His dim-witted tank of a partner, on the other hand...

Marcus D'anatello sat at the back of the room, his eyes on the floor, his bald head a rosy pink. The last time I'd seen the hulking bruiser, I'd saved his life. Of course I beat him halfway to death while doing it, but that's beside the point.

He fidgeted in his chair, his knuckles a bright white as he clenched his fists in his lap. He obviously didn't want anything to do with me.

Too bad. That only egged me on. "Where's he at, Marcus?"

"Unavailable, Mister Trigg." Poe stepped between us, his words fierce but still composed. "Time for you to leave." He gestured to the door where Scarlett stood, her arms overlapped in front of her chest.

Meeting Poe's steely gaze, I saw his eyelid twitch subtly. He was brushing me off. There was more going on than he was telling me. I looked past him to the weakest link. "Tell me where he is."

Marcus shook his head, the muscles in his jaw clenched in a visible knot. Poe told me to leave again, but I ignored him.

"Don't make me come over there, Marcus. Tell me."

"We don't fucking know, all right?" Marcus screamed as he jumped to his feet. He looked ready to explode, his face a deep shade of red.

Poe snarled and Marcus dropped back into his seat with a graveled huff. Poe glared at me with open hostility, and I realized what Marcus said was true; they had no idea where Baalth was.

"He just up and disappeared?"

Poe stood there without answering, the vein at his temple throbbing as though he were sending a message in Morse code. I stayed quiet as well, meeting his withering gaze. At last, he sighed and his eyes dropped away as though letting go of a burden that had been too heavy to bear. He ran his hand through his thinning gray hair and gave a shallow nod.

"When?"

"About a week, now." He went around the desk and sunk into Baalth's chair. He stared down at his hands. "He'd sent us on an errand and when we returned, he and Veronica were gone. He left no word as to where he was going or when he'd be back. He gave no operating directives." Poe met my eyes once more, his calm expression returning. "Outside of Mister D'anatello and I, only you two know he is gone."

The warning was clear. Baalth's presence was a major factor in minimizing the supernatural hijinks in the area since God and Lucifer sauntered off for parts unknown. Only the bravest, or dumbest, stirred up trouble anywhere near the demon's territory. If word got out he was missing, all Hell would break loose—literally.

"He picked a great time to go on walkabout. You hear about Heaven?"

Poe nodded. "Our network is still in place, so our information lines remain constant. Though without Baalth, our resources to respond are limited."

"What about The Gray?" I hated the redneck, Santa Claus lookalike, but there was no denying he had the power to go toe-to-toe with angels. He'd done it before. We could use him.

"Unfortunately, Mister McConnell has yet to recover from our adventure in Limbo. Were he to summon his magic, it would kill him."

Torn between laughing at The Gray's misfortune and sighing at ours, I chose the latter. The already short list of help was getting shorter by the minute, and we were running out of time. I could be a vindictive ass later. "You know anything about the weird storm that hit the city?"

Poe shook his head. "None of our sources have seen anything like it before, nor do they have any idea what might have caused it." He leaned back, rubbing at his chin. "No, that's not entirely truthful. There is one who *might* know something, though he would never deign to tell me. Perhaps he might be more willing to speak to you."

"Who?"

"Asmoday."

Scarlett hissed and pushed past me, nearly knocking me over. The wounds on my back burned as her elbow dug into them. I clenched my teeth to keep from screaming.

"Where is he? I'll cut the answers from his entrails, I'll—"

Poe raised a warning hand. "He is under Baalth's protection."

While that might have deterred me, Scarlett was 100 percent Old Testament when it came to revenge; an eye for an eye. Actually, she was probably closer to 130 percent. She'd go for a limb too, while she was at it.

Worse still, when it came to Asmoday, she was harboring some serious hate. Not too long ago, the Archangel Gabriel had captured her and handed her over to the demon lieutenant. Chained with manacles that inhibited her power, she was helpless until I came along and freed her. She was probably madder about that last part than anything.

Given the opportunity, she'd take a piece of Asmoday home with her; one of the warm and juicy ones. It'd be dangling over her fireplace by nightfall.

"Where is he?"

Shaking his head, Poe looked to me. "Not with her here. Baalth will have our heads if any harm comes to Asmoday."

She drew her sword and leaned over the desk, setting the tip at Poe's narrow throat. "Tell me or *I'll* have your head right here and now!"

Marcus jumped to his feet with a growl. "Put the sword away, bitch!" He aimed his gun at Scarlett. It was one of my old ones, stolen from me a while back, and it was loaded with DA slayers. Things were spiraling out of control fast.

As unnatural as it was to be the voice of reason, I had to step in.

"I know how you feel, Scarlett, but this isn't helping. Poe would die rather than betray his master, and I would bet my balls that Marcus has no idea how to reach Asmoday." A confirming smile flashed across Poe's lips as Scarlett glared, her sword arm steady. "Your people need your help. Would you condemn them for the sake of petty revenge?"

She stood rigid, the point of her blade drawing a dot of blood from Poe's throat.

"Damn you." At last she relented, a quiet sob slipping from her. She covered her mouth and stumbled back into the wall, sheathing her sword with a clack. Tears welled from her eyes as she crumbled into a ball on the floor, hugging her knees.

Relief colored Poe's face and he sunk deeper into the chair, his hand massaging his throat. He waved Marcus away with the other. Sweat trickling down his face, the bruiser holstered his gun and stormed out of the room without so much as looking back. So far, that was the best thing to happen all day.

"I'll take you to him, but she stays here," Poe said, one eyebrow raised, waiting for an answer.

I glanced at Scarlett, her body trembling as she rocked back and forth. The guilt card played without mercy, I couldn't help but feel bad for her.

A sensitive soul, Scarlett suffered the slings and arrows of life far deeper than most. She couldn't imagine hurting those she loved and I'd laid it out for her in graphic detail, setting the full weight of blame for what might happen on her shoulders; the image was too much for her to bear. I watched her for a moment longer, her body trembling in time with her tears, then nodded to Poe.

"Fair enough." I turned to Scarlett. "Stay put. I'll find out what we need to know and be right back." She didn't bother to look at me. "We'll save Heaven, I promise." The words sounded hollow, but they seemed to work. She glanced up at me, her reddened eyes daring to hope. I had to look away.

A plastic smile covered my lips until I'd followed Poe out of the room and down a short hall, where it cracked and fell away. We wound our way through a minor maze of rooms and doors until we hit the basement. Inside, the gentle glimmer of power hung in the air. A small, simple pentagram was etched inside a circle on the concrete floor, its lines drawn in gold. Poe gestured to it.

"Hop in, Mister Trigg. I'll direct the gate."

The need for expediency outweighing trust, I stepped into the circle without question and held my breath. In what was a telling moment, Poe closed his eyes and I sensed the subtle waves of energy that emanated from him, triggering the gate.

As the dimensional vortex whisked me away, I stared at Poe until he faded from sight, my mind whirling. He'd never shown any inclination toward magic before. Though operating a portal isn't exactly high-end craft, it took a solid measure of mystical competency that couldn't be mastered overnight. Poe had done it without a hitch.

My arrival cleared that revelation from my head. A brimstone tang met my nose, giving away my destination as clearly as any sign could. I was in Hell.

Far from the prison cell quaintness I'd expected, the room I appeared in was cavernous. I recognized it immediately as a part of my uncle's private chambers, a section squirreled away in the deepest recesses of his old quarters. A quick glance to my left made it clear the area had been sealed off from the rest of the rooms. Where once a massive archway had led out to a series of uninhabited rooms, there was now a seamless wall of stone. There'd be no *Shawshank Redemption* with that hunk of rock.

Amused that Baalth had chosen to imprison Asmoday in Lucifer's old dominion, I took a look around at what'd been done to the place. Comfortable furniture littered the open space, the walls buttressed with overflowing bookshelves. Works of great art, clearly stolen from the world above, hung in a rigid array along the walls. Their bright colors threatened to overwhelm the dull tones of the rest of the room.

"Has the prodigal son come home at last?" a smooth, quiet voice asked from behind me, interrupting my sightseeing.

I spun to see Asmoday leaning in an arched doorway, a glass of wine dangling at his fingertips. Always lean, he looked damn near anorexic, like a piece of wood chiseled to its bare essence. His jet black hair and beard were unkempt and greasy, brown specks floating in them. A connoisseur of fine suits, it surprised me to see him dressed in flowing black robes that had seen better days. Dark stains marred the bulk of them, and the sleeves were tattered and frayed at their ends. Powder gray dust was visible on the loose threads. The mangy sandals he wore on his feet were speckled in what looked like dried mud, his feet nearly brown.

The iron stare that had long inspired fear amongst the Angelic Choir flitted dull and fidgety; his brown eyes little more than murky puddles in sallow sockets. His presence, which had once wafted from him, thick with steel and arrogance, was the wispy breath of a barren grave. His power was gone.

My mind jumped on the last part, my eyes glancing to his wrists and dirty ankles. Seeing no manacles, my stomach twisted into a knot. If ever I needed some kind of benchmark to comprehend just how powerful Baalth had become after inheriting

Glorius's magic, Asmoday was it.

As one of the first Fallen, a top lieutenant to Lucifer himself, Asmoday was power incarnate. In the top ten of supernatural entities, he was a god amongst men; *was* being the operative word.

Without any artificial assistance, Baalth had shut him down as easily as flipping off a switch. That reality settled over me like tsunami.

"Hardly." I fought to keep the satisfaction from my voice.

He didn't seem to care as he strolled to a velvet couch and plopped down, waving me to a seat across from it. He stared at the stone floor. "Then to what do I owe the great pleasure of your esteemed company?" He knew why I was there. Even banished to Hell, robbed of his magic, Asmoday was a demon lieutenant; there wasn't a war he didn't know about. Each and every battle was a song that rang clear through his blood.

I sat, my wounds reminding me they were still there, and took a second to collect my thoughts. Having lost everything he valued, Asmoday wasn't gonna be swayed by a sob story, so I played to his ego. "I need your help."

Though he sat a little straighter, taking another sip of his wine, he didn't lift his gaze. "I have none to offer."

"Actually, you're the only one who does."

His eyes peeked up at me from under drowsy lids. "Why not ask Baalth? Surely he can assist you."

"Baalth has his own agenda, and I have mine. They rarely coincide conveniently to my benefit."

Asmoday straightened, his wine glass hovering at his lips as he stared at me. "So Baalth doesn't know you're here, Triggaltheron?"

I shook my head, cringing at the use of my given name, but I let it go.

He sighed, his shoulders slumping. "Then I can expect nothing for my assistance."

Settling back into my seat, I tried not to smile. While he might have seemed uninterested, I knew the game well. We'd reached the bargaining stage. "I can certainly speak with Baalth to see what I can manage..." He shifted on the couch and looked to his glass. I waited a moment, letting the line trail out a little. "Though I believe I have a more...accommodating solution."

He glanced up, his brown eyes curious at last.

"While Baalth may hold all the cards at the moment, fate has a habit of reshuffling the deck." I leaned forward as though confessing. "As I'm sure you've heard, Longinus is back among the living."

Asmoday gave a curt nod as though it were old news, motioning for me to continue.

"What you may not know, is that I helped get him there. He owes me."

Expressionless, Asmoday waited for me to sweeten the pitch.

I did my best, though I couldn't help but twist the knife a little. "Though Gabriel seems to have turned his back on his former allies, I have no doubt Duke Forcalor, and his newfound friends, would be more than willing to reward your loyalty to the right cause."

He drained his glass and sat silent. I knew what he was thinking so I headed it off. "Away on business, Baalth would, no doubt, be appreciative of someone looking out for his interests, especially if things in Heaven are as bad as they seem. It's only a matter of time before the war spills over and affects the rest of the realms." Though I shouldn't have told Asmoday that Baalth was gone, he probably already knew. Besides, he wasn't in a position to take advantage of the info. While it might come back to bite me in the ass later, I could worry about it then, if I was still alive to care.

He laughed, a hint of life finally coloring his voice. "It already has."

"The storm?"

He nodded, accepting our arrangement by default. His powers bound to Baalth, there could be no contract between us. He had only my word. With no other offers on the table, it was apparently enough.

Asmoday stood and went to refill his glass. "Lucifer once told me a story." His wine replenished, he sipped at it and returned to his seat. "After a fierce argument with God, he stormed through the Garden of Eden, on his way to Earth. As he neared the Tree of Life, he noticed small black dots spring up and speckle the trunk. As he moved closer, the dots grew, the blackness spreading.

"Intrigued and curious, as Lucifer had always been, he set his hand upon the tree and the trunk split about his fingers, a festering wound exploding beneath. In the wake of its ashes, life around the Tree withered." Asmoday smiled, his face becoming animated. "Uriel, perhaps sensing the Tree's distress, arrived and chased Lucifer from the Garden before he could experiment further, but the damage had been done. Soon after, we were cast from Heaven, barred from setting foot in Eden, forever."

My mind spun in dizzying circles as it tried to piece everything together. "So, it's not something Gabriel is doing directly, but rather a consequence of the war in Heaven?"

Asmoday raised his glass in a mock toast. "Created in paradise, the Tree is sensitive to its environs. Assailed by hate and rage, bathed in the bloodshed and death of war, it suffers. The blood of angels wears upon its sensitive bark. As its roots are woven through the entirety of existence, as it suffers, so shall we all."

"Which means there's gonna be more storms."

"Unless tranquility is returned to the Garden, they'll grow worse, devouring everything in their path."

Damn. Why can't it ever be good news? It's always the end of the world, the Apocalypse, Armageddon—blah, blah, fucking, blah. Just once I'd like to wake up and hear, "*Today's forecast will be mostly happy, with no chance of death.*" Or maybe there could be a blowjob storm. I'd drag my fat ass out of bed for that.

"I guess this means I'm going to Heaven." Asmoday and I both chuckled at that. "The only problem is, Gabriel has barred all the portals and the Nephilim have plopped their asses outside Eden's gate. It's not like I can just stroll up to it and knock." I thought back to what the old warrior had said. "Is there some way to open the gates from the outside? A key, maybe?"

Asmoday raised an eyebrow. "Perhaps." He set his glass aside and walked to one of the cluttered bookshelves, his finger leading the way as he read through the titles with a bored casualness. At last, he pulled out a thick leather tome and flipped through it, the pages creaking in the bind. "Ah, here it is." He lifted the book to show me the page, and then began to tell me what it said.

"It was rumored that during his exile, after the murder of his brother, Cain longed for God's forgiveness. However, as he was banished from His heart, Cain's prayers no longer reached God's ears. As such, he devised a plan to confront God in person, so to speak. It was said he learned of a way to enter Eden. He had found a key of sorts, but ultimately chose not to go through with his plan. His reasons for not doing so are unclear, but it is implied the cost was too much for him to bear."

"Is it true?"

Asmoday gently placed the book back on the shelf. "Honestly, I know not." He returned to his seat. "Outcasts as we were, the Fallen had no interest in a Heaven we could never attain while God still ruled. If there was such a key, its location died with Cain."

The information was like a striptease; just when you got to the good part, the show was over. "Thanks for the help."

Asmoday smiled and a flash of his old demon self lighted up

his pale face. "I'll look for you when the crisis has passed."

Anything but subtle, I got the hint. "I'll stay true to my word, Asmoday. You have my...uh, word." I smiled back, thinking Scarlett might not be so honorable. "See you soon."

Frustrated by how little I'd actually learned, I returned to the gate. Once inside the circle, I felt the portal trigger and I was on my way back to Earth. Scarlett wasn't gonna be happy, but at least I had an idea where to start.

It could only go downhill from there.

Chapter Six

After rounding up Scarlett and dropping by the house for a quick fix of my uncle's blood, I put in a call to DRAC for help. Not ten minutes later, Katon and Michael were at my door and we were on our way, courtesy of a Rachelle portal.

While it wasn't common knowledge, though I guess it could be presumed, my uncle had a soft spot for Cain—at least until he became repentant.

Back in the early days, when Lucifer was still pissed at God, Cain was one of his early successes at getting under the Big Guy's skin. He was pretty proud of it. It was one of those stories that got him animated when he told it; and he told it often.

Though it all went south once Cain was sentenced to wander eternally, Lucifer kept tabs on him and even secretly helped him to settle down as a kind of thank you. When Cain died, Lucifer sent the family some gold to build him a monument. Rough as life was back then, they ended up spending most of the money to get by. They did save enough to construct a small cenotaph for Cain, though they chose to leave his name off of it to avoid God's wrath. My uncle was a little miffed by that, but he let it go. In the grand scheme of things, he had bigger issues to worry about around that time.

That made our starting point easy. We packed our bags and headed for northern Iran, just a short distance to the west of the Caspian Sea. Once we arrived, the oppressive heat of the desert settled over us. Though we had come from our own little desert of El Paseo, there was no way to compare the two. It was like stepping into an oven or standing too close to Jessica Alba. It was that hot.

Despite that, it was nothing like home. Low grasses and tiny shrubs stretched out as far as I could see. Surprisingly green, it was like stepping into a Hallmark card. There were none of the imagined wastelands of sand you see so often in movies depicting the Middle East. The Caspian within spitting distance, the area didn't lack for water and it showed.

The time difference screwed with me. It was morning when we left and now it was late afternoon. I took a second to catch my breath and get my bearings.

Surrounding us was an open plain, with several large hills popping up to the south. Just to the north, in stark contrast to the flatness of the plain, giant poplar trees sprung up tall and verdant orchards circled a small cluster of mud-brick huts. Dark shapes could be seen shuffling off in the distance, the sun at our backs as it crested over the sea.

"Here we are...the village of Noqdi." The row of blank stares told me my fellow travelers were impressed, or so I pretended. I gestured to the land behind us for a little bit of clarity. "Behold, the Land of Nod."

When Scarlett realized where we were, her eyes narrowed and glanced toward the distant mountains to the west; toward the earthly gate to Eden.

"Relax, cuz. Unless you can take out a hundred of the Nephilim, we've gotta find another way in."

Katon sighed, taking a gentle hold of Scarlett's sword arm. "It's more like a thousand, now."

Scarlett's head snapped toward Katon and he tightened his grip.

He nodded, daring her steely gaze. "It seems Gabriel has decreed amnesty for those who take up arms in his name. He intends to reward them with a piece of Heaven for their loyalty."

"Betrayer!" Scarlett shrugged loose of Katon. Her shimmering wings, the manifestation of her power, sprung from her back, their light blinding. She crouched, ready to leap into the air, an angel of fury.

Fearing for my balls, I stepped in front and blocked her. It was like using a Volkswagen Bug to stop a tank. I had to think fast or she'd bowl me over. "Ten or ten thousand, they can't do shit from outside Eden. As long as the Nephilim are sitting there, we know Uriel and Forcalor still stand." My hand on her chin, I pulled her fiery eyes to mine. "Twice now, we've been told of a key. That means, somewhere out here, there's a way to get into Heaven. Regardless what you believe your duty is, if we're not the ones to find that key then Heaven is lost."

She snarled and shoved me away, but she didn't take off.

Arguing with Scarlett was like tea-bagging a wolverine, only usually more fatal. It wasn't that she wasn't smart, quite the opposite, it was just that she was ruled by her emotions and had a hard time rationalizing things on the fly.

Unlike the Demonarch, angelic society had a rigid structure;

they followed God's commands, they smote His enemies, they defended Heaven. God led, they followed.

Now that He was gone, they struggled under the concept of free will, something they'd never tasted before. They'd only seen it in man, and you know how that turned out. It wasn't something they thought much about until it fell into their laps.

For Scarlett, whose bloodline was tainted by her father's devilish heritage, she had to go above and beyond to prove to the Choir she belonged. She turned her back on her past, and she'd succeeded in gaining their trust. With God out of the picture, the angels were all she had. That was until Gabriel struck them down in their sleep.

I understood her rage, but we needed her. Waving Katon over for support, I told her, "Save the Kamikaze antics. There's always another good day to die."

A willing Katon stepped alongside and gave her a warming smile. "We'll save them, Scarlett. Just give us some time."

Their eyes met and her wings dispersed as she loosed a quiet sigh. She nodded, giving his hand a quick squeeze. Much less likely to set her off than me, I was more than happy to let the enforcer take over. After a minute, they dropped down onto the grass and started to talk, Scarlett still somewhat aggressive in manner, Katon keeping his voice low.

Hopeful she'd stay put now, I turned to Michael. "Somewhere around here is a monument to Cain. Head over to Noqdi and *ask* the villagers what they know. We'll wait here." In the interest of avoiding unwanted attention and an international incident if we could help it, Rachelle had gated us in a little ways from the village.

"You got it." Michael gave a quick wave, a crooked smile on his lips for the length of the walk ahead of him and then drifted off. After just a few minutes, he was just another of the black shadows in the distance, his merging with those of the village.

The sun beating down on us like a masochist's wet dream, I watched Katon and Scarlett as they chatted. I felt a strange pang of something weird well up in my gut as they sat close, whispering. I felt the irrational urge to insert myself in the conversation or to break it up. Watching them talk so comfortably, Katon's hand on her knee, I wondered if what I felt was some twisted sense of jealousy.

Nah, that couldn't be it. It wasn't like I had feelings for Scarlett, certainly not romantic ones—she was my cousin after all—but the situation nagged at me for some reason. There was something about Katon's attention, even as oblivious as Scarlett was, that riled me up.

Then it hit me what it was—

—Katon blocked my view of her cleavage.

I stepped to the left a little and felt much better. We stayed that way until Michael came strolling across the grass toward us. Katon and Scarlett, seeing the mentalist, got to their feet as he arrived, my view once again obscured.

"It's just over that way." He pointed to the hills and trudged off. "Apparently, it's not much of a secret."

Thinking that was too easy, despite Michael's telepathic insistence, I went after him quick, my hand on my gun. Katon and Scarlett followed behind. In less than a minute, we crested the hill.

Just on the other side, a barren patch of scrubby land stretched out before us. Weather worn, wooden posts lined an area about thirty feet square. Set at its center was a pile of gray stone slabs, raised to about three feet high. Wholly unimpressive, it didn't give me much hope we were even at the right place, let alone that we'd find something.

As we approached the ancient cenotaph, shapes appeared on the stones, carved in bas relief on their faces. The colors having long since dried and cracked off, the images blended into the stones, their edges worn away by time.

Gently, I ran my hand across the nearest of the stones, clearing away the dust of centuries. The gritty sand fell away in little brown puffs, my confidence with it. Out in the open, with no barrier to defend it from the wind and rain, a number of the carvings had been smoothed to almost nothing. They were but whispers of what they'd once been.

Katon and Michael joined me in dusting off the cenotaph, while Scarlett stood back, her lip curled up in a sneer. After just a few minutes, the stones were clear of clinging dirt, the images displayed in all their muted glory.

The carvings abstract, made even more so by wear, they had no discernable pattern, their rhythm broken and scarred by centuries of weather. Unable to make heads or tails of what I was seeing, random biblical images abound, I circled the cairn examining what remained. As I stepped around to the right, my eyes lighted on a vague image set near the top of the stones. I ran my finger over it, clearing the remaining dirt from its face, believing

I recognized it.

Sudden context coming on like a light, I stepped to the back and smiled as another familiar figure stood out. Once more around the other side, everyone wondering what I was smiling about, I was rewarded with yet another carved representation I knew. Then returning the front, located as the others were, was one last carving that cleared my brain like a fart in a sauna; the gates of Eden.

Having been known to be an idiot, I examined the cenotaph for any obvious signs of it being more than just a monument. After a few minutes, I was satisfied it wasn't, the stones smooth and solid, leading me think my first instinct was right.

The hunt was on. "Grab your fig leaves, kids. We're gonna visit Mom."

Chapter Seven

While all I had to go on was a hunch, it made sense...to me at least. So, after a short portal trip, Rachelle dropped us off in Jeddah, Saudi Arabia; the burial place of Eve.

Night was settling in. Though doing little to stifle the overwhelming heat, it did cut down on the likelihood we'd be seen considering the cemetery we'd come to visit was set smack dab in the center of a residential area.

The pockmarked street that ran alongside the cemetery entrance was quiet, its traffickers having long since returned to the safety of home. Dilapidated houses lined the block, their cracked and crumbling walls little different from the rows of tombs that lay in the cemetery across from them. Darkened windows faced the street like dead eyes, seeing nothing.

In the distance beyond them, shadows of larger buildings loomed, their white tiled roofs standing out like the eyes of giants. A haunting male voice drifted through the air, a blanket of religious faith settling over the city.

Scarlett glanced about, her eyes scanning the gloom as the voice droned on. "You sure about this?"

I shook my head. "No, but it's all I've got." Adding together what Asmoday told me, and what I'd deduced from Cain's cenotaph, our search options were pretty limited.

However, common sense tells you, if you're looking for a key to a house, you look to the people that live in it, right? In our case, it was more like lived. This particular house only ever had three people call it home: Adam and Eve—*and* Lilith.

The representation of Lilith on Cain's monument is what clued me in. Gone from Eden long before Cain had even been conceived and never a part of his life, there was no reason for her image to be on his cenotaph. There wasn't any connection between them except that Lilith had once been married to Adam, and she had lived in Eden.

Unfortunately though, thanks in part to me, Lilith was dead. There'd be no asking her about anything. Her body lay in cold storage at DRAC, and none of her personal belongings were there. Of course, Adam and Eve were also long gone, which posed its own problems. As the burial place of Adam has never been confirmed, that left us with Eve. We could only hope she'd been buried with her worldly possessions and the key was among them.

"Let's get this over with," Scarlett muttered, darting across the potholed street.

Katon followed her and sidled up to the battered, closed green metal doors as Michael and I raced to catch up.

Unlike most cemeteries, this one wasn't fenced in with big metal gates out front. The entrance was through a plain, dusty tan building, which circled around in both directions before finally resolving into rock walls that enclosed the rest. A small alcove up front gave us a place to hide as we waited to get inside.

Katon fiddled with the simple lock while Scarlett looked away, trying to appear innocent as we actively broke into hallowed ground. She wasn't doing a good job of it.

Michael ran his hand over the light blue sign posted on the wall beside the entrance and chuckled low. "The mother of humanity is buried in a slum. How's that for respect?"

Scarlett turned on him, fire in her expression. "Did you expect something more from your people?" She didn't wait for an answer, slipping through the door Katon had propped open.

Michael feigned hurt, his hand on his heart, and went in behind her, chuckling quietly. Last, I slipped inside and eased the door shut.

The mausoleum portion of the cemetery ran in a half circle around the edge of the property, the inner section opening up and leading to the common graves arrayed outside. The outer wall was stacked flush with plain marble tombs, three high. They seemed to run on forever, vanishing into a white blur as they curved with the building and disappeared into the darkness.

Michael groaned. "None of them are marked. How are we going to find hers?"

I waved him forward as I got as close to the crypts as I could. "Don't worry, it'll stand out."

Even dead and gone to ashes, Eve's presence would still linger, a spiritual memory of times long past. It would be subtle, and we'd need to be close to sense it, but it'd be obvious in its uniqueness.

As I moved along the lines of tombs, I gestured for Scarlett to follow my lead. Her senses far more sensitive than mine, she'd pick Eve's footprint out if I missed it.

We'd traveled about halfway around the circular mausoleum when there was a crash off in the distance, muted hisses following it. Like a choreographed dance move, all of us drew our weapons and crouched low. We crept forward, quietly frantic voices drifting to us through the marble corridor. As we drew closer, I saw about ten figures huddled in front of the wall of crypts. Small chunks of concrete were scattered about their feet. One of the figures loomed over the rest, her massive frame impossible to miss: Venai. Twigs and the behemoth were nowhere to be seen. They were probably off somewhere licking their wounds.

Scarlett growled low in her throat when she saw the big woman and started forward. Katon and Michael followed her lead and flanked off to the left. No point in bothering to be slick with them rushing in, I went ahead and took the center track. We weren't doing subtle.

"Lose something, Venai? A key maybe?" I asked.

The Nephilim jumped and spun about as one, eyes wide. Venai snarled when she saw me and limped away from the crowd in a hurry, drawing a blue symbol in the air. In an instant, she had a portal open and was through it and gone, leaving her buddies behind as it vanished. As I glanced over their pissed off faces, they didn't seem to mind she'd abandoned them. They were looking for a fight.

So was Scarlett. Without a word, she dove at them. The Nephilim scattered before her. Two brilliant flashes and the closest of the group fell—more like flopped—to the floor looking like a morbid puzzle; the perfect gift for a mortician who's got everything.

Armed with a variety of weapons, the Nephilim pressed their number advantage. Unlike their pure-bred parents, they'd been amongst humanity long enough to value the effectiveness of a good gun.

Bullets whined past us, their reports thunderous in the confined mausoleum. Michael returned fire, his left hand raised in the air, fingers spread out. He shimmered and became hazy, his image distorting and becoming unclear. Though I knew he hadn't moved, it looked as though he were in ten places at once. Each reflection was a perfect copy of the first, but each appeared to be doing something different. It was confusing even for me.

Katon, a fan of the up close and personal, waded into the crowd, his blade a silvered blur. Its poison an afterthought, DRAC's enforcer cleaved his way through the Nephilim, his victims dead before the paralysis could even begin to take effect. After just a couple more, he and Scarlett would meet in the middle, the numbers already even.

Not to be left out of a winning fight, I let my gun loose. One of the stragglers caught a few bullets to the face and dropped without a sound. Unfortunately, because of the Nephilim's banished status, there wasn't a soul transfer, their energies not transferring over to me at death.

That sure didn't stop me from tying to kill them though.

I hit another just as Scarlett reached him, the shots whipping him into her blade. He went down in bloody heap, a patchwork of circles and squares—Live Action Tic-Tac-Toe.

In just seconds, the fight was over. Scarlett stood above the carnage, her face splattered in red, blood dripping from her blade. Katon, the more graceful of the two, looked immaculate. Not a drop of blood stained his leather outfit or ruined the sparkle of his spikes as he surveyed the ruin of the Nephilim. Not a body in the bunch twitched.

Michael came over and let loose a deep sigh. Not used to showing up until after the mess was made, he looked a little pale as he surveyed the scene. "You guys sure know how to handle yourselves."

"These are the runts of the litter," I told him as I put my gun away. "They were sent to do the grunt work while the big boys wait by the gate to stake their claim." My eyes went to the crypt they'd been tearing open, my senses drifting loose. I felt a tenuous tingle as they hit upon a gentle presence. "At least they made the searching part easy."

The marble face had been torn from the crypt and cast aside. Behind it was a wall of concrete, the tomb filled with it. The Nephilim had just started to chip away at the mass of concrete, jagged hunks broken loose and littering the floor.

I looked around and spied a sledgehammer, sighing as I picked it up. "We should have waited a few minutes longer."

"I'll watch the entrance," Scarlett said as she headed off, no doubt offended by our intended grave robbery.

Katon glanced from Scarlett to the crypt and back again, his hands stuffed deep in his pockets. He had it bad.

While I'm the last person who should ever give advice regarding women, I couldn't help myself. He looked lost, so unlike his normal self. "Go on, Katon, Mike and I have got this."

He stared at me a moment, then nodded, heading off after her. Once he was out of earshot, I turned to Michael. "She doesn't even know he's interested and he's already whipped."

To the soundtrack of Michael's throaty chuckle, I went to work. The hammer slammed into the concrete, shards flying as the sound reverberated through the room. Again and again I struck the concrete, cracks appeared and chunks crumbled away. After a few minutes, the concrete gave way and the hammer punched a hole in it, blackness appearing beyond. I knocked the hole bigger and peered inside.

It took a second for my eyes to adjust, and when they did, my stomach sank. There was nothing inside the tomb but dust. If there'd ever been anything there, it had long ago been looted. No symbols or signs stood out against the gray walls to lead us to the key. Only the wispy tingle of Eve's presence remained.

"Fuck!" I growled, hammering furiously at the concrete, my one lead turning to shit. Slabs gave way under the onslaught and crashed to the floor. Michael stepped back to avoid the flying debris.

I swung with intent, adrenaline and anger fueling my attack. The hammer plowed through the last few feet of concrete, showering me in dust and gray rock.

"Frank!"

I glanced over my shoulder to see Katon staring at me, his eyes narrow and red. Distracted, my swing went wild and smacked into the marble plate of the crypt above Eve's. It broke loose of its moors and fell to my feet, shattering with a loud crack.

Katon stormed over. "Can you be any louder?"

"Probably." I shrugged, motioning to the tomb. "It's empty."

He growled and looked past me, shaking his head. Taking the hammer from my hand and tossing it aside, he stepped over the wreckage on the floor and peered into Eve's tomb. Grunting, he then stretched and leaned into the crypt I'd accidentally opened.

After a moment, he sighed and stepped away, brushing the dust from his jacket. "There's nothing but a bone in the top one."

His words stuck in my ears, tickling my brain.

"A bone? Just one?" Michael asked as he came over to us, apparently catching the same vibe as me.

Katon nodded as I stepped past him, peeking into the crypt. My heart fluttered when I saw the ivory white thigh bone that lay inside. Untouched by time, the bone stood out from its gray surroundings, everything else withered away. I snatched it up and felt my senses tingle at the contact. The Nephilim had opened the wrong crypt.

"This is Eve." I held the bone out for them to see.

Scarlett returned right then and glanced at the bone before averting her eyes, but nothing could hide the smile on her face.

"So, this is the key to Eden?" Michael asked.

I thought about it for a second, then shook my head. "I don't think it's all of it."

Scarlett snapped her head around. "What? We desecrated a grave, Eve's no less, and you're telling us this isn't the key." Her words were a hurricane, stinging spray and bluster.

"I didn't say that, and technically, *I* desecrated a grave, well... two if you want to be picky." She put her hands on her hips and glared at me. "Asmoday told me Cain chose not to seek the key because he felt the cost was too high for his conscience to bear."

"As the key is clearly the bone of his mother, I can see why he thought that," she argued.

"Then why would his family put Lilith and Adam on the monument?"

"Because it's all three," Michael answered, catching on to what I was getting at.

I nodded. "That's the most likely presumption." Katon said nothing as Scarlett started in again. I waved her quiet. "If it were just one of the three he needed, Cain could have gone after Lilith. Given that he intended to beg for forgiveness for what he'd done, the last thing he'd want to do is murder his parents on the way to God's house. However, as Lilith was *persona non grata* in Heaven, mixing it up down under, Cain could have gotten away with killing her, perhaps even been rewarded for it."

Scarlett grumbled and looked to Katon. He met her gaze and nodded as he followed the line of logic. She stuck her bottom lip out and stayed quiet. She just liked to argue.

"If we're right, this gives us a big advantage," I said.

"Because we have Lilith in cold storage back at DRAC," Michael finished my thought.

"Exactly. Now all we need to do is figure out which bone is the one we need and we've got two of the three."

"How are we going to do that," Scarlett asked.

I shrugged. "I'm not sure, but we'll fig—" The loudspeaker blare of a telepathic connection tore through my head. Judging by the pained look on everyone's face, they were receiving the same message.

Abraham's voice broke in through the shrieking static. "Rachelle is coming to get you. DRAC has been attacked!"

Chapter Eight

The carnage was absolute.

We arrived in the middle of it. Blood pooled on the floor, thick and black. The air was pungent, the slaughtered meat stench of an *abattoir.* Crimson dripped from the ceiling in a fetid rain, the walls painted in claret. Pieces of DRAC security and office personnel were scattered in a macabre display, recognizable only by the remnants of their uniforms. There'd be no identifying these bodies.

Scarlett took one look and scurried through the shattered front doors. While no stranger to death, or the blood and guts that came with it, she knew these people had died because of what was going on in Heaven. Knowing her, she felt responsible.

Not a front line kind of guy, Michael followed her out gagging, his hand over his mouth. Katon stood there taking it in, his face carved deep with fury. His feral eyes burned as he looked to Abraham.

The appearance of contentment Abe had worn the last time I'd seen him was gone, six feet of metaphorical dirt piled over top. His eyes were red through his glasses, their lenses magnifying his sorrow. His lips trembled as he surveyed the scene, the bodies at his feet friends and co-workers; family. Once it all settled in, the toll on his spirit would be devastating, but he was a trooper. He'd make it through, for now.

He gestured further into the facility, as though barely able to lift his arm. "This is where we kept Lilith's remains." He confirmed what I'd already surmised. With a reedy sigh, he told us, "There's more."

Katon bowed his head and trudged deeper into the building. Though I didn't want to see what else had been done, my feet fell in line. A soldier does what he's told.

We made our way down a long hall that led to a pair of double doors, which had been torn from their hinges. They lay broken on the ground just inside the warehouse-sized room beyond.

On the other side, the slaughter continued. Though the body count seemed less, the abandon with which they'd been dispatched appeared to have doubled, at the very least. My math is a little shaky.

Nearly unidentifiable parts littered the entryway, slabs of meat and sheets of wet flesh stuck to the walls and floor. Fingers and toes, and the occasional manly vestige, were visible amidst the wreckage. Sightless eyes stared at us from broken orbits as skeletal grins sat on skinless faces.

We moved slowly through the ruin, the footing treacherous. At last we happened upon Lilith. Her body lay on the floor outside the cooler, discarded like so much trash. For whatever reason, they'd left her intact...mostly.

Her shirt had been torn open, exposing the grandeur of her marbled torso. While normally I'd have spent a few extra minutes on a sightseeing tour, death having failed to make a dent in her beauty, the gaping wound in her side drew all of my attention.

Brutal, with no hint of surgical influence, her side had been ripped open, exposing her ribcage. From its bony line a single rib had been snapped free and removed, exposing her desiccated heart. It lay sunken in the blackened well beneath.

At least it answered the question as to what bone we were looking for.

"Seems you were right," Katon told me, his voice subdued.

I turned and caught his eyes. "Yeah, give me a second to pat myself on the back."

Though it was somewhat vindicating to realize I had been on the right track, my conscience didn't need any more ghosts. Unsure of the specifics of Lilith's connection until we'd found Eve, I hadn't thought to warn Abraham, believing her body was safe where it lay. It never crossed my mind someone would come to DRAC looking for her. I hadn't expected people to die, but they had. I could have done something to stop it from happening.

Katon set his hand on my shoulder, apparently reading my mind. "This isn't your fault." I started to argue and he gave me a gentle shake. "Even if we had known what the Nephilim had planned, Lilith's presence here was supposed to be a secret. No one should have known where she was."

Our eyes met as I realized what he was getting at. "Great. So on top of everything else we've got going on, you think there's a rat inside DRAC, feeding the half-breeds information?" I started to pace. "So where does that leave us?"

"The same place we were before we arrived here." He gestured to Lilith. "We know the key requires the bones of the three original residents of Eden. We have one and the Nephilim have one, so we're still in the running. Now all we need to do is find out where Adam is entombed and retrieve the last of them. Once we have that, it won't be long before the Nephilim come to us."

Buried beneath all the black leather and spikes, the mean looks and bad attitude, Katon was an optimist. "Yeah, Adam's grave has been hidden away for some four thousand plus years and we're just gonna stumble across it after a few minutes of looking?" I couldn't help but laugh.

"You're telling me you don't know anyone who was alive back then who could point you in the right direction?"

"Normally there'd be Baalth, but he's incommunicado, and Forcalor is in Heaven, out of reach obviously. Plus, I'm already up to my ass in favors to Asmoday and I don't have anything else to trade that doesn't involve me grabbing my ankles. So, no, all my sources are..." A thought came into my head, warm and sticky. "Hmm, maybe I do have someone I can ask."

Before I could elaborate, Rachelle burst into the room, her narrow face flush. Her normally flighty demeanor was replaced by one of cold urgency. "There's another storm coming."

My stomach sank at the news, remembering Asmoday's warning that they would only get worse. I hurried after her as she fled the room, Katon right behind me. There wasn't anything we could do but pick up the pieces, and I didn't really want to think about it.

Like a Kansas trailer park during tornado season, I was going along for the ride.

Chapter Nine

Rachelle plopped us into a downtown alley near the edge of the storm, just as the thick white clouds began to form. Purple flashes of lightning crackled to life overhead as the roiling mass washed over the sky like torrential waves. In just seconds, they filled the horizon with light, the ashen snow drifting down, the air still.

Scarlett winced and bit her lip as the storm's spiritual decay washed over us. She stood strong this time. Michael stumbled and nearly fell as his psychic sensibilities fell under siege. Katon steadied him.

"Take this and go back with Rachelle," I told Mike as I handed him Eve's bone. I quickly explained what I wanted Rachelle to do with it, then shoved him toward the portal.

Grateful, with only a hint of guilt on his pained face, he leapt inside the glowing tear. Rachelle sealed the portal behind him, her eyes downcast as she disappeared. The muffled crack of preternatural thunder drew my attention back to the storm.

I'd hoped we'd be able to rescue people before things got too bad, but the fall had already become a blizzard, downtown a whitewash of murderous snow. We moved out onto the street, a morbid magnetism drawing us closer to the edge. The acrid scent of decay, a lifetime of rot compressed into a single moment, burned my lungs and settled bitter on my tongue.

Though it was Saturday, the traffic downtown was only slightly less than it would have been during the hectic week. People milled about in the kill-zone, looking up in awe at the falling snow, a rarity in the desert climate. Their amused smiles and cheerful banter turned to terror as the first of the flakes settled over them. Screams erupted as death gnawed at their flesh. Panic set in.

Though I knew there was nothing I could do, my conscience screamed at me to act. Unable to go to them, I called them to me. It was little more than nothing, but it was all I had to offer.

"Come this way. Hurry!" My voice cracked with the force of my words as I waved them on.

Katon and Scarlett joined in as those nearest the edge bolted in our direction. Those in vehicles whose metal roofs sheltered them just long enough, made it out, the smell of burning rubber mixing with the harsh air. Those just a little further back were caught in the chaos. Cars slammed into one another as the fall ate its way inside. Many scrambled free only to meet their fate under the wheels of their fellow victims or at the hands of the relentless storm, no mercy shown by either.

The people on foot had it the worst. Instinct driving them to cover, they huddled in doorways and under flimsy awnings. They clutched to their wounds as they stared wide-eyed toward the sky. Death delayed but a moment, those who couldn't make it inside fell beneath the white ash, their screams seared from their mouths as their bodies disintegrated into ash.

The few who made it out of the storm, after the snow had struck, were no better than those who'd fallen beneath it. Scored, blackened rot festering in bloodless wounds, they lay screaming in the streets, agony in their every movement as they were eaten away. Shock settled in for many, thankfully numbing their last few moments.

We helped all we could, pulling them free in a pitiful attempt, but death would not be denied.

Above us, the buildings that towered over downtown were gnawed away. Floor by floor they disappeared under the drift of white, dust and smoke heralding their destruction. As the snow built up, the buildings came down faster, their supports collapsing beneath them. To a background of purple flashes, they fell from the horizon, dust and debris adding to the chaos and death in the streets.

My stomach a mass of churning acid, I turned away and stumbled back into the alley, eyes on the ground. I couldn't watch it any more. Gasping for clean air, I made my way toward the back of the alley when my senses suddenly lit fire. I whipped my gun out and looked up to see a black mass gathering before me.

My heart stuttered a beat, and then slowed as the darkness coalesced, its form becoming humanoid. As the figure took shape, adrenaline sparked a wildfire and my heart thundered back to life.

Before me hovered Azrael—the Angel of Death, better known as the Grim Reaper.

Unlike the rest of the archangels, Azrael lurked behind the scenes, out of sight. Save for rare exceptions, were you to see him, he would be the last person you ever saw. He was the death of the party.

Dressed in the stereotypical flowing black robes, he floated a foot above the ground, a swirling abyss of obsidian roiling beneath his feet. His pale hands were crossed before him and he stared at me through crimson eyes, literal flames flickering in the deep sockets. His face was gaunt, skeletal features pressed tight against paper thin flesh.

"Greetings, Triggaltheron," his voice drifted to me, the smell of the morgue.

Stunned he knew who I was, I didn't immediately realize he'd used my given name. "Here for the show?"

He glanced up at the storm a moment, then back to me, his narrow lips set in a grim line. "Though it does make for a pleasant view, I'm here to pass on a warning. Leave the affairs of The Kingdom to the denizens of Heaven. End your search for Cain's key and do not join the war. It is not your concern."

"In case you haven't noticed," I gestured to the clouds, "Gabriel's pissing match has extended way beyond the boundaries of Heaven. He's made it my concern by bringing it to Earth. If he wanted to keep it private, he shouldn't have whipped it out in public."

Azrael stared at me, his gaze frigid—an amazing feat considering the fire in his eyes. "Destiny has been set in motion. You cannot bring it to heel." He floated closer, his hands held out before him. "I have no desire to harm you, Triggaltheron, but I will do what I must, though it would pain me to betray your father's trust."

My world turned red. "First off, don't call me by that name. Secondly, don't you ever fucking mention my father again!" Unbidden, my energies came to the front, my hands glistening with power.

Azrael stood his ground, a cadaverous smile crossing his pale lips. "There is so much you don't know about him. Your history is a revisionist's myth."

"I know he died at my hands for what he did to my mother, his soul forever condemned. That's all I need to know."

He chuckled. "You prove my point, little demon. That's but a sentence in the tome of your father's life, though you cannot see it, blinded as you are by the lies you've so eagerly swallowed. You know nothing." He floated a step closer, the flames in his eyes flaring up. "Mind my words and turn your back on Heaven so you may live. Then, when your heart has shed its woeful burden, come to me and I will tell you of your father's truth."

"You can shove *that* truth up your ass." While I knew I was pushing my luck, I didn't care. He couldn't hurt me any worse than he already had.

The sperm donor who fathered me was dead. I'd stared into his hollow eyes as I carved him apart, piece by bloody piece. His life, his history, his everything, was erased in a frenzied bloodbath, and then cast to the pyre. The look of terror on his dying face was the only memory of him I kept; there wasn't room in my heart for any more.

Azrael bowed his head and drifted back, his hands once more clasped at his waist. "You choose to remain blind and deny who you really are. Such a pity. Your ignorance will cost you your life one day, or perhaps worse." He grinned feral. "Our paths shall cross again, Triggaltheron. I pray it is under better circumstances."

The last word his, he took his leave. Dark billowing clouds welled up from the maelstrom beneath his feet, their blackness enveloping him. In but a moment, his figure was obscured, the obsidian shifting to gray, then to nothing. He was gone.

My head in a fog, I left the alley to find Scarlett and Katon where I'd left them. They still stared at the storm as though I'd never left. While its bright clouds were fading, its fury spent, theirs still boiled on the surface, peppering my senses with rampant bee stings.

Unlike the first storm that erased four city blocks as though they never existed, there'd been too much here to completely wipe away in the short time the storm had raged. What had once been a panoramic view of steel and glass was gone, the clearing sky flooding in to take its place.

Whittled away, all of the top floors were missing, some of the lower sections having crumbled underneath. Many of the mid-floors still stood, no doubt filled with people too terrified to even go near the windows, let alone come outside now that the storm had ceased.

Where the streets had been, a murky lake had begun to form, disintegrated water pipes spewing their loads unchecked. Several geysers erupted like volcanoes from where there'd been fire hydrants just minutes before. Water flowed into the exposed sewers, filling the air with the rancid stench of downtown's collective ass. Fortunately, it appeared as though the power to the area had been severed at some point, otherwise we'd have been looking at the world's largest—and most horribly fragrant—hot tub.

Scarlett looked terrible. Her face was pale and stained with red blotches of disgust. Her hands, clutching to Katon, were bone white and trembling. They stood out like spotlights against the enforcer's blackened leather arm. She looked as though she'd fall over if he weren't there to support her.

He didn't look much better. His jaw was clenched so tight I thought he was Glenn Danzig. The vein at his temple throbbed a blast beat, speed records broken in its wake. He clung to Scarlett, staring at the destruction through the tiny slits of his eyes, feeding off her discomfort. Torn between duties, they stood rigid, likely waiting for a sign as to what to do. Though my stomach still sang with bile and my heart hung so low it was in my boots, I wasn't so conflicted.

Most of the people still inside the remaining buildings would be fine, sheltered as they were from the storm. As for those in the ones that collapsed, well...let's just say we hadn't come equipped to deal with them. I'd left my mop and bucket at home.

A realist, I knew our time would be better spent hunting down the key pieces, but I also knew that wasn't gonna happen.

"Why don't you two take care of the survivors while I track down Adam's grave?"

Scarlett turned to me, her face a wash of surprise and uncertainty. Questions loomed in her big green eyes.

There wasn't any point in lying about my reasoning. "Look, you're too caught up in all of this to be any use to me." I motioned to the ruin of downtown. "Do your good deed and get it out of your system, so when I come back, you're ready to focus on what we need to do to stop all of this."

Her look turned to a glare at my honesty, but she knew what I was getting at; her effort would be a Band-Aid on a severed limb—useless. Despite that, she couldn't help herself. It was in her nature and nothing was gonna convince her otherwise.

A sliver of a smile graced her lips and she nodded. Then with Katon in tow, she ran off toward the nearest building that hadn't yet come down. Once they were gone, I let out a big sigh.

The continued search for Eden's key was gonna put us at odds with Azrael, and that was a sobering thought. Even with the power Baalth had gifted me, plus Katon and Scarlett at my side, we didn't stand a chance if the Angel of Death chose to step in.

While the threat of abject failure and horrible death were par for the course in my life, it didn't stop my asshole from puckering up in brown-eyed fear. Once more I was sticking my neck out and risking slaughter in order to save the day and keep from being killed.

Irony is a motherfucker sometimes.

Chapter Ten

My whirlwind day a case study in the effects of sleep deprivation, I stopped off to grab a stout cup of coffee on my way to meet the one person who might know where Adam had been buried: Longinus, the Anti-Christ, newly resurrected thanks in part to yours truly.

A quick phone call put me in touch with his daughter, Karra, my first true love. It was an awkward call, the sound of her voice triggering all sorts of sloppy memories, but I muddled through it without having to change my jeans.

She arranged for me to meet her father at my house, which made things easier. With the backroom gate, he could pop in without drawing the attention of my neighbors.

After McConnell pulled his *Three Little Pigs* routine and blew my house down, they kept a wary eye on me. Even with Michael Li smoothing things over, his mental adjustments made with a light touch, there'd been enough weird crap in the area to make them suspicious. The storms would only make things worse.

Despite DRAC's best effort to keep things under wraps, news of the annihilation had hit the networks. Appearing worldwide, the storms left havoc and death in their wake—and a whole butt-load of questions no normal human could reliably answer. Though, to give the networks credit, they were doing their best to bullshit their way through it.

The people in my neighborhood were no doubt wondering what I'd done to cause this, so it would be best if no one in full plate armor and satanic regalia, wielding a sharp pointy stick, came knocking on my door in broad daylight. You can only use the medieval re-creation excuse so many times before people start to ask uncomfortable questions about where you're sheathing your sword at night.

So, back at home, I hung out with Chatterbox as I waited for Longinus to arrive. To lighten the mood, I popped a Nasty Savage CD in the player. Me and the zombie head rumbled our way through *Fear beyond the Vision*. Chatterbox, sans balls, or anything from the neck down for that matter, provided the air raid siren falsettos. For a head without lungs, he sure could belt out the tunes.

We'd just gotten into *Metal Knights* when my senses pinged on my gate becoming active. I shut the CD off, much to Chatterbox's wailing chagrin, and willed the portal to receive our guests.

A few seconds later, Longinus moved down the hall, his arms tucked in front to keep them from becoming wedged against the walls. Karra was a little ways behind him. Chatterbox glanced at them, then lowered his eyes, his chin tucked as though he were attempting to bow.

Even more massive than I remembered, Longinus moved with leonine grace, his wild mane of black hair flowing down his back. As he entered the living room, he straightened out and it was like having a door slam in my face, the light dimmed in his presence.

The deep bronze of his face made him look like he was made of rich leather, his dark eyes ageless. He took a moment to look me over, then smiled wide, his face coming alive above his thick black beard.

"Triggaltheron." He proffered his hand and I took it, his steely grip a humbling experience. "I had not expected you to seek me out so soon." There wasn't any censure in his tone, but I suddenly felt guilty like I'd called a girl before the three day rule was up.

Suddenly unsure, I cast a quick glance at Karra and saw an easy grin brightening her lips. She winked and it did a lot to assuage my uncertainty.

"Well, neither did I, but it seems a couple of rogue archangels had other ideas." I waved them to a seat, hoping my sofa would survive his bulk.

He laughed softly, letting Karra take her seat first. Once they were settled, I plopped down in my old Lazy-Boy, which let out a loud squeak.

"I presumed your call had something to do with that mess up there." He gestured skyward. "While I knew I'd returned to a different world, I would never have imagined a Heaven overthrown by Gabriel."

"Times have changed, and not for the better. At least in the old days, you knew who the bad guys were. Nowadays, it's every supernatural for himself."

Longinus nodded and settled back with a chuckle. Karra slipped into view, no longer blocked by his barrel of a chest. I found myself staring at her, the past washing over me in pleasant waves that prickled my skin. She met my eyes with a sweet smile and leaned forward, her lithe body uncoiling. My face heated, I looked back to her father before my body found another way to show its appreciation.

"I wouldn't have come to you with this, but I had nowhere else to go. Gabriel's war is turning the world on its head and I need to stop it before it tears Earth apart. I need some information that might help put an end to it all."

"I'm loath to involve myself in the affairs of Heaven, but I will honor my pact to you and tell you what I can." He stood and paced to the middle of the room, his face sullen. Karra's expression seemed to echo his. "I cannot, however, bring myself to assist you directly. Though the old order has been cast aside, I have no forgiveness in my heart for those of the Kingdom." His steely gaze settled on me. "With that in mind, ask of me what you will and know that I will answer truthfully in gratefulness for your part in my resurrection."

I didn't even bother to sigh, having expected no less. Things never came easy when you had to deal with demons, no matter what they said they'd do for you. "I need to know where the earthly remains of Adam are buried."

While I knew I might be blowing my favor and breaking a part of my promise to Asmoday, there were more important things to consider. Besides, he was a demon...he'd understand getting screwed, even if he didn't appreciate it.

Longinus looked at me through narrowed lids. "An unexpected request, for sure." He stared at me for a moment longer, and just when it became really uncomfortable, he continued. "You seek to enter Eden?"

No point in lying, I answered, "Yes. I hope to offset the balance and help Uriel and Forcalor drive Gabriel away from the Garden and out of Heaven."

A crooked smile fluttered to his lips. "For certain, a valiant plan, Triggaltheron, but there is something you must know before you throw yourself upon the willing spears of your enemy."

That sounded positive.

"As it is, the Tree of Life struggles to maintain its integrity. The insertion of additional forces into the Garden may well be the tipping point that sounds its knell."

Hey look, another challenge. Never enough of those in my life. I sunk deeper into my chair, rubbing at my temples. "Will the storms worsen?"

He shook his head. "They will end with the Tree's death."

He paused and I could imagine the guillotine slicing down. "However—" *Kchunk*! "—the ruin of Earth is the least of our concerns. Should the Tree of Life fall, the children of Heaven *and* Hell will suffer for its destruction." A slow, deep sigh oozed from him. "We will all become mortal."

It took a second for his words to sink in, my mind unwilling to register their meaning. Thoughts tumbled from my mouth, in no particular order, and I took a second to string them into a coherent sentence. "We'd be human?"

"Not quite, though certainly close enough that the difference would be negligible. We would fall sick and age, become infirm and die as all mortals must. Though we'd retain our magic, it would be limited by the frailty of our bodies, its use a grindstone upon our remaining years. Given the aggressive nature of our kind, we would likely soon become extinct."

My stomach churned as I thought about that, my head spinning like I'd been on a three-day binge. While I didn't have a whole bunch of power to give up, my magic humble and only recently acquired, I had gotten damn used to the idea of living a long, sexually-unfulfilled life. As rarely as I got laid, another eighty years just wasn't gonna cut it. That'd be like three more times.

"So now, all I have to do is figure out a way to end the war in Heaven in order to stop the storms from devastating Earth while at the same time, I have to keep the Tree of Life from dying or we become mortal." I sank further into my chair, my brain threatening to commit suicide by leaping from my eyes. "Maybe I missed the memo, but I don't remember being promoted to the savior of the universe. I sure as Hell didn't get the pay raise or the sexy spandex outfit." In it just as deep as me, I looked to Longinus, hoping he'd throw me a bone; one that didn't require me to get on my knees. "You're willing to bet your immortality on me succeeding?"

He smiled and shrugged. "I am not the man I was once, Triggaltheron. The cold embrace of Death has sobered my perspective. While I do not relish the loss of my strength, I believe I can find peace growing old with my daughter." He turned to her, his smile beaming off his face.

Karra hugged him quick and mussed his long beard playfully.

The sweetness of it almost made me gag. I hid the look of disgust as they turned back around, cheese plastered all over my face.

Though I couldn't fathom the changes that had turned Longinus from conquering lion to sedate lamb, I had to respect his decision, even if I didn't like it.

After he'd given me the location of Adam's grave, I thanked him and prepared the gate for their departure. Longinus ushered Karra toward the backroom, his hulkish form blocking her from sight once more. It was just one more disappointment piled on top of an altogether shitty day.

I sighed as she pulled open the door and motioned her father inside, her eyes catching mine with a sideways glance.

"Go on ahead, I want to talk to Frankie for a minute," she told him.

My heart stuttered at her words. We had a lot of history, the most recent not so great. No matter where the conversation went, it would be awkward.

Longinus narrowed his eyes and looked back and forth between us a couple of times, then gave an amused chuckle.

"Good luck in your quest, Triggaltheron. I suppose we'll know soon enough if you succeed." He bowed shallow, and then went to the portal.

Power flickered in the room as the gate amped up and whisked him away, though I can't say I actually saw him go. Uncomfortable about checking out Karra while her father was around—the threat of horrific death a surprisingly effective deterrent—I took full advantage of her watching him leave, her back turned to me.

Dressed in a pair of blue jeans that took form-fitting to new depths, and my imagination with it, I admired her shape in the fluttering light of the portal. Oh, what I would have done for a jar of Vaseline and a Slip N' Slide.

Her pink T-shirt fit snug, the toned muscles of her back defined by its tightness. Her wild blond hair, the tips dyed black, ended just above the gentle curve of her neck. The pale flesh called to me and before I knew it, I had taken several unconscious steps toward her.

Longinus gone, she spun around and I shut my mouth quick, covering it with my hand to hide any drool that might have run amok. She smiled and took my other hand, leading me back to the living room. There, she pushed me down onto the couch and dropped beside me. Our thighs pressed together, mine tingled at the contact. The subtle scent of her perfume entrenched itself inside my nose and I found it hard to concentrate. I found a lot of things hard right then.

"I'm sorry we haven't had a chance to talk since...you know, but it's been hectic catching my father up and getting him settled.

Now's probably not a good time either, but I wanted to speak with you before you ran off, just in case..."

Even though she'd let the last part hang, the words flowed over me like a gentle breeze. Like a politician in an off-election year, I didn't hear a single one of them. My peripheral vision combat-honed, I stared into her hazel eyes, but all I could see was the glory of her ample chest. It was a pleasure in pink.

"Yeah...busy...uh huh."

She just laughed at me and leaned back in the couch to look over at Chatterbox. "I see you've kept the old boy. How you two getting along?"

"*Maaaassssstttterrrrrrrr*," he mumbled in an airy voice, once more doing his best to bow.

My eyes suddenly focused, I looked to Chatterbox then back to Karra, the door of realization slamming into place. I'd never really thought about how Karra had managed to manipulate me in her quest to resurrect her father. She'd always been a step ahead, but there it was right in front of me; Chatterbox.

We'd chased the clues Michael had picked from his undead brain, ultimately finding the trap by following his directions. They'd all been programmed in from the start. The sudden sense of it all settled over me. I sat back and whistled low.

"You dropped Chatterbox into the grave with me on purpose." I'd presumed Reven had set up the resurrection spell and Karra had simply triggered it by dousing Longinus in Lilith's blood, but it never occurred to me that it was Karra's spell to begin with. "You're a necromancer." It explained why Chatterbox was still animate, having survived Reven's death.

She gave a half-nod-shrug as an easy smile graced her lips. "A useful profession when you're trying to bring your father back to life, don't you think?"

Couldn't argue with the logic, but necromancy wasn't an easy skill to master. It took a lifetime to become powerful enough to raise someone like the Anti-Christ. Things started to make sense. "Is that why you disappeared, to learn how to bring him back?"

She nodded. "Among other reasons. While he never said anything, I couldn't imagine your uncle letting me stay close to you in Hell, after what he'd done to my father. I was scared and angry, and I wanted Lucifer to pay. At the same time, I was worried he'd sense that and come after me, maybe even hurt you in the process. There was no way I could have lived with that." She loosed a quiet sigh, her thigh pressing harder against mine. "I fled Hell and took up with Reven to learn necromancy, but I never wanted to leave you behind."

The past rushed up and kicked me in the balls. My chest thundered like stampeding cattle as I remembered how my uncle had dismissed my pain at losing Karra. He'd done so because he knew he was to blame. He'd chased her away as a convenience to himself. His petty revenge against Longinus had torn her from me and he had waved it off as inconsequential, as acceptable collateral damage. It had meant nothing to him, but to me, it had been my whole world. Melodramatic as it may sound, she had been everything then.

I felt my face flush as I hopped to my feet, the urge to destroy something burning at my fists. My eyes steamed with memories, fury leaking down my cheeks. In the span of an instant, my mind flittered back in time to question every decision Lucifer had made on my behalf. I couldn't help but wonder for whose benefit they'd really been made. Had they ever been for me?

I jumped when Karra closed her hand over mine, not even realizing she'd come up behind me. She pressed hard into my back, her arm tight around my waist. Her heartbeat thudded against me, insistent in its steady thump. My breath caught in my chest as she settled her chin on my shoulder, her nose nuzzling into my ear.

Goose bumps took wing in flocks down my arms as Karra's breath wafted over the nape of my neck.

"I'm sorry," she whispered, the words soft caresses. My anger crawled away to die, its death unnoticed in the tumultuous inferno of my thoughts.

She pulled me in even closer, gentle kisses peppering my ear, the line of my jaw, and cheek, stealing my tears away.

Rigid, in more ways than one, I couldn't move. My arms and legs were locked in place. It was if I had been transported back in time, my dead and buried shyness reborn, excitement winding a suffocating coil around my body. My vision flickered as waves of butterfly tingles shot through me, my hands trembling. My thoughts exploded and reformed, then exploded again before they could reach coherence. The gooey corpses of logic and reason were spewed against the walls of my irrational, terrifying lust.

Then she bit me.

That was all it took.

The twin drum beats of my heart and crotch rumbled a rally and kicked the shit out of my passive inner child. The little fucker deserved it.

My own man again, at least to the extent my penis would allow, I spun on Karra and kissed her fierce, my hands entangled in her soft hair. Her insistent lips were a siren's call, luring me ever deeper as we pressed into one another. Male directives asserting themselves, my hands drifted across her shoulders and down her arms to settle on the firm curves of her ass.

In that moment, the key of bones was forgotten, but one Heavenly gate I wanted to pry open. I already had the key for that.

So much taller than Karra, I lifted her into my arms and settled her crotch against mine, the fit electric. She ground into me as transient images of someone starting a fire flickered in the background of my mind, driven by the repetitive *fwip* of rubbing jeans. Shudders trembled through me as she moaned into my ear, whispering things you normally need to pay $3.95 a minute to hear. Her tongue stung my neck with wet serpent kisses.

Unable to contain myself any longer, I moved to the couch and dumped her onto it. Romance run out of town with a bullet in its ass, I yanked her boots off and tossed them over my shoulder. The tinkling crash of glass sounded behind me, but I barely noticed as I went toe-to-toe with the button on Karra's painted-on jeans. At last, I managed to pop it free with a grunt. Her zipper barely down, I whipped her pants off and sighed at finding her pantyless. Like an altar to the god of all mans' gods, I felt compelled to kneel and worship, to loose my tongue with flickering songs of the coming rapture. Hallelujah!

Karra had other ideas. She latched onto my belt and undid it with nimble hands, her fingers at my zipper a second later. They were inside a split-second after that.

I nearly fainted as her hand wrapped around my erection. What little blood I had left in my brain made a mad dash for my dick, unwilling to be left behind. Light-headed, I let her have her way with me as Chatterbox stared on with obvious and unabashed glee. He winked at me and licked his blackened lips in lascivious circles, cheering me on in a misguided effort to draw out the show.

"Baassseeeeeebaaaaallllll. Miiiiiicccccckkkkkeeeeeeeeeeeey Maaaaaantllllllllllle. Roooooooosssssssiiiiiieeeeeeee Oooooo oooo'Donnnnnnnellllllll."

The last sent a sickened shiver down my spine. Not wanting to ruin the mood—nothing like the view of a decayed and severed head to take the wind from your sails—I locked my sights on Karra.

Her eyes narrow slits, her lips pursed, she yanked my penis out without bothering to unbutton my jeans. The quick scrape of zipper against skin did nothing to lessen my excitement. In fact, the sharp contrast only spurred me on. A groan slipped from me as she slid me inside her, our pelvis's colliding in our rush. Her warm wetness enveloped me as flash fires of ecstasy sparked out from my crotch in concentric circles, its heat searing.

Holding my neck, she pulled me to her, nose to nose, and stared into my eyes as I found my pace, her hips driving me on. Her panted breaths huffed in rhythm with mine, the air between us shared in shuddering gasps. After just a moment, a tiny whimper oozed from her lips and her eyes closed tight. Her hands shook at my neck as she drew my face to her still-clothed chest, her heartbeat thumping wild against my cheek.

Pressed against her heaving breasts, the barest hint of her fingernails biting into my sensitive flesh, the moment overwhelmed me. Unable to hold back, I clutched Karra to me as the rattle of orgasm crept over my skin. My face buried in her neck, her raspy voice urging me on, I let loose with a growl.

I twitched atop her as she ran her hand over my sweaty scalp, her teeth nipping at my ear lobe. We lay there quiet for several minutes, the only sound our receding pants. After a bit, I rolled to the side to take my weight off her and she turned into me, our faces just inches apart. The heat of her breath warmed my skin.

"I'm sorry," she whispered.

I put finger against her lips. "Don't." My anger at my uncle washed away in the flood of our passion, I didn't want to think about him or what he'd done. All I wanted was to revel in the closeness of Karra, to steal back the years as though she'd never been gone.

Not wanting to let go, I pulled her into me. Nestled into her neck, the light sheen of sweat stirred up by our sex felt cold against my face. The flowery scent of her hair filled my head with dreamy thoughts as I tightened my grip around her.

Her hand stroked my cheek, her finger tracing my ear in lazy circles. After a moment, far too short for my liking, she pulled away. "As much as I'd like to stay here with you, you're needed elsewhere." She slid off the edge of the couch and stood before me, the image seared forever onto my retinas.

Reality intruding once more, I groaned and sat up, my eyes unable to leave Karra as she rummaged through the wreckage of my living room to find her pants and boots. She tiptoed limberly through the shattered glass of my bookshelves and bent to retrieve her clothes. The visual reignited my waning crotch and I sprang to full mast again. With a sigh that was almost a sob, I watched her slide her jeans back on. I'd gotten all I was gonna get.

Dressed, she returned to the couch and gave me a firm kiss, her tongue lingering at my lips. "Put that thing away before you hurt someone." She poked its head with a finger and grinned at my reaction. I felt like Moby Dick in miniature. "Go save the world. There'll be plenty of time for us after that."

She laughed and ran her hand over my cheek as she stepped away. Unable to say anything, I watched her make her way down the hall and into the portal room. The sudden flux of energy and flickering lights signaled her departure, the dissolution of both filling me with an agonizing gloom.

Thinking back on what I'd said about Katon earlier, I apologized out loud. "We men are weak." Apparently he wasn't the only one heading down the road toward Whipsville. Oh, how the mighty have fallen, one split-thighed encounter sealing the deal.

Though I was reluctant to wash away the smell of Karra, which clung so pleasantly to my skin, I needed a cold shower or I'd never be able to zip my pants back up. At last, I dragged myself to the bathroom and climbed under the frigid spray. It took several long minutes, my penis bound and determined to resist, before icicles started to form on my balls and it gave in, a limp, defeated shade of blue. My teeth clacking together, I climbed out of the shower and dried off. Back out in the living room, Chatterbox greeted me with catcalls and lurid commentary.

"*Twennnnnnnnttttttttyyyyyyy-oooooonnneeeeee, Twennnnnnnnttttttttyyyyyy—ssssssspppllaaaaaaaaaaaaaat!*"

So what if the shower took longer? I gave him the finger and got ready to go.

My gun loaded, ammunition stockpiled, I slipped a wrapped vial of my uncle's blood in my pocket, all while trying not to think of who it had come from. Despite the angry thoughts that crept to life unbidden, its value outweighed my petty misgivings. I could be stupid later. You could almost set your watch by it.

The pleasure of Karra soured by Lucifer's unexpected betrayal and the slaughterhouse I was about to return to, I ground my teeth and headed out to collect Scarlett and Katon. It was time to do what I do best.

Stumble into danger and hope I make it out alive.

I should really start thinking about a plan B.

Chapter Eleven

After I'd rounded up the Wonder Twins, their moods dark and palpably angry, we hitched a ride with Rachelle to where Longinus had told me Adam had been buried.

The Temple of the Holy Sepulchre; Golgotha.

The old Jerusalem site but one location of a number rumored to contain the mortal remains of Adam, the stories have always downplayed Golgotha as unlikely because it contradicts what is universally accepted as the truth of Christ's confirmed history. The Bible states he was buried in a tomb never before occupied. For Adam to be there first, that would have to be false, thus the location was discounted.

That's what you get when you have humans keeping track of things way beyond their lifespan and understanding. It's all conjecture and bullshit after a certain point. The most unlikely of options becomes reality.

So, there we were. Once again, the time factor played into our favor. Nighttime darkness in full swing, we wouldn't have to worry about sightseers tromping through the place. The most we were likely to run into would be a janitor or two, maybe a security guard. With all the storms battering the world, it was more likely we wouldn't see anyone.

While the church was far from modern, its historical and religious relevance precluding a high tech security system, trying to sneak in from the outside would have been a hassle we didn't need to attempt. So thinking, Rachelle dropped us inside the main chapel, into the Basilica of the Sepulchre.

Amusingly enough, we arrived right around the corner from a chapel dedicated to Longinus. I got a good laugh out of that and earned a vicious stare from Katon. Some people just don't see the humor in things, but I guess I couldn't really blame him.

Scarlett had been in Heaven when Longinus was resurrected, and probably didn't even know he was alive because of the war. There hadn't been a whole lot of time to chit chat and catch her up on things. Considering how sensitive Scarlett was at the moment, I guessed Katon didn't want me to drop that bomb just yet. It made sense. So when she looked at me with suspicious eyes and wondered what I was laughing at, I just shook my head.

"I never thought I'd be here, that's all," I lied, gesturing to the chapel around us. "Not really my scene, you know?"

The Basilica was awash in gold and reds, hints of white splattered throughout to limit the gaudiness of it all. The altar at the end of the chapel was dark and the numerous golden candle holders arrayed near the dais were unlit. The elaborate chandelier that held court over the center of the room glistened, ambient light reflected in the multitude of its crystal faces. A quiet creak echoed through the empty hall as it swayed in the gentle breeze that circulated through the chapel. The air was cool despite the heat outside, air conditioning most likely the one modern convenience that hadn't been overlooked.

Above our head, set at the very apex of the dome, was the Pantokrator mosaic. The illuminated image of a gloomy Jesus glared down upon us through brown eyes, a leather-bound book held in his hand. He didn't look pleased to see us. Can't say I blame him.

An angel, a demon, and a vampire walk into a church...

Stop me if you've heard this one before.

The yellowish-oranges of the center image, circled out to a ring of angels and saints, most of whom I recognized. It was kind of spooky considering our goal there, the likenesses of Gabriel and Michael hovering above us as though waiting to pounce. It sent a chill down my spine.

No time for sightseeing, we slipped out of the chapel and crept down the hall toward the stairs, which would lead us to the tomb of Adam. Off to our right was the Stone of Unction, where Jesus's body was said to have been bathed after his death. Displayed above it were eight, white crystal urns with gilded crosses set upon their faces. The golden slab beneath them lay empty, which was probably a good thing.

Thanks to the modern miracle of the internet—and no, I'm not talking about free porn, though that certainly ranks right up there—we were able to look at blueprints of the church. It made finding Adam's tomb so much easier.

Right across from the stone was a stairwell, which led below the chapel that contained The Rock of Calvary, where Jesus was said to be crucified. A little before my time, I'd have to take their word for it. If I remembered and survived, I'd ask Longinus about it.

We slipped down the stairs, noticing the chapel below was

bathed in darkness. Not that it was a problem, all of us able to see pretty well, it was just unexpected considering the rest of the church was somewhat lighted. As we neared the bottom landing, we heard a quiet thud, as though something heavy had been set aside.

I looked to Katon and he gave a grim nod, his sword already in hand. He gestured for me to swing to the right while Scarlett was to go left. That left the center for him, which was okay with me.

My gun out, I waited until Katon gave the signal, then shot out low. As I entered the room, my spidey senses gently tickled my neck. Near the far end of the chapel I spotted an elaborate marble sarcophagus raised on a short dais, its stone lid open and leaned against its side. Hunched over it was big, dark, and furry, his paw digging around inside the crypt as though it were a cookie jar.

"*Hey, Boo Boo. What do ya think is in that pic-a-nic casket*?"

Grawwl spun around and snarled. His voice rumbled like thunder in the acoustics of the chapel. He looked at Katon and Scarlett before the reddish glimmer of his eyes landed on me. He rose up to his full height and smiled pointy.

"Eek, you caught me. Whatsoever will I do?" A guttural chuckle rumbled up through his throat as he raised his muscular arms in mock surrender. "Guess you're not as dumb as you look."

Maybe I was. For the life of me, I couldn't figure out why Grumpy Bear was there looking for the key to Heaven. Outside of the chaos factor, I had no idea what the shifters and vamps had to gain by helping overthrow Heaven. Maybe Gabriel made them an offer too. It was all I could think of.

My brain on overload, I watched as Scarlett and Katon advanced slowly and I matched their pace to keep from being left behind. I was missing something. It was gonna nag me until it kicked me in the ass.

"Why don't you step away from the crypt and we can discuss your peaceful reintegration into polite ursine society."

His smile grew wider, his teeth brilliant white in the dimness of the room. "No need to worry about the key piece getting damaged, mutt. We've already taken steps to make sure it's safe and sound." He gestured over his shoulder.

Through an archway on the far side of the chapel, a werewolf strolled into the room, its reddish-orange eyes glimmering. It had a whitish streak of fur shaped kind of like a lightning bolt running vertically across its forehead. Though nowhere near the size of Grawwl, the new arrival had the same shit-eating grin stretched across its lupine face, which made them look like twins; at least as much as Danny DeVito and Arnold Schwarzenegger did. Cradled delicately in its clawed hands was a human skull, the empty-socketed face turned toward us.

"I'd like you to meet Rumble." The werewolf winked and held up the skull. "The little guy there is Adam, the first of his oh-so-tasty kind. No pictures, please."

Grawwl took a step forward, his smile resolving into a snarl. "Now, if you'd be so kind as to hand over Eve, we can get on with our business. Make it easy for us and we'll go easy on you."

A cold chill wriggled down my spine as it became quite obvious the *we* he referred to wasn't limited to just him and pooch holding Adam.

From the same alcove Rumble had waltzed through, a pack of similar looking lycanthropes spilled into the chapel. All toothy smiles and sharpened claws, I stopped counting at around fifteen. Really, all the ones beyond that were just overkill.

Behind us, the multitudinous click of claws coming down the stairs and spreading out across the tile floor made it clear we were probably looking at about the same number of puppy dogs at our back. Grawwl had stacked the deck in his favor.

More of a cat person, I looked out over the sea of furry bobble-heads and sighed. Someone was gonna end up with fleas, no doubt about it.

I glanced at Katon and he shook his head when our eyes met. To his left, Scarlett had dropped into a defensive stance, a fierce grimace on her face. She was ready to go out with her boots on.

Me...not so much.

While I'm always up for a good scrap, and don't even mind racking up a few bumps and bruises along the way, I'm not really the martyr type. I have sensitive skin and there's nothing that irritates more than nails being driven through it.

Besides, with only one obvious exception, martyrdom isn't exactly the ideal route toward longevity beyond the mythological ideal. As a realist—he who runs away, lives to screw another day—I never saw the point in playing odds like that.

Grawwl glared at me and huffed, waiting for an answer. I huffed back as I mulled over my options and realized I really didn't have any. It made my decision easier, for what it was worth.

"I'll take Fuck the Big Brown Bear for $200, Alex." If I'm known for nothing else, I hope people can look back on my life and see me for who I truly was: spiteful to the end.

His muzzle rippling around his dagger-filled mouth, Grawwl growled low in his throat and shook his furry head. "You'll regret this, mutt."

For anyone keeping score, I already did.

The werewolves loped forward, all gnashing teeth and bad attitude. No room to go up, Scarlett spread her fiery wings and dropped low. Everto Trucido was a malevolent blur in her wake, hacking through the ankles of the wolves that were too slow, or too dumb, to get out of her way. They hit the floor howling, thrashing about as they clutched at their oozing stumps. They were pretty lucky that was all she cut off.

Katon, smooth as ever, stepped in to reenact the *Matrix* movies. Minute shifts in positioning helped him avoid the legion of flashing claws that whipped toward him. He lashed out lightning fast to counter. The air around him exploded in a crimson rain. The rich scent of blood filled the room within seconds.

Not to be outdone, I turned my attention toward the sea of werewolves behind us. Given the width of the chapel, its wide open spaces, I was at a tactical disadvantage as well as a numerical one.

So, in essence, it was pretty much the same as every other fight I'd ever been in. Good times.

Still exhausted, and pretty sure I didn't have the energy to just napalm their ranks like Rahim would, I had to be subtle. Too bad I don't do subtle well.

Fortunately, magic is all about imagination and I have that in oodles. So, before any of the werewolves got close enough to rip me a new one, I pictured thousands of tiny little spheres, like mystical ball bearings, and focused my energy into creating them. In an instant, they came to life, hovering in a coalesced, glowing bunch before me looking like a bundle of ugly grapes. The pack slowed when they saw them, the line spreading out, wary. They didn't know what the spheres were, but they had to know they weren't good; for them.

I just smiled and waved. "Boom!"

I'll leave out the part where I nearly shit myself worrying if my trick would work. Fortunately, I didn't have to wait long to find out.

At my command, the spheres exploded outward like an anti-personnel mine. Tiny projectiles of pure energy ripped into the ranks, penetrating through until they ran out of steam. Red dots appeared on the werewolves as though they'd contracted chicken pox. Those closest dropped instantly. Those behind them stumbled as the tiny red holes began to bleed, then gush. Crimson waterfalls sprung up in abundance, bathing them all in their own, thick red blood.

The wounded critters howled and screamed and stumbled about on the slippery floors, the puddles beneath them growing fast. Those who avoided the blast, or were wounded less gravely, struggled past their injured and dead companions and renewed their charge as best they could. Feeling generous, I rewarded them with bullets.

More tired from my magic act than I would have expected, I moved back and picked my shots to give me time to recover some. My ammunition just as effective on lycanthropes as it is on angels or demons, I put a bullet into the head of every wolf that got within clawing distance. They dropped fast. Unfortunately, the clip emptied even faster.

As I ejected the first and reached for another, there was a loud crash to the left, and just behind me. Instinct took over and I leapt to the side...right into the statue of the Virgin Mary that had been swung at me like a baseball bat.

Stupid instinct.

The marble statue crashed into my face and chest and I heard all sorts of things crack and pop—most of them probably belonged to me. The world went white and I felt a second, dull thud, followed by a third as my head went from a full gallop to a lazy trot. Something warm and wet spilled down my face and into my throat, choking me.

Gagging, my already opened eyes reengaged somewhat, I realized I was on the other side of the room from where I was just a moment ago. Grawwl trundled toward me, surrounded by a bunch of bloody and pissed off looking werewolves. Nothing left of his makeshift bat but the legs, he tossed the remnants of Mary aside. There was a merciless grin on his snout.

Suddenly remembering the Wonder Twins, I looked for Katon and saw him just past Grawwl, being borne down by a dozen lycanthropes. A whirlwind of teeth and sharpened claws tore at him as he was hauled to the ground. He was making them pay for it but he wasn't winning. Every blow was answered in stereo, and then some.

Nearby lay Scarlett, her blond hair dyed red from spattered claret. She lay on her back with a pile of critters pinning her down. Her one free arm lashed out vicious, but it wasn't more than a few seconds before the werewolves got a hold of it, her resistance drowned in a furry wave of violence.

My heart pounding to the rhythm of an early 80's Slayer song, I hopped to my feet to go to her. At least that's what I told my body to do.

What really happened was I twitched and fell over onto my side in what amounted to slow motion. The broken shards of the statue embedded in my face were ground in deeper as my cheek smacked the ground. It was a little unpleasant.

While my face stung and my skull throbbed like I'd been out all night with the boys, and it was a little hard to breathe, I really didn't hurt too much. All that being pretty minor considering the shit I've been through, I couldn't figure out why I was having such a hard time getting up. Nothing made sense.

I raised myself up with the one arm that would still somewhat listen and took a second to survey the damage. Interestingly, I was looking down over my left shoulder and could see my ass sprawled out kind of Playboy-esque behind me. A bit disconcerted, I turned my head and bolts of lightning shot through my eyes, obscuring the world in a sudden flurry of snow. My head filled with static, the white noise between radio stations. When it finally cleared, I was laying on the ground, my hand twitching under me like Pee Wee Herman's in a dark theater.

Without moving my head, I pieced together the images that were flooding into the murky swimming pools of my eyes. Though I recognized what I saw, it still didn't make any sense. Flat on my stomach, I was able to look past my shoulder blades and watch over my heels as Grawwl came stomping towards me. It was really quite disconcerting.

That's when it clicked. My neck was broken.

I like to think I'm a pretty tough guy. Busted into more pieces over the years than most modern mathematicians can count, I'd seen just about every injury imaginable. No matter how many broken bones, punctured lungs, or exploded rectums I've experienced—you don't want to know—there's nothing that says helpless quite like a broken neck or spine.

You can fight through the rest, drag a shattered leg behind you, shove a roll of toilet paper up your ass, but there's not shit you can do when the drive shaft is broken. You just flop about like a landed fish until things knit back into place.

As a demon, I was fortunate; it'd happen after a while as it hadn't been a magical weapon that hit me, all dogma aside.

Though from the snarky look on Grawwl's face, I wasn't gonna have that kind of time.

"Aaaaaah, the poor little mutt fell down. Ooh, that looks painful." A snide laughed grumbled from him.

He hovered over me, his eyes glistening with the kind of excitement you only saw at Christmas and in the prison shower. I tried to tell him where to go, but my inner GPS must have been on the fritz; I only blew a spit bubble.

Grawwl chuckled as the bubble popped and cold spit splattered across my face.

"You look like you're having a real hard time. Here, let me help."

His massive paws reached for me and I screamed, but I don't think anyone but the voices in my head heard me. Though in their defense, they're usually more helpful getting me into trouble than out.

Undeterred, he sniggered as he latched onto my skull, his claws clacking together as they settled into position. Then one good twist later, WWII was reenacted in the span of an instant within the confines of my head. In that instant, my consciousness disappeared like the concept of French pride.

Poof.

Chapter Twelve

Through the blackness, which pressed down on me more uncomfortably than a Tyler Perry marathon, I became aware of a steady, whooshing breeze that blew against my tingling face. It carried with it a fetid stench, which brought to mind chicken gizzards dipped in unwashed ass.

The stink invaded my nose and settled in my throat as though I were a porn shoot fluffer. Choked into a full and painful consciousness, I opened my eyes to see Grawwl's wet snout just inches from my face.

"Guess that answers the question of where bears shit."

My eyes watering, I didn't dare move my head for fear of the pain that'd accompany it. Through my peripheral vision, I could see my crotch was once more in its proper position with respect to the rest of me, and that was a good thing. I still felt nastier than a used tampon though.

Grawwl grumbled and leaned back, his paws on his hips as though posing for an anthropomorphic calendar. The worst part was that he wasn't a Ken werebear, he was a fully developed fuzz-bucket who happened to be in frightening proportion. The furry thing was jiggling about like a cat toy as he laughed and I was feeling rather self-conscious, not to mention a little inadequate.

"Welcome back. Feeling better?" He stepped away and I had to admit I was as the chapel came into view once more, sans bear penis.

A ways behind him sat Scarlett and Katon, their arms and legs trussed up mummy-like. They'd been beaten ugly, blood leaking from between the ropes. Both of their faces were puffy and battered and their eyes were almost invisible behind swollen, black eyelids. I could feel the little daggers of their gazes as they glared at me through the tiny slits. Something fun must have happened while I was out.

"It's nothing personal, mutt, but I can't seem to get any answers out of your friends, so it's your turn in the hot seat."

I think I whimpered, though I won't swear to it. "If you wanted to play *Trivial Pursuit*, all you had to do was ask. How's next Friday sound?"

He grinned vicious and moved in close once more, the rancid stink of his breath washing over me again. "I don't have time for this, demon. Where is Eve?"

Right then, the circular train of illogic rolled into the station once more. His reddish-orange eyes pulsing right in front of me, I just couldn't make any sense of his need for the key or why he would be working with vampires to get it. Neither race had a stake in Heaven now that God was gone. Their lives wouldn't be benefited or harmed should The Kingdom fall. Then what Longinus had told me wiggled to the fore.

That's when it all came together like a bukkake birthday cake.

"I'm not telling." My chin stuck out as far as my wobbly neck would allow, I told him where he could go; detailed directions followed.

Grawwl roared and stomped over to Scarlett, lifting her into the air by her throat. She clenched her jaw and snarled at him through gnashed teeth, but I could see fear in the slivers of her eyes.

Dying in battle was one thing. It was part and parcel of the supernatural world we inhabited. Being torn limb from limb, or worse, while tied up and helpless was an entirely different kind of death to face. There really wasn't any way to take that with dignity or honor.

"Tell me or I'll start tearing pieces off." His massive claws settled on her breast, their points making tiny indentations in her shirt. Tiny dots of blood welled up underneath.

My stomach seized and filled with weighty bricks of disgust as I made up my mind to stay the course. While I would forever regret—forever likely only gonna last a few seconds—being the cause of Scarlett's death, the alternative would be far worse.

I shook my head. "I'm sorry, Scarlett. I can't give it to him. If he gets the key, not only is Heaven lost, but all of humanity will end up laid out on a dinner plate for him and his bloodsucking, asshole vampire buddies. No offense, Katon."

Grawwl stomped his foot and tightened his grip on Scarlett. Her eyes bulged from her face. "Do you think I'm bluffing?"

Fighting the urge to shake my head, I met the fury of his gaze, doing my best not to look at Scarlett dangling in his paw. "I have no doubt whatsoever that you're telling the truth. For the humans to stand any chance of making it out of all this in relatively one piece, you can't have it."

The muscles of his arm flexed beneath his fur and I narrowed my eyes to keep from seeing my cousin used as a scratching post. Katon cried out, his wordless scream pure murderous rage. Grawwl screamed back and slammed Scarlett into the floor. There was a moist cracking sound and she lay there in a heap, unmoving. Blood began to pool around her head.

A pitiful groan slipped from Katon as he struggled to get up. A number of the werewolves piled on and held him in place.

Grawwl, foaming spittle dripping from his maw, dropped to all fours and barreled to a stop right in front of me. Our noses touched. "When I'm done with you, you're going to wish you were dead."

I met his stare without flinching. I'd like to think it was because I was brave, but being mostly paralyzed helped. "I'm already dead. All of us are." My eyes flitted toward Katon and Scarlett. "It took me a while, but I finally figured out why you want the key so badly. It has nothing to do with the Nephilim or Gabriel's rebellion against the angels. It's all about the Tree." The look on his fuzzy face told me I was right. "Take out the Tree of Life and all the angels and demons become mortal. That leaves the vamps and the shifters at the top of the food chain."

With a rancid huff, Grawwl backed away and dropped down on his haunches. He continued as though I hadn't spoken. "I know your human friends have it, mutt. You don't really think I'll have any problem killing them until I get it, do you?"

"Nope, but it doesn't matter what you do. By the time you find Eve, assuming you've tracked down Lilith's rib, which I doubt, it'll be too late. By then, the storms will have devastated Earth and you along with it." Pretty much damned no matter what I did, I smiled at Grumpy. It was a gallows smile, empty of any real emotion, but it was the best I could do given the circumstances. "While this might come off as a little defeatist, I'm thinking I'm just gonna hang out and watch the plans of wolf and bear crumble down around us. Got any popcorn?"

At that point, I really didn't care what happened because the nuts-in-a-bear-trap look on Grawwl's face made it all worthwhile. No threat he could think of would change my mind and he knew it. Somewhere in the back of my mind, my mother cheered. That made things a little easier to bear, no pun intended.

Grawwl spun and went back to the audience of werewolves who circled around him, gathering close to hear what he had to say. They grumbled and howled as they discussed their plans, until at last the majority of them began to nod. Grawwl turned back to us, his snout pulled back to show his monstrous teeth.

"Before we're done, everyone you know and love will die."

"How about you start with me?"

If I hadn't recognized the voice, I would have thought Barry White had come to rescue us.

Every head in the room—except mine—snapped to see Rahim standing less than twenty feet from us. Out of the corner of my eye, I could see his hands shimmering with red energy that danced along his fingertips. His smile beamed as though he had a miniature lighthouse on his face. He'd gotten the drop on the weres and he loved it.

The werewolves loosed a symphony of guttural howls and leapt toward Rahim. His smile only got wider as he unleashed his magic. The first rabid wave disintegrated just like you'd see in a nuclear war movie, blown backwards in a vaguely humanoid puff of dust. Most of the pack scattered to weather the storm, the second wave bursting into flames before them. The rank stench of burnt fur rose up thick.

All of a sudden, I had a feeling of weightlessness. I glanced down to see the floor beneath me was disappearing, a whirling blue vortex opening in its place. As I started to fall, I saw the same type of portal opening up below Scarlett and Katon. His eyes were wide despite the swelling.

I looked back quickly to see Rahim stumble as his power gave way, his wide grin replaced by an agonized snarl. He'd expended too much energy for his battered body to handle.

The very last thing I saw before my vision turned blue was Grawwl plucking the wizard out of the middle of the howling pack, his dagger-like teeth sinking deep into Rahim's shoulder.

The closing of the portal silenced Katon's helpless scream.

Chapter Thirteen

The void swallowed me for two agonizing heartbeats, then Katon's ragged voice exploded, made even louder by the confined room we were dropped into.

Though I still couldn't turn my neck to see where we were, the almost overpowering scent of old books made it obvious. We were in Abraham's office at DRAC. Rachelle, who had violated every security protocol DRAC had by bringing us there, stood in view, leaning against Abraham's desk. Her moist eyes were locked on something behind me.

"Free me!" Katon shrieked, a razorblade sharpness to his voice. "I have to help Rahim."

Abraham shushed him, his breath hurried and shallow. Unable to see him, I could only imagine he was freeing the enforcer from the tangle of ropes that held him immobile. After a moment of grunts and swearing complaints, there was a dull thud, then Katon popped into sight, stopping just inches from Rachelle.

"Send me back!" He reached and grabbed her by the arms, stooping so their eyes were aligned. "Please, send me back."

Pity was draped across her face as she looked down, unwilling to meet his gaze.

"No," Abraham's answer was forged in steel.

Katon released Rachelle and spun, the begging sadness transforming into deep-lined rage. "What? How dare you? After all Rahim ha—"

Abraham appeared, silver tears leaking out from beneath his glasses. Fearless in the face of the enforcer's fury, Abe wrapped his hand around Katon's neck and pulled him forward until their foreheads thumped together.

"You think me heartless? See for yourself."

Katon went rigid, the raging glimmer in his eyes melting away into a blank stare. His arms dropped to his sides as Abraham pressed his vision into his mind. Katon's hands opened and closed spasmodically, then they went limp. His shoulders slumped as his resistance gave way with a whispered sigh.

"Do you understand now? He sacrificed himself so that you would live. He would have it no other way."

A quiet sob slipped from Katon, so horribly pitiful I felt my eyes moistening in sympathy. He collapsed into Abraham's arms. The old man held him close as Katon broke down. Tremors racked his body so violently that Abe struggled to keep them on their feet. They swayed in each others arms in the dance of sorrow.

I couldn't watch it. Unable to turn away, I closed my eyes and thought of porn.

It makes me happy, all right?

Some people think of home, others of their loved ones or a song that always makes them smile. Me, I think about boobs. It's a primal thing encoded in male demon DNA, so don't judge me.

After a while, Katon composed himself and I dared to open my eyes. He separated from Abraham and squeezed the old man's shoulder before looking over at Scarlett. Already emotionally battered, I could see the guilt on his face as he realized he'd been so caught up in mourning Rahim that he'd left her tied up, unconscious, and bleeding on the floor.

Hoping to spare him, I called him over. "I've got a vial of my," I caught myself, "of Lucifer's blood in my pocket." Abraham looked at me with an eyebrow raised, but said nothing. He knew when to let things lie.

A look of relief flashed across Katon's face and he rushed over and gently slipped his hand into my pocket. It was probably a good thing I was numb from the neck down or he might have found a little extra something in there, a side effect of all my happy thoughts.

He pulled the vial out and unwrapped it, popping the cork.

"Just a couple of drops."

Seeming grateful, he gave me the first two, then ran out of sight where he probably did the same with Scarlett.

It wasn't but a few seconds before I felt the warming rush. The blood's energy prickled my skin as it lavished its attention on me like a well-paid hooker. Where only seconds before numbness had reigned, I felt a gentle surface tickle as the nerves were repaired. The bumps and bruises were already gone. The shards of marble still stuck in my face clinked to the ground one by one, pushed out as the wound beneath sealed shut.

Though I wasn't real thrilled about it when it happened, I was kind of glad Grawwl had straightened my neck. It made the whole process quicker, not having to rely on the blood to adjust my head, and then heal it. That could have turned out real ugly if something knitted together wrong.

My body almost back in one piece, I heard Scarlett gasp and glanced over at her, elated that I could do so at all. She popped up with wide eyes, the bruises and swelling on her face replaced by angelic beauty once more. She looked around the room, then to Katon, who held her in his arms.

"What happened?" she asked, clearly sensing the mood of the room.

"Rahim," Katon whispered, explaining everything with that simple utterance. He shook his head, unable to continue, a fresh wave of tears running free.

Her hand went to his wet cheek and she pulled him in close. For a moment, they just sat there, Scarlett gently wiping his sobbing tears away. Then without a word spoken, Katon stood and disentangled himself before stumbling for the door. He set the vial on the desk as he passed. Scarlett gave me a sad smile and followed him out.

"Hey, we're not—"

Abraham cut me off, offering me his hand as they slipped from the room. I knew better than to argue. On my feet, I looked from Rachelle to Abe and filled them in on what we'd learned.

They both took it in and seemed to shrink right before my eyes as the entirety of what we were facing settled over them. Between them, they'd seen a lot, but it was starting to wear them down. To realize it might have all been for nothing, their lives dedicated to combating the supernatural threat that had emerged after God's disappearance, was too stiff a blow to just roll with.

After a few tense moments of silence, I asked, "What now?"

Abraham shrugged and went to his desk, dropping heavy into his chair. "There have been more storms. They're spreading across the globe and getting worse," he said. His voice was little more than a whisper. "There's nothing we can do to contain them. The world is slipping into chaos, believing the end has come. Perhaps, this time, it truly has."

Rachelle wiped tears from her eyes and slid into his lap. She buried her face in his neck. His throat muffled her quiet sob.

"I'll do what I can to see a path through this, but for now, there is little we can do without the key." He wrapped his arms around Rachelle and held her tight, his eyes closing as his own tears streamed with silver dignity down his cheeks.

Hopelessness hung thick in the room. It was a deathbed vigil, the end riding in fast on the ticking hands of time. We were just waiting on the corpse to figure out what everyone else in the room knew; it was dead.

With no way to enter Heaven, there was nothing we could do to stop the war before all life was wiped from the planet. In a nagging bit of irony, the key parts split between us, the Nephilim, and Grawwl, what I'd told Grumpy Bear as he held us hostage was just as true for us as it was for him.

With an army of lycanthropes on one side and an army of half-breed angels on the other, there wasn't any chance to separate the parts from either before everything went to shit. We simply didn't have the power, especially considering Azrael had made his stance clear.

While used to being an underdog, the odds were stacked too deep for us to land on our feet this time.

A defeated sigh slipped loose as I looked at Abe and Rachelle. Their arms entwined, they'd forgotten I was even there as they staved off their misery with their love for one another. It made my heart hurt that I stood there alone.

The end of the world coming, Rahim dead, I snatched up the vial and headed for the door. Right then, I could only think of one person I wanted to spend my last few minutes alive with. The one person who knew me inside and out and who'd never let me down.

Jack Daniels.

Chapter Fourteen

Half way into my fifth bottle of whiskey, I'd wandered out to Old Town on autopilot. A creature of bad habits, my body seemed to think that drunk equaled Fiesta Street. Can't really blame it; there are boobs there.

Well, probably not tonight considering the storms had been busy tearing away at existence, but there usually is. That's good enough for me.

My walk was quiet, eerily so. The streets were deserted like I'd never seen them before, with only the occasional emergency vehicle disturbing the unnatural still. The end of the world being prophesized on every news channel across the country, the people of El Paseo had apparently taken it to heart.

All the businesses downtown were boarded up or just plain abandoned. Even the bars and liquor stores I'd passed were shut down and empty. Much to my surprise, I didn't see any sign of looting, which renewed my faith in humanity. Better late than never, huh?

The roads were clear of traffic and even the homeless had fled the impending doom, finding shelter elsewhere. They couldn't possibly know it didn't matter where they were, the storms were coming. They were coming for us all.

The only place I saw any sign of life was at the church I passed. There, the people gathered in rabid hordes, the arched doorway packed thick as they struggled to get inside. Some sobbed and looked to the sky while others trudged in, zombie-faced and silent. Children scampered about, some catching onto the gloom of their parents, others oblivious; like kids should be. Their end was coming too, and there wasn't gonna be anyone to save them. Not their parents, not their grandparents, and certainly not God. They'd all come there in vain.

Even with my tongue soaked with liquor, I couldn't bring myself to tell them they were wasting their time. God was out of the office. If it made them feel better to end their days clamoring for a seat on a pew, then good for them, but there weren't gonna be any miracles today. I certainly didn't have one in me.

So, to the rhythm of the sloshing bottle, I turned my back on the throng and made my way around to where Baalth had fricasseed the neighborhood. Once there, I stared at the ruin, made more poignant by my whiskey-addled brain. It was a bitter preview of things to come. My stomach churned with disgust and I chugged another mouthful of Jack to help keep my inebriated perspective.

Half devil, it took an awful lot to get me drunk, and a whole Hell of a lot more to stay that way. My recuperative powers burned away the alcohol just a smidge slower than I was consuming it so I had to keep sucking it down or I'd sober up.

While I didn't have to worry about hangovers, my bar tab had a lot in common with the national deficit; way too many zeroes. The good part of the end of the world lurking around the corner was that I wouldn't have to pay it. That was a plus.

Maudlin, I pulled my eyes from the scorched earth and stumbled down the road. It felt weird to see how abandoned it all was. It was if the world had given up, just like we had. It didn't inspire confidence.

Driven on in mindless motion, my feet kept on slapping down, one after another, as they steered me toward the red light district—my own personal place of worship. As much as I wanted to pretend I could die alone and be all right with it, the truth was I wouldn't be. I hoped there'd be some brave—or stupid—souls out tonight with whom I could commiserate.

My thoughts swirled to Veronica and our life together. It'd been Hell sometimes, but there'd been plenty to smile about, despite it all. I wondered where she was and what she was doing, though the more I thought about it, it probably didn't matter. She wasn't exactly the snuggly type. Were she around, we'd only fight until the world blew up, and probably for a little while afterward.

Then there was Karra. Nothing would make me happier than wrapping my arms around her and telling her how much her coming back into my life meant. It was like I was fifteen all over, minus the constant erection.

Well, things really hadn't changed much in that department.

That aside, her presence had reawakened something in me I'd thought dead and buried long ago. Maybe it was just the whiskey making me emotional, but I couldn't help but feel like there was something there between us, some hint that we had a chance at something special. Something more than we'd made the first time around. She had her father though, and he was ready to go down with the ship. There wouldn't be any room in her life for the both of us if things went to Hell. There was no way I was gonna win out over daddy. I hadn't the first time, and no amount of liquor made me think I would the second.

I swallowed the rest of the bottle and let my feet do their thing. So deeply alone it hurt, I let them guide me toward the only sanctuary this city held for me; the dregs of society. Unable to spend my last moments with my own kind, I'd spend it with my mother's. While I can't say she'd approve of my choice of locations, it gave me a kind of solace to think of dying amongst the humans. It would be the closest thing I'd ever have to being with her again.

Moist eyes on the sky, I stumbled on and tossed the empty bottle away. It took me a second to realize I hadn't heard it land.

My heart surged with adrenaline as I drew my gun and spun around. Two grim, blue and blurry eyes met mine.

"I presume by this you haven't you've had much success?" The weathered old man held my bottle in his hand, the bronze of his armor reflected through the thick glass.

Taking a deep breath, I stuffed my gun in my waistband and glared at him. "I know I'm supposed to respect my elders and all that, but I'm not really interested in whatever it is you're selling."

It was obvious he wasn't human, but strangely, he didn't ring back on my senses like any supernatural I've ever known. It was if he wasn't even there. The blood on his armor was definitely real though. Splatters coated his right side in crimson and there were streaks running the length of his right arm. Seeing that, I regretted putting my gun away.

He tossed the bottle aside and smirked as it smashed into a million pieces, glistening shards skittering across the asphalt. "Is there no room for salvation in that calloused heart of yours, demon?" His voice had that raspy bite that lifelong smokers develop over the years.

"Look, I don't know who you are, or how you factor into all this, but can you get to the point? I'm kind of in the middle of something here." The alcohol was wearing off and I was starting to give a shit again.

"The middle of quitting is what it looks like to me, boy. I'd have figured you for sterner stuff considering your bloodline."

If there's one thing that pisses me off more than anything else, it's when people know who I am but I have idea who they are. His vague reference to Lucifer didn't help my mood much either.

"If you've got something to say, old man, spit it out while you still can."

A smile exploded onto his face, the Grand Canyon cut between the not so grand. "I knew there had to be some fire left in there somewhere." He raised his hands to warn me off as I went for my gun. "I'm on your side, at least until our current crisis passes." He looked at me for a moment and shook his head. "There is so much you don't know."

"No shit, Sherlock. How about we start with your name?" That's the problem with supernaturals–they live so damn long that paranoia becomes a way of life. They hoard their knowledge and squirrel away every myth and legend just to prolong their miserable existence, hiding the truth from the world. Every great once in a while, they give a drop of it away, for a price of course, just to make themselves feel important; remembered.

"I have many names, but you may call me Akrasiel, if you must."

Didn't recognize him, but that wasn't a surprise. Most angels and demons had a handful of different names they used, each buried in deeper mystery than the last. There wasn't room in my head to remember them all. The fact that I didn't care probably didn't help.

"Well, Akrasiel, mind telling me what your stake in all this is?"

"The same as yours. Should the Tree of Life die, it's only a matter of time until all of existence follows it to the grave."

"Wow. You should be a motivational speaker. I've got chills. I mean it, seriously. The way you're telling me what I already know is just amazing. Where do I sign on?"

His cold blue gaze met mine as his leathered lips dropped into a grim line. It looked like I pissed him off a bit. Good. It's the little things that make life fun.

When he spoke, it was in a rough-edged monotone. "There is a faction not yet represented on the field, which may sway the battle in a favorable direction." He motioned toward Heaven. "The end looms, but there is still time for one who knows how to use it. The last guardian of the throne lies inert. Stricken by the loss of God, he is blind to what is happening in the Kingdom. He must be made aware."

"Just a shot in the dark, but I'm guessing he's in Heaven."

The old man nodded.

The circle jerk continued. "Maybe you haven't been paying attention, but I don't have any way to get in up there. They've revoked my passport."

A crooked grin cracked the hard leather of his face. "You'd be surprised by what you're capable of, Triggalt—"

My given name not even all the way out of his mouth, I waggled my finger and growled at him. "Don't say it."

He chuckled and took a step back, his arms raised in mock surrender. Then he stood there silent, just staring at me as though it were my turn.

"Is that it? No more words of wisdom, no prophecies to lead me? No bridges or beachfront property?"

He nodded again, his smile inching wider.

"You're a snake oil salesman, you know that? You show up selling hope, but it's all just bullshit and broken dreams." He hadn't told me a damn thing that would help. "What about the key parts? Can you at least tell me where I can find them?"

"Do you not want the same thing as those who hold the other pieces?"

The obvious hit me between the eyes like a brick. Akrasiel just laughed at me and bowed, disappearing in a flash of golden light.

The old bastard was right. We did want the same thing. Both the Nephilim and the were-critters were looking to get into Heaven just like us. That meant the key pieces had to end up at the gate soon for them to be any use. Now all I had to do was figure out how to take advantage of that fact. Clearly that would be the easy part.

Yeah right.

Presuming the two groups were quicker on the draw than me—which is pretty much a given—they would be prepared to defend their piece and had probably worked out a plan to relieve everyone else of theirs. So, while it was an opportunity I hadn't thought about before, it wasn't much of one. It would put us smack dab in the middle of both factions, and that was the last place I wanted to be.

My head running in circles, the remnants of the alcohol still tripping it up, I needed to sober up and think. The melancholy having eased just enough to let a glimmer of sunlight through, I headed off to find a portal back to DRAC. This problem needed a greater mind than mine.

Caught up in my head, I didn't notice the car that pulled alongside me until I heard the distinctive clack of a bullet being chambered. Before I could look to see who it was, the cold steel of a gun barrel was pressed hard against my skull. There wasn't even a tremble in the manicured hand that held it.

"If you so much as breathe, Mister Trigg, you're dead."

Chapter Fifteen

Someone behind me yanked my pistol roughly out of my waistband with no regard for the wedgie he'd given me. His rapids huffs warmed my nape.

It didn't take a genius to figure out who it was from the smooth voice of the gun wielder and the gorilla breath of his helper wilting the hair on my neck.

"Hi, Poe. There a problem?"

"Fuck this!" D'anatello's voice rang out over my shoulder and I cringed. To no surprise, I felt the grip of my own pistol crash into my skull.

Dots of light flickered in my eyes and the next thing I knew, I was hugging the ground. There was a heated conversation happening overtop of me, but the words didn't make sense. They buzzed and hissed incoherently. Blinking tears away, I peeled my face off the asphalt and rolled over to see Poe and Marcus had finished their argument and stood there glaring at me. Poe held two guns, one in each hand. One of them was pointed quite rudely at my face.

Marcus started to say something, but Poe silenced him with a low growl and a withering look. His eyes flickered with malevolent red energy. He turned his stare on me and my subconscious mind immediately starting flipping through the Rolodex of my memories to see if it could remember having done anything to make him mad since I'd seen him last. I couldn't recall.

"I can't believe you, Trigg." He'd dropped the ever-present mister. He was seriously pissed. "I let you in to see Asmoday so you could stop the storms, not so you could exact vengeance for your cousin. I thought we had an understanding."

My brain addled from the blow, not to mention the five bottles of Jack Daniels, I had no idea what he was talking about.

"Huh?" I majored in smooth. Admittedly, my test scores really weren't that high.

Poe dropped down beside me and pressed the barrel hard against my cheek. The lines of his face were drawn tight, the tiny slits of his eyes like murder holes. "Don't play stupid. Why did you kill Asmoday?"

The words ricocheted around inside my head for a few seconds before finally striking home. "I..." I had to work hard to think back, drawing my memories of our encounter to the forefront. "Wait. What do you mean? I didn't—"

Poe leaned in closer, his weight on the gun grinding into my face. His eyes flickered back to their normal ice blue. He stared into me. "Tell me why you killed him."

"I didn't touch him," I gasped, my tongue finally finding enough traction to spit out my thoughts. "He was alive when I left."

He just stared at me for a minute, no hint of mercy on his face. The barrel felt like a cattle brand against my skin as he held it there. At last, he pulled the pistol away and stood, drawing in a deep breath. It reminded me to breathe too.

"Don't let him trick you. Shoot that demon son of a bitch," Marcus howled as he stomped back and forth in a tight circle. "He used us, and now Baalth will—"

Poe glanced over at Marcus and finally let his breath out. "Do you think me so incompetent?"

As a mentalist of amazing power, perhaps even more so than DRAC's Michael Li, Poe might not be able to read my mind, but he sure could tell whether I was lying. He knew for absolute fact I hadn't been the person to kill Asmoday.

Probably just realizing what he'd implied, Marcus stopped pacing and swallowed hard. "I didn't mean—"

Poe didn't give him time to finish, cutting him off with a wave of a pistol. "He's telling the truth, Mister D'anatello. He didn't kill Asmoday." He slid his gun into his holster beneath his suit jacket, and then held his free hand out to me. "The most likely suspect proven innocent, it makes finding his murderer more difficult. I assume your cousin was with you after you left."

A bit tentative, I locked onto Poe's hand and he pulled me up. "Yeah she was, until about a half hour ago."

He nodded as he spun my gun in his hand and passed the grip to me. "I apologize for our presumption, but after your earlier visit, you have to understand our suspicion."

Seeing how Scarlett tried to skewer Poe, I couldn't really hold it against him. I shoved my pistol back into my pants and yanked my underwear out of my ass. "We're good. Now tell me what happened?"

"It's best we do it on the way." He snapped his fingers at Marcus who hopped in the driver's seat and slammed the door, looking like a beaten puppy. Once the gorilla was inside, he motioned me to the car.

I climbed in on the other side of the sedan and slid deep into the comfortable leather seat. The base of my skull pounded out a tribal rhythm as Poe got in the back beside me, Marcus taking off the second the door was shut.

"The storms worsening, I'd gone to speak with Asmoday in the hopes of pressing him for information. The moment I'd arrived in his chambers it became clear something was wrong." He took a second to regulate his breathing. "The smell of fresh blood and burnt meat filled the chamber. I found him on the floor. He had been torn apart." He gave me an apologetic half-shrug. "With no way into his quarters except through the gate, which is synched to only me, I have no idea how it happened."

Nodding, I sunk even lower in the seat. It was weird thinking of Asmoday as dead. As much as I'd wanted to put a bullet in him during his quest to bring about Armageddon, he'd always been too much of a force to take out. With Baalth holding his power in check, he was little more than a haggard drunk.

For him, that must have been the worst part of dying. Taken out like a common human, knowing death was coming for him and not being able to do a damn thing about it. It was a bitter kind of poetic justice that visited him, but I couldn't bring myself to gloat. I sure did want to though.

Whoever, or whatever, killed him had to be powerful, given they'd bypassed the security on the gate. That alone implied a serious threat. I didn't mention it to Poe, but I had an idea who it might have been.

We rode the rest of the way in silence until Marcus came to a sudden stop outside the office whose portal led to Hell. We hopped out and Poe took the lead as Marcus drove away, tires screeching. Inside, we worked our way to the portal room and the mentalist motioned to the gate.

"I've no interest in an encore performance, so if you don't mind, Mister Trigg, I'll remain here."

Caught off guard by his reluctance, I nodded. I'd never pictured Poe as the squeamish type, so his sudden decision to send me down alone made me nervous. The power in the gate coming alive, I looked to the mentalist and saw tiredness in his eyes, but no hint of deception.

Besides, he had a gun to my head just a few minutes ago. If he'd wanted to kill me, he could have done it with a twitch. No need for an elaborate trap. No matter how much I wanted that rationale to make me feel better, it just kept falling short. There was more to it.

A servant to Baalth, a demon with no qualms about doing things the ugly way, Poe had to have seen a lot of really, really, really disturbing things in his time. So saying, his not wanting to go into the chamber again said volumes about the horror I was walking into. Alone.

Lucky me.

Materializing in Hell, I resisted the urge to take a nostalgic deep breath and held it instead. Boy was I glad I did.

Poe's description of Asmoday being torn apart didn't come remotely close to explaining what had really happened. No horror movie I'd ever seen could match the viciousness on display inside his chambers. It brought to mind what had gone down at the DRAC installation, a similar cruelty at work.

The walls and ceiling were stained in the thick redness of his blood, stalactites of dripping flesh hung from the roof. Slabs of meat were everywhere. Chunks oozed down the walls and sat wedged amidst the books on the shelves. Bone fragments littered the room as though they'd been through a wood-chipper, glistening white amidst the moist crimson.

The portraits on the walls were soaked with splattered blood, the paint running with it to blur the once priceless images. Most of them were hardly recognizable, their beauty forever marred; their value measured in dust.

The chair I'd sat in when Asmoday and I spoke was soaked in seeping red, the couch beside it the same. Everywhere I looked there was a piece of Asmoday, some grisly remnant of the demon lieutenant.

While most of it was unrecognizable, I spied a few fingers here and there, and a toe or two. My stomach doing its best to run out of my ass and flee, I eased across the floor, trying not to slip. Every step squished as I crossed the chamber toward the arched doorway that led to the back half of the quarters. The short walk seemed to take forever, the lurid scene splayed out before me.

Finally through the arch, I exhaled hard and coughed, choking a bit as I drew in a breath. The air tasted like death; a bitter, vile stench that latched onto my lungs and assailed my nose and throat.

My back to the main room, I felt my lungs begin to adjust, the carnage out of sight. The only trace something had gone on here was the trail of blood, which led to the king sized bed...and of course, Asmoday's severed head.

A look of shock carved into his stiff face, Asmoday's head sat propped upon the mattress. His bulging eyes stared at me sightless, the blanket beneath soaked in black.

My heart pounding, I glanced around the room expecting to see a killer leap from the shadows, despite the reassurance of my senses telling me I was alone. I tried to survey the quarters, but my eyes kept flitting back to Asmoday's.

Even in death he annoyed me.

Finally, I went over and yanked the blanket up to cover his head, but it had other ideas. Before I could stop it, the head tumbled off the bed and hit the floor with a moist splat before rolling underneath it. Honestly, I'd have just left it there, out of sight, out of mind, but a second wet squishing sound a moment later caught my attention. I kneeled down and glanced under the bed to see what looked like a hole dug into the floor.

Adrenaline spiking my veins, I tossed the bed aside to find the hole was actually a tunnel, dug through the floor to an almost invisible chamber below. Asmoday's head sat about ten feet down, looking up at me.

So much for my thinking he couldn't dig his way out.

My mind tripped over that thought. While the location of the hole suggested that Asmoday did indeed dig it, it could very well be the source of whatever killed him. Since Poe hadn't noticed the gate being used, that made more sense than anything. Worse still, Asmoday's murderer could still be lurking down there.

Less than excited to go jumping in, I listened for a few minutes while working my courage up. After not hearing anything, I made up my mind and dropped inside, hoping I hadn't just committed suicide.

I landed in a crouch, my gun held out before me. The room I'd arrived in was small, little more than a ten foot square. An unlighted tunnel loomed ahead of me, the only apparent exit. A quick glance at Asmoday's severed head made me wonder if I should be going it alone. I decided not to.

"Here's your chance to be a hero," I whispered to the head.

A quick kick sent Asmoday rolling down the corridor, bravely charging into the unknown as I covered him from behind. He flopped into the darkness and came to rest about twenty feet away. I waited for a few moments, but nothing jumped out in response.

Comforted by that a little, I followed the head into the tunnel. About five feet past him there was an opening to another chamber. At the edge, I peeked inside and nearly shit myself. The massive room beyond was filled to the brim with dread fiends.

I stumbled backward and fell to my ass beside Asmoday's head, my back against the cold rock wall. My hand shaking, gun trained on the tunnel entrance, I held my ground, ready to blast the first ugly face that burst into the tunnel.

Sweat ran down the back of my neck as I waited...and waited... and waited, my knuckles aching from holding my gun so tight. At last, my brain registered there hadn't been so much as a peep from the chamber the whole time I sat there. So, I waited a little longer, just to be sure.

Finally thinking maybe I just hadn't been seen, I urged my balls out of my ass and got to my feet as quietly as possible. I crept back to take another look. My heart floundered for a second as once again I saw wave after wave of dread fiends.

The shock troops of Hell, the fiends were built for devastation. Thickly muscled, they could snap a man in half without effort. Their mouths are filled with rows of serrated teeth, reminiscent of a mutant piranha. Backed up by an arsenal of sharp claws that grew like bony saws from the tips of their fingers, it wouldn't take but a few seconds for one to rip you apart. I could only imagine what thousands of them could do. Actually, I could probably just look to Asmoday and get a pretty good idea. Longinus would know too, though I'd never have the sack to ask him.

My heart drummed a retreat, but somewhere in the abyss of my mind I realized there was something strange going on. Though I could hear them breathing, whistled breaths humming in rhythm, they hadn't moved. The glimmers of their orange eyes stared straight ahead without blinking.

As close as I was to them, I could see the yellow-green bile that oozed across their leathery skin and smell the rancid stink of their unwashed flesh. If I could smell them, they most definitely could smell me, their natural senses far greater than mine.

I looked out across the sea of fiends, and other than the gentle tremble of the porcupine spikes extending from their bony faces, there wasn't a hint of movement. It was freaky.

While my experience with the fiends was limited to the few encounters where they were trying to rip me to pieces, their current state seemed way out of character. They were obviously alive, so I had no idea what to make of it all.

Logic dictated that if they had wanted to attack they'd had plenty of time to do so. Deep down I knew logic didn't mean shit when it came to the supernatural world. The rules weren't the same.

Dread fiends weren't wild creatures who acted on instinct. They were bred to serve, to kill. I couldn't predict their response because it all came down to whoever had raised them, impressed their will upon them. So, while my presence might not incite them, I had no idea what would. It could be anything; a wayward fart could send them into a murderous frenzy.

A smidgen of confidence emerging at their continued immobility, I looked over their heads to the other side of the room. Well over two football fields in length, I couldn't see anything clearly in the gloom, but I spotted an arched doorway at the far end, of course. A narrow path between the fiends led straight toward it.

No idea what lay beyond the arch, I tried to picture the layout of Lucifer's chambers in the hopes of gaining some perspective. It wasn't happening. The chamber was obviously built underneath, but I'd never heard so much as a whisper about it. Even with all the secrets Lucifer had shared with me, I'd never known about this place.

That meant two things: I wasn't meant to know or they were built after Lucifer took off for parts unknown. It was likely the former, if recent revelations were any indication.

Either way, it meant that whatever was down here was here for a reason. Like a kid admonished not to peek, I suddenly felt an overwhelming desire to find out what was so important it had to be guarded by an army of dread fiends.

Have I mentioned I'm a tad bit on the impulsive side?

I put my gun away and covered it up with my shirt. Not sure what the trigger might be for setting the fiends off, I didn't want to risk looking like I was there for a fight. Besides, if the horde woke up on the wrong side of the cave, it wouldn't matter if I had a million guns. There just wasn't a win buried anywhere in that massacre. It wouldn't be but a couple of seconds before I ended up as a chunky, red coat of paint on the walls.

A quick tap to my head cleared that thought away before it could dissuade me. I drew in a deep breath and took one step into the chamber. Nothing happened. I took another and still nothing. By about the tenth step, my ass threatening to turtle, I had passed the point of no return. If they sprung awake then, I was dead.

My pretend optimism fueling my advance, I sped my pace and moved as nonchalantly as I possibly could while running my ass off. The orange shimmer of their eyes stayed on me as I passed, but they never turned their heads or moved to intercept me.

About ten yards from the archway, I nearly barreled into a wall of fiends that blocked the way. My attention on the ones behind me, I hadn't noticed the ones in front. Breathing like a locomotive, I felt panic start to well up, but it subsided just as quickly when the fiends didn't so much as blink.

The path cluttered, I peered over them to find a new way to the arch. There wasn't one. Wedged tight against each other, the fiends formed a solid barrier. I thought about backing up and diving over them, but I highly doubted I'd make it. Ten yards is a long way. Ask any football team.

Flying crossed my mind, but that was a pipe dream. It went up in smoke the second it popped into my head. Images of me crash landing in their midst sprung up unbidden. Even if I managed to figure out how to fly, I couldn't be sure they wouldn't take offense to the use of magic. So, limited in options, there was only one more thing I could try.

Tentative, I reached my hand out and touched one of the fiends with the tip of my finger. The ooze felt warm as I yanked my finger back to keep it from being bitten off. The fiend just stood there.

A little braver, I did it again, this time laying my palm on its arm. Once more it did nothing. Its lack of response was encouraging. Thinking I could make it, I gave it a try.

My courage tucked between my legs, I squeezed between the closest two fiends, their stench making my eyes water. Neither moved, but their bodies were so rigid they didn't even sway as I pressed against them. The greasy pus slathered across their bodies made it easier to slide past, though I felt like I was crawling out of an infected boil.

In the second rank, I slipped between two more and found myself surrounded in the third. Packed even tighter, there wasn't any room for me to get by. Since it didn't make any sense to go backward, it would have to be forward.

Careful not to bump the fiends, I gently leaned my shoulder against theirs and exerted some pressure. It was as though I were pushing against a brick wall. I'd managed to slide through a couple of inches, but they weren't budging. As I got to my chest, it was like squeezing a watermelon through a dog's ass; it just wasn't happening.

Determined to get through, I put my weight into the move and I slid a few more inches but was unable to go further. While not quite the immovable object, they were as close as I would ever see. Worried I might wake them if I pushed any harder, I tried to back out only to find I was stuck.

Wedged between their arms, I had one elbow grinding into my spine while the other pressed into my stomach, the fiend's hand grazing my crotch. Even as easy as I am, it didn't feel good.

Unable to go either way without a jolt, I got up on my toes and tried to save some space that way. It didn't quite work out as planned. Only able to lift up a little, I was still stuck, only less comfortably.

The stifling air was filled with the stink of dread fiend, every breath was torture. I could taste the decay. My stomach grumbled, compressed as it was between pointy elbows. To make things worse, an oozing pustule broke open on the shoulder of the fiend before me.

Yellow-green goop boiled out of it and ran like a putrid caterpillar down the fiend's arm and onto my chest. It soaked through my shirt, its pulsing warmth lapping at my skin. Spurred on by the biochemical assault upon my sensibilities, I tried one last time to slip past, but I remained stuck. I pushed harder and then harder still, squirming to be free. They didn't budge.

"Move damn it!" The words were out of my mouth before I'd even realized I said them.

To my horror, they did. The pressure suddenly relieved, I fell on my ass as the fiends stepped away, the room filled with a horrific symphony of snarls and rumbling growls.

On the ground, surrounded by dread fiends, I did what any self-respecting hero would do in my situation. I curled up into a ball and pleaded for my life.

To my utter and complete surprise, it worked.

After a few moments of me sitting there with nothing being gnawed off, I suddenly realized the room had gone quiet again. I dared a peek past my forearms to see the fiends were still there, but they'd gone rigid once more.

I uncovered my face completely and glanced around the room to find they'd stepped to the side, pressing into an even tighter group than before. Amazingly, the path to the arch was clear.

A tentative sigh of relief slipping out, I got up and willed my feet forward before they changed their minds. The last few yards flew by and I reached the doorway, casting furtive glances inside to make sure I wasn't walking into an even worse situation.

The room beyond free of dread fiends, I went inside in a hurry. As I crossed the threshold, magical flares along the walls flickered alive, filling the room with gentle light. A closet in comparison to the fiend room, the walls of the chamber were carved at odd angles, sharp corners jutting into the room. It took me a second as I moved around, but I realized it had been cut in the shape of a pentagram.

On the furthest wall was another tunnel that had been recently dug judging by the rough edges. Broken rock and gray dust sat at the mouth, piled several feet thick. I ducked around the opposite side to keep the tunnel in sight as I surveyed the rest of the chamber.

In the center of the room, upon a raised dais of blackened marble, stood a trophy case, kind of like the ones used to showcase sports uniforms. Its muted gold frame was intact, but the glass that made up the front wall was shattered. Pieces lay on the ground before it, glistening in the light.

On its remaining walls were elaborate, mystical symbols etched into the glass. The writing flowed along the breadth of the glass and seemed to segue seamlessly from one to another, its sequence lost only at the shattered pane. Though I couldn't read a word of it, it was written beautifully.

That meant bad.

In general, magic is ugly. Based in a primal brutality, it comes to life in fire and fury through sheer force of will. It's the battering ram and the bullet.

Now when you get into symbols and scripts, it means the mystical energy has been harnessed to a specific use, which is most often defensive or meant to counter offensive magic. Crude symbolism limits its potential, the essence of magic born of imagination and creativity. Like art, the more beautiful, the more transcendent, the more effective it is; the more versatile.

The artistic script on the case told me it was meant to hold or protect something powerful. The broken glass *outside* of the case meant whatever was inside had let itself out.

That's real bad.

A spider-like shiver ran down my spine. Coming down here, I had a pretty good idea who might have whacked Asmoday, but now I wasn't so sure. If whatever was in the case was sentient, then that only added to the suspects and muddied the water.

Honestly, I didn't really care who killed him. As a matter of fact, that person did me a favor as it cleared my debt to Asmoday without me having to welch. That point aside, the empty case was just another problem I had no idea how to fix.

Feeling a bit exposed with the dread fiends at my back, I made my way to the tunnel. A quick peek told me it curved upward. Once more attempting to picture the rooms above, I thought I could guess where it would come out at.

No sounds echoing through the tunnel, I pulled my gun out and headed in. The slope wasn't too steep, but it still rose quickly. After just a few minutes, I'd reached the other end and let my senses loose for long range recon. They didn't pick anything up. It seemed I was alone.

Out of the hole, I popped up into what could be considered the foyer of Lucifer's quarters. The massive stones that sealed the chamber after Lucifer's departure had been removed by Asmoday and never been replaced. Now, the archway led out into the open expanses of Hell. From there, a knowledgeable person could get anywhere.

That didn't bode well.

Despite my anger at my uncle, I couldn't help but feel a bit proprietary about his quarters. It would nag at me until I made sure there wasn't anyone hiding in them or messing with his stuff. Besides, I had Rachelle hide Eve in Lucifer's God-proofed room and I needed to make sure the bone was still there.

A quick search of the place eased my mind, finding Eve right where Rachelle had put her. The place being empty made it even more so. Able to do it myself this time, I stashed the bone where no one would find it. Hopefully I could remember where I put it when the time came to retrieve it.

Getting ready to leave, I had an idea. As one of the first beings to come into existence, Lucifer had a wealth of knowledge on tap. While he wasn't around to ask questions—not that I would right now anyway—there was still plenty of information stashed away in the books he kept in his chambers.

In the off chance I might learn something useful, I returned to his room and plopped down in front of a stack of ancient texts.

Reminded of my lessons as a child, I wished I'd paid more attention then because cramming for tests never works out.

Chapter Sixteen

Time running out, my research job was half-ass at best, but I did find out a few things.

The last guardian of God's throne, who Akrasiel alluded to, was none other than the Archangel Metatron. The highest in the hierarchy of angels, he was God's personal scribe and right hand wingman. It was his job to pass on God's word to the rest of the Choir until the Big Guy up and poofed. He would definitely have the power to alter the course of the battle.

If what Akrasiel said was true, we were still pretty much screwed. Stationed in Heaven, right beside God's throne no less, I had no way of reaching him, or even getting a message through. Even if I could, I had no idea what it would take to spur him into action. If an angelic revolt in Heaven hadn't woken his ass up, then what the Hell was I gonna do to top that?

I'd also managed to dig up a little info on Akrasiel. He was actually the Archangel Raguel. Apparently, it was his place to keep all the other angels in line.

He sure wasn't doing a good job.

With God gone, I couldn't be certain that was still his angle. His cryptic commentary made me think he didn't really want me to succeed, but at the same time, you never know with supernaturals. There's always a hidden goal in everything they do, which is why they never just come out and say things plainly. As such, there just wasn't any way to be sure whose team he was playing for.

Worn out, my mind a useless jumble of nonsensical theories and ideas, I headed for the gate to leave Hell when a burst of static exploded inside my head. Recognizing the faint sputter of a telepathic connection, I answered, but no one replied.

Without warning, a glistening blue portal appeared in front of me. Already on edge, I jumped back with a squeak; I might have even tinkled a little. My fright turned to anger a split-second later as I recognized the source.

Rachelle peered out of the gate, her face ashen. "We need you, Frank. The Nephilim have attacked DRAC again."

She turned and exited the other side and I nearly ran her over in my haste to get through. We popped out in the cool desert night and I could have sworn it was the 4th of July.

Flashes of red and blue energies seared through the air, lighting up the sky as though it were day. Screams of rage and agony joined the cacophony of battle sounds. Over by the DRAC installation that was buried deep beneath the desert sand to avoid detection, stood what remained of the organization's military force.

Scarlett and Katon were a blur on the front lines, wreaking havoc upon the enemy. The gleaming trails of their mystical swords were conspicuous in their absence, but that didn't stop them. They barreled into the lines with a fury, blood and bodies flying in their wake.

At their sides were the few remaining DRAC wizards with any real power. Although nowhere near the might of Rahim, their spells were taking a heavy toll on the Nephilim. They'd opted for explosive magic that left black smoke and flash fires behind, helping to confuse those who survived the initial blasts.

The human security force, while immensely underpowered compared to the opposition, used the DA slayers to help even the odds. Set up smartly to take advantage of the Nephilim's clustered formation, deadly, magically-enhanced bullets peppered the half-breeds like sideways rain. It was surprisingly effective.

While not a tactician, Rachelle did great by bringing us in behind the gathered Nephilim. Though they hadn't brought but a fraction of their army, they still had us way outnumbered. Unfortunately, my being able to sneak attack them wasn't gonna be enough to even things out. It'd have to do though.

Too exhausted to pull off any more magic, I was gonna have to do it the old fashioned way. Committed, I left Rachelle behind and charged forward to put bullets into their backs. Amid the chaos, it took them a while to even realize I was there. I'd emptied two clips before I even got an ugly look. When they finally did notice, they responded with a vengeance.

A dozen bolts of mystical energy sizzled toward me at once. Fear and adrenaline kicking my body into overdrive, I managed to avoid the first volley, ducking and dodging as the glowing spears whipped past.

Their surprise worn off, the second barrage was more on target. I slipped the first two by jumping over them, but a third grazed my side and sent me into a spin; right into the path of the rest. Unable to get out of the way, I tucked into a ball to minimize the target space and hoped I didn't get hit anywhere vital.

Just before they struck, a shimmering blue portal appeared in front of me. It swallowed the bolts in one hungry gulp. I hit the ground at the same time Rachelle opened up a second portal in the midst of the Nephilim army.

The bolts exploded from the portal and crashed into the unsuspecting half-breeds with a resounding boom. My maniacal laugh was probably louder.

Obviously clueless as to what had happened, the Nephilim focused on me continued to blast away. My eyes on Rachelle to be sure she was still paying attention—she had a habit of wandering off mentally—I stood and fired. As the spears neared, they were once again intercepted and turned back upon their force.

Magical explosions bombarded the Nephilim from all sides as the slender mystic varied the locations with a thought. I continued drawing their attacks to me as Rachelle stayed out of sight and redirected everything tossed my way.

Katon and Scarlett realized what we were doing and ordered our folks to advance. Random blasts tearing at their flesh and morale, the front line violently cleaving through their ranks, the Nephilim broke. Those capable of dimensional travel ported away, leaving their friends to find their own ride home.

No longer being bombarded, I surveyed the field until I saw someone I recognized. Thinned as it was, it didn't take long.

Less than fifty feet from me, I spied the massive bulk of Jorn. Braver than most of his companions, he stood his ground, his meaty fists wailing away in a circle at anyone who came close. Shirtless—a sight that will forever live on in infamy in the annals of my memory—his arms and shoulders were covered in pustulant, bubbled wounds. The side of his face, I could see, was seared black, pieces molting off as he moved.

Scurrying around his feet was Zellick. The little guy stepped out quick from behind Jorn's shielding mass to lash out with his dagger, before leaping back to safety.

Venai was probably another fifty feet past them. She held a flickering portal open at her back as she screamed for Jorn and Zellick.

An idea sprang to mind. I called for Rachelle to pass on a message for Katon to follow me and headed off. As quick, and as low, as I could, I closed the intervening space. Venai spotted me just as I came up behind her companions. She shrieked a warning, but it was lost in the white noise of battle.

A smile plastered across my face, I waited until the weasel

popped up for another round of hit and run before doing anything. He saw me just as I pulled the trigger.

"Remember me?"

His eyes went wide as the bullet pierced his cheek. They were wider still when the back of his head exploded in a conflagration of red and gray. The spray showered Jorn in warm chunks as Zellick dropped at his feet. Venai screamed again and left the portal, racing toward us as fast as she could manage, her wounded leg slowing her down.

Jorn spun around to see Zellick crumpled in the sand. A horrible look of despair washed over his round face as he fell to his knees without even looking at me. He picked Zellick up like a child, and pulled him to his chest, showering him with tears.

Seeing the big guy crying, I felt a little bad about shooting his buddy; but only a little. The bastard had no problem going after my cousin or sticking me in the back, so why should I care? He'd reaped what he'd sown.

Venai almost on top of me, I leveled my gun toward Jorn's head and waggled a finger at her. Katon arrived right then, moving to stand beside the big guy, his hand on his huge shoulder.

"We've got some business to discuss," I told her with a wiggle of the gun, making sure she understood I would do the same to Jorn as I had Zellick.

She froze, but her glare was hot enough to melt steel.

"C'mon now, you don't get to be a hypocrite. You and your buddies were looking to whack my cousin, so get down off your high horse."

Venai growled, but her glower took on a shade of resignation. "I won't give you the key piece."

Before I could say anything, Scarlett stepped up behind her. She wrapped her arms around Venai's thick waist and lifted her into the air as though the half-breed weighed nothing. Venai's eyes popped wide as Scarlett took her for a ride, flipping her head over heels before slamming her hard into the ground. She hit with a manly grunt.

Scarlett stood over her with a vindictive grin, her fists clenched. "Bitch!" She didn't look like she was done.

Katon, catching the imploring look I gave him, left Jorn where he was kneeling and went to pull Scarlett off Venai. She put up a little bit of a fight, but it was halfhearted.

Once Scarlett was away from her, Venai looked up at me, her face dusted in sand.

"I don't want the piece," I told her, continuing as if we hadn't been interrupted.

She looked at me like I'd just outed Brad Pitt. "You lie!"

"Of course I do, I'm a demon, but I'm serious this time. You can keep the damn thing. In fact, you can have ours too."

"What?" The question was asked in triplicate. Katon and Scarlett stared at me like I was out of my mind while Venai just stared in disbelief.

"We're not giv—"

I waved Scarlett quiet. "Look, Venai, as things stand, we're at a three-way standstill. You have a piece, we have a piece, and the weres have a piece. What that means is none of us are going anywhere near Heaven before the world goes *kaboom*." Gesturing to the Nephilim who lay dead around us, I laughed. "We can do this all day and it won't change the outcome one bit. Seeing how we're all gonna die anyway, who cares?"

Her eyes met mine and I saw a tiny crack of reason squirreled away in there. I went to work on it.

"The Nephilim are in just as much danger as the rest of us. If the weres win, they'll cut down the Tree of Life and we'll all become mortal. That includes you. At that point, it won't matter how many of you there are; you'll all die. You won't pass Go, you won't collect $200, and you won't be going to Heaven."

The crack slit wide. "What do you want?"

If only getting laid were so easy. "A truce of sorts."

Scarlett shouted and stepped forward. Though Katon pulled her back, he looked a bit reluctant. He stared at me with questioning eyes, wondering what I was up to. Scarlett just looked like she wanted to kill me.

Venai shook her head. "Why? What do you get out of giving up your piece?"

"First off, I get to live. That's pretty high up on my things to do list. I'm not gonna get to do it much longer if something doesn't change soon." I waved my hand in the general direction of Eden. "Second, your people aren't looking to commit genocide like the weres. While it's not the ideal solution, from our perspective, letting ya'll win is easily the lesser of the three evils we face. We can always renew hostilities later." My gun still trained on Jorn, I shook it to make my point.

Though she didn't even blink, I could tell she was thinking it over. "So, you just hand the bone over and we go our separate ways?"

"Kinda, yeah, but I won't be giving it to you, at least not here."

The glare back on her face, Venai got to her feet. A finger of warning to Scarlett let her stay there.

"Then what do you propose?"

"You go back to your people and tell them I'll be at the gate shortly to hand over the key piece. You have to make sure they're ready to deal with the weres though, because the second I pull the piece out, it's gonna rain furballs."

"That's it?"

I nodded. "I'm not greedy. I just want to wake up alive tomorrow."

She looked to Scarlett, then back to me. It was clear what she wanted to know.

"I'll never hear the end of her bitching, and you can guarantee she'll be kicking down your door after the dust has settled, but she'll go along for now. Won't you, Scarlett?"

Venai looked to Scarlett again and I nearly disfigured my face trying to get her to agree with me. Scarlett went back and forth, glaring at both of us, but she finally relented. She knew me well enough to know I had a plan. Unfortunately, she also knew me well enough to realize it probably sucked and would likely end up getting us killed.

She was probably right.

A quiet sigh slipped from Venai as she looked to where Jorn kneeled, cradling Zellick's body. "I'll do this, but you and I aren't finished. You will pay for Zellick's death."

A wise-ass remark hopped onto my tongue and I nearly choked swallowing it. Though I rarely listen to my own advice, it wouldn't help things to antagonize. So instead, I took a handful of steps back and lowered my gun.

"I'll be around." At least I hoped I would be.

Venai didn't waste any time. She summoned a portal beside Jorn and pulled it over them, Zellick still in the big guy's arms. In just a second, all three were gone. Less than a second after that, I was on my ass, staring up at the spinning desert sky.

Scarlett stepped over me, a vicious snarl marring her beauty. "What the Hell are you thinking?"

"That this would be a lot less awkward if you weren't trying to put your foot in my ass."

She kicked me. Hard.

"How dare you give away Heaven." She pulled her fist back to finish the job.

"Whoa, whoa, easy there." I raised my hands in surrender. "I'm not giving anything away. Help me out, Katon."

The enforcer walked to my cousin's side and stared down at me. He didn't look any more inclined to listen than she did. Rachelle came up behind them, and peeked around. It was hard to tell if she meant to rescue me or just watch.

"If you'll stop beating me, I'll explain."

Scarlett growled, but she relented and slowly lowered her fist.

I climbed to my feet. "We don't stand a chance against either army, let alone both. We got lucky here because they underestimated our abilities." I pointed to the remaining members of DRAC who stood huddled together like refugees from a liberated concentration camp. "That won't happen the next time. If the were-critters are busy fighting the Nephilim though, we can sit back and pick our moment."

"Doing what?"

"Stealing the key out from under them."

Scarlett drew in a deep breath and let it out slow as if I was starting to make some kind of sense to her. It's happens every once in a while. "How?"

I nodded toward the mystic. "With Rachelle able to open a portal pretty much anywhere, we wait until the pieces are together, then port there and hit whoever has it with everything we've got." A toothy smirk on my face, I continued. "Once we have it, we open the gate to Eden and make a mad dash for it, key in hand. As soon as we're in, Uriel can seal Eden behind us to keep the rest of the clowns out."

It was obvious Scarlett liked the idea, but she wasn't sure. Katon voiced his concerns and Scarlett's as well, no doubt.

"We're not much in the way of reinforcements. Are you thinking we can turn the tide against Gabriel?"

"No, not really." Scarlett started to complain, but I cut her off. "There is someone who can and he's already there; Metatron."

Scarlett whistled, a bemused smile crossing her lips. "I always knew you were crazy, but this plan of yours confirms it. Metatron has been comatose since God left." The smile melted away as her voice hardened. "He couldn't be bothered to help when Gabriel and Michael were slaughtering angels at the very heart of Heaven, so what makes you think he'll care if a few more die?"

"You don't think we can wake him?" I'd hoped for some optimism.

Scarlett shook her head, a tear rolling down her pale cheek.

"It would take the return of God to draw him from his emotional slumber."

That wasn't gonna happen, but I couldn't think of anything else we could do. "Do you have a better plan?"

Rachelle stayed quiet as Scarlett shook her head. I looked to Katon, who stared at the ground.

Sighing, I climbed up on my soapbox. "Look, I don't want to die, but if I have to, I'd rather do it thinking we had a chance. Even if that chance is as slim as me getting to sleep with Megan Fox, it's got to be better than nothing. The last thing I want to do is sit around and mope until the Winter Wonderland of Death comes to wipe me out of existence. Is that how you want to die?"

Katon raised his chin and met my eyes. There was fire there. "I'm in."

Scarlett grinned at his approval and nodded. "If there is a chance I can spill Gabriel's blood then I'm in as well."

Rachelle just smiled. I'd probably have to remind her of what we decided later, but for now, her smile was good enough for me.

"Hey, Rachelle, I need a lift."

"Where are you going?" Katon asked.

Scarlett looked at me, the same question etched across her face.

"I need to do a couple of things, plus I have to get Eve. Besides, somebody needs to tell the weres they're invited to the shindig. You can't trust those party animals to show up on time." I smiled and waved. "Stay here and get the troops ready. I'll be back in a bit."

While Rachelle whipped up a portal, I grinned. "Take me to Hell."

Chapter Seventeen

After a few minutes spent digging around in Hell, I'd rounded up Eve and confirmed a hunch. Finished with that, I used the gate in Asmoday's cell to pop into Baalth's office. Poe met me with a gun aimed at my head.

"I'm either experiencing *déjà vu* or we've done this before."

Poe growled and lowered his weapon. "You've been gone for hours. I was getting ready to come after you. What happened?"

"Got a little distracted. Oh, and I'd advise against using the gate anytime soon. In fact, I'd suggest locking it down. Turns out, you've got a pretty big varmint infestation down there."

He raised an eyebrow. "Varmint?"

"Varmint, dread fiend, same thing."

He stared at me a moment, no doubt waiting for the punch line. When he realized there wasn't one, he sent a spike of mystical will toward the pentagram to seal the gate. Sparks glimmered along the golden lines and the lights flickered for second, then the star turned black. Finished, he turned back to me.

"Are they what killed Asmoday?"

Unsure if I should tell him about the empty case, I shrugged. "I'm not sure."

His eyes narrowed at my answer, but he didn't say anything. Having not been definite, even though I doubted the fiends had butchered Asmoday, he couldn't get a bead on my true feelings.

Before he could start asking more questions, I got to my reason for being there. "Hey, you got plans for tonight?"

He looked at me and I swear I saw a flash of red color his cheeks before his mask of neutrality washed it away. "You're asking me why, Mister Trigg?"

A once in a lifetime opportunity in my grasp, I bit my tongue and let it slip away. Damn. "We're a little short on the Save the World Committee and I was hoping we could enlist your help."

He swallowed deep before he answered, "What do you have in mind?"

"We'll be storming Heaven a little later, and if you don't have anything better to do, we'd appreciate your assistance."

He sighed, knowing full well I was serious. "I'll clear my calendar."

I told him we'd swing by and pick *him* up when everything was in place, making it clear I didn't want Marcus tagging along. That done, I headed for the house.

* * * *

A hop, skip, and a teleport later, I was home. Chatterbox greeted me with happy giggles as I entered the living room, bouncing up and down on the table beside the couch. The TV was on and *Dawn of the Dead* screamed from the screen. A quick flick of the remote dropped the volume to a reasonable level.

Both Chatterbox and I grumbled at the same time, though for different reasons. He complained because I'd turned the movie down. I was annoyed because the remote was covered in zombie tongue-slime. He got the better end of the deal.

"You can turn it back up in a bit," I said to keep him quiet, my hand unconsciously wiping the slimy, gray-green nastiness off on my pant leg.

The screams and howls of the dying and undead—those on the screen and those in my house—muted well enough I could think again, I headed for my room when there was a sudden, loud knock on my front door. Chatterbox and I whipped our heads toward the door at the same time. The security camera monitor in the foyer was filled with static, so I couldn't see who was outside. It got me thinking.

Neck deep in paranoia, I pulled my gun out and let my senses loose. It's not like I expected my current crop of foes to politely knock at the door, but you never know. Stranger things have happened.

My senses relayed back a lack of any substantial mystical aura, but there was a glimmer of confusion in what I felt. It was as if they couldn't read what lay beyond the door, an uncertainty in their report. Not encouraged by that, I probed a little deeper as the knock rang out again, a little more insistent this time.

Not able to pick up anything I could construe as a magical threat, I whispered for Chatterbox to sit by the phone just in case. To be safe, I ran to my room and stashed Eve with the blood vials, then I went to answer the knock.

"Who is it?"

A muffled, but polite voice answered, saying something I

couldn't understand, though I picked out the word neighbor. Still unsure, I cracked the door open and peeked outside, my gun just out of sight and ready to go.

Two men stood there in simple black suits. My eyes instinctively went to their hands and saw they were empty and relaxed, so I drifted back to their faces. The men smiled at me in stereo.

One was dark skinned, though it seemed more from exposure to the sun than natural pigmentation, and the other was so pale I could almost see through him. Both were shaved bald and neither had the slightest hint of facial hair. Their twin brown eyes sparkled with excitement and their perfect teeth seemed to glimmer in the dim light, their smiles wide.

The shorter of the two, though neither of them could be called short—both easily six feet plus—proffered his hand.

"Mister Frank Trigg?" His voice was smooth; a salesman's modulated tone. The use of my name sent a shiver up my spine. Once more, everyone seemed to know me, but I had no clue who the Hell they were. It was getting seriously annoying.

My glance flickered back to their hands. I'd been looking for weapons the first time, but now I was looking for pamphlets.

"Out a little late to be selling salvation, aren't we?" At the risk of appearing rude, I didn't take the man's ashen hand.

He lowered it easy, not looking the slightest bit bothered, as though it happened all the time. "My name is Jonas Black and my partner here is Ethan White. We'd like you come with us."

My eyes shifted back and forth between the two and I shook my head, trying not to laugh. Someone in their family trees had a wry sense of humor. "I'm not sure who you gentlemen are, but I really don't have time for this right now." The politely disguised order made me think they were government agents of some sort. If that were the case, I definitely didn't need to be talking to them, let alone going anywhere. "Come back in a couple of days and we can chat all you want." If the world still exists, that is.

White took a step forward, the smile still on his face. "I'm afraid we must insist."

My finger on the trigger, I went to close the door. "Some other time, thanks."

Jonas Black stuck his hand between it and the frame, the door thumping against his knuckles as though they were made of brick. Despite my leaning against it, he left it there and the door stayed cracked.

A quiet voice called out from the other side. "We need you to come with us now, Mister Trigg. This matter cannot wait." There was no change in his inflection, but the words seemed somehow harder, fiercer.

No clue what these guys wanted, or who they were working for, I didn't have time to be nice anymore. My foot against the door to hold it in place, I swept down with my pistol grip and smacked Black's hand. It was like banging two steel pipes together.

A sharp metallic clack rang out and his hand popped free of the frame, the door slamming shut once it was out of the way. The house wards came up instantly, their energies prickling my skin as I ducked around the corner to be out of the line of fire.

Turns out that was a good idea, though not for the reasons I'd expected.

A thunderous explosion shook the house and my front door was blown off its hinges. It flew backwards down the hall and through the living room until it crashed into the adjoining kitchen wall. The impact devastated both. Shards of plaster and wood flew everywhere, a gray dust kicking up.

Chatterbox rolled for cover as the door hit, dropping off the table to cower behind the couch. I made sure he was safe before tucking my head. Then waiting until the pieces settled, I cast a glance down the hall.

The two men were out by the street, flat on their backs where the explosion of the defending wards had tossed them. Smoky whispers drifted from them as they quickly got to their feet. The house unprotected, I hunkered down and took aim.

Their smiles gone, they ran straight toward the missing door. The move was so obviously stupid, it made me wonder if there were more of them behind me somewhere, waiting for me to take the bait. They couldn't possibly be that dumb.

"Watch my back," I called out to Chatterbox, just in case. He moaned an affirmative.

The men closing, I waited to make sure my shots counted. Just as they reached the threshold, I put two in the chest of Ethan White. The impacts rang out as though I'd shot a steel plate.

He stumbled back into his buddy, slowing their momentum, but he didn't fall. His lips screwed up into a crooked sneer, he caught his balance and came forward again.

Surprised by the quality of his flak jacket, it took me a second to steady my hand and put a shot into his skull. Once more the bullet rang out, metal on metal as I caught him in the forehead. White fell to his knees and wiped the protruding bullet away as though it were an annoyance. His buddy slipped past him and charged.

Suddenly realizing why they chose the direct route, I emptied the clip on Jonas as my mind scrambled for a plan. The bullets did little more than piss him off. Driven to a snail's pace, he growled as he waded forward through the hail of fire. A smug smile broke out on his marbled face when my gun clicked empty.

The wiser of us, my asshole puckered and signaled a retreat.

To the sound of stomping feet, I stuffed my gun into my pants as I swung around the corner and headed for the back door. It crumpled on its hinges before I could make it there. White smiled at me through the ruin of the door, looking like a reject out of a Stephen King novel.

The run-n-gun approach out the window, I figured I'd take a page out of their operating manual and go through rather than around. My shoulders stooped, I barreled straight toward White, who only smiled wider at my approach. At the last second, I faked left and dodged right.

It almost worked.

White shifted toward my feint, but even off balance he managed to get his hand in the way as I ran past. It was like running into an I-beam.

A loud bell went off inside my skull and I felt my feet fly out from beneath me. A second later, my back slammed into the ground, my head following it down with a thump. My momentum slid me across the floor as wooden splinters poked me in places a Penthouse Letters reader might blush to hear about. The slide ended ten feet down the road after I'd bumped over the small doorstep and tumbled into the yard.

My eyes swum in their sockets as I stared up at the star-filled night sky. Not sure which were real and which were a byproduct of having my brain scrambled, I decided it best not to lay there and try to figure it out. Rolling over, the world swaying around me, I reevaluated that decision. It probably was best just to stay there.

Of all my bad habits, I really need to give up getting smacked in the head. I wonder if there's a patch for that.

Black and White stood just outside the doorway, their amused smiles grating on my battered nerves. They looked down at me and White shook his head.

"Care to come with us now?"

"Yeah, I'm starting to think that might be a good idea." White went to help me and I waved a hand at him. "I got it, just give me a second. At least let me get up on my own."

A silken chuckle eased from his mouth as he stepped back to Black's side. "By all means. I wouldn't want to impugn your manhood, such as it is."

"Thanks," I told him, forcing a couple of coughs.

My head resting on the ground, I pulled my left knee under me and kind of leaned to the right. Hoping my body blocked my movement, I slid my hand into my right pocket. As soon as my fingers wrapped around the vial, which was miraculously intact, I slid it out and pulled my other knee up while coughing a couple more times.

"Any time now."

"Just a sec—" Mid sentence, I broke out in a fit of coughs, my hands going to my mouth. I rolled to my side as though I were choking, and turned my back on Black and White. Almost frantic, I popped the stopper on the vial as I heard them coming toward me. With a little lean to raise my head some, I emptied the contents of the vial into my mouth and swallowed fast just as I felt their cold hands latch onto me. With a gentle push, I left the vial slip from my hand and slid it across the grass, toward my feet.

"Come on now, surely you aren't that hurt."

They pulled me up and held my arms, not even bothering to restrain me. I squirmed a little and stumbled forward and they tightened their grip to keep me from falling over. My feet barely touching the ground, they led me across the yard and through the gate to the front, the vial still on the grass behind us; unnoticed.

As we neared what I presumed was their black van, I felt the warm rush of Lucifer's blood as it merged with mine. The gentle tingling ran through my veins, easing away all my aches and pains. A pleasant tickle played at my groin and I fought the urge to give in to it, knowing it was just foreplay for the mind-fuck to come. The feelings growing more intense, I clenched my teeth and waited.

Suddenly my body went rigid, my muscles screaming in agony as they surged with mystical energy. A rabid, foam-mouthed scream slipped loose from my mouth as molten lava ripped through my innards. My vision went white and I could feel myself twitching like an epileptic.

Though I couldn't see them, Black and White held on. Snippets of their words pierced the haze of my whirling mind, but I couldn't follow what they were saying. It was all gibberish to me, like watching Oprah.

Then just as suddenly as it hit me, the pain passed and I dropped limp in their grasp. They set me down on my knees but kept ahold of my arms. White leaned over to look me in the face.

He huffed, irritation finally tainting his smooth delivery. "No games, Trigg. Go with us peacefully or we'll do this the hard way."

I focused my eyes on his and broke into a wide grin. "Let's go with the latter."

Confusion stampeded across his face and I didn't let it go to waste. A quick jerk of my arms pulled them around in front of me, the men crashing into each other with a kettledrum boom. They fell to the ground in a tangled mess of thrashing limbs.

Their hold on me broken, I stepped away and summoned my energies as they fought to get to their feet. Unlike before, my horse and buggy magic needing a steep hill to get going, the power roared to life like a Ferrari. The feeling was orgasmic.

Black and White, now back on their feet, eased away, clearly realizing something had changed.

"Leaving so soon? I thought you wanted to chat."

White spun without a word and ran for the house. Black went the opposite direction, racing across the yard. Not wanting to damage my house any further, I went after Black.

Envisioning a sword, my magic complied. Made of pure mystical energy, a shimmering blade appeared in my hand, illuminating the night.

Though Black had a head start, it wasn't much of one. A quick leap put me at his back as he scrambled to get into the van. While he dug in his pockets for the keys, I grabbed his shoulder from behind. There was a clank as my hand latched on, my fingers sinking in a little with a muffled metallic squeal.

Without hesitation, he threw an elbow at me, but with Lucifer's blood flowing in my veins, I saw it coming. The shimmering blade of my sword met his triceps midway and cleaved clean through. His severed arm boomeranged passed to land in the yard behind me.

Black didn't scream, but I nearly did.

I'd expected to see spraying blood and hacked up meat, but there wasn't any of that. Instead, the stump of his arm was a solid mass, one big hunk of reflective steel. Inside the fleshy cocoon, it flowed like water, swirling in the wound. No clue what Black was, my eyes were transfixed.

He took advantage of my hesitation and yanked his shoulder free. He took another swing at me, my mind waking up, and I moved to defend, but it had been a feint. He spun and bolted down the street as I regained my balance. I watched him go. He wasn't so fast I couldn't catch him, but I didn't want to waste the energy. Having used some of the blood to heal Scarlett and me a couple of times, I wasn't sure how much longer I'd be Super Frank on the lower dosage. If White was still in the house, I was gonna need the boost.

Spurred on by the thought of powering down, I raced inside. Chatterbox whistled and hopped up and down to get my attention.

"*Doooooooooorrrrrrrrrrr,*" he said as I charged into the living room.

I looked to my shattered back door and let my senses go. While they hadn't exactly been on the money earlier, I'd been able to feel Black and White. That feeling wasn't there now. They were gone.

The timing was perfect. I could feel the magic of the blood slipping away, a subtle tiredness trickling over me. My mystical blade flickered and died, no longer needed.

Certain I didn't want to be in the house when I came all the way down, exhaustion too mild a word to describe the feeling that awaited me, I ran to my bedroom. There, I retrieved the last of Lucifer's blood and wrapped the vials in one of my pillowcases for safekeeping. Eve came next, then I remembered the power-dampening manacles hidden under my bed. I grabbed them and flung them over my shoulder before heading back down the hall to the living room.

My energy wavering, I picked up Chatterbox and set him on the table facing me. "Send a message to Karra. Have her meet me near the mausoleum at Rest Land as soon as she can." Still connected to Karra through the psychic link that kept him animated, it was the quickest way to reach her. It also kept me from having to touch the zombified phone.

While he was doing that, I went outside and grabbed Black's severed arm. It twitched as I picked it up, a subtle spasm that weirded me out, before going completely rigid. Not sure what to do with it, I really didn't want to leave it laying around for someone to find should the world make it through the crisis. Besides that, it would make a groovy trophy. I decided to keep it, at least until I could dig up some information on the bastard it belonged to and what him and his partner wanted. It didn't hurt to think Black would be a little easier to deal with, minus a limb.

So thinking, I added Black's stiffened arm to my baggage and went back inside.

"You done?" I asked Chatterbox.

After a few seconds, he nodded—well, he actually rocked back and forth, but we're talking semantics here. A black-lipped smile plastered across his face, he hopped into the pillowcase I held open and sniggered like Muttley as he got comfortable.

Through blurry eyes, I took one last look at my house. I'd lived there for over eighty years, and though the rebuild had taken some of the old charm away, it was still my home. Thinking I might never see it again, I sighed and made my way to the gate room in back. The portal powering up, me powering down, I clutched my loot tight to make sure I didn't lose any of it in transit.

Whisked away to Chatterbox's off-key warble of *Jump in the Fire*, I couldn't help but think he was psychic.

Chapter Eighteen

Wanting nothing more than to close my eyes and pull a Rip Van Winkle, I paced along a line of graves with Chatterbox in my arms, silently reading the names of each to keep my mind somewhat active. The steady rhythm of the sprinklers filled the night air, the gardens just to the north being watered.

The mausoleum closed and locked down, I waited for Karra behind it, sticking to the shadows to avoid being seen by the night guy, Marvin.

He was a jumpy fella with bad cholesterol and an inflated beach ball for a belly. The last thing his overworked heart needed was to stumble across me in the middle of the night, holding an animated zombie head. There was enough blood on my conscience already.

On about my fiftieth loop, I felt the zombie head go rigid and I turned to see Karra walking toward us, her shape defined even in the darkness. Not wanting Chatterbox to feel alone, I started to go rigid too.

Karra closed the distance and wrapped her arms around my neck, pulling me in toward her. Her lips met mine and I forgot all about the end of the world, swept away in her kiss. A squirming lump between us, I felt her tongue flicker into my mouth and that's all it took; I was at full mast.

Her mouth pressed hard against mine, I leaned into the kiss and heard her moan, deep and throaty. Though it sounded a little odd, she didn't pull away. Encouraged, I reached around and grabbed her ass and felt her slide a hand down my stomach, to my crotch. Driven by pure male instinct–kill, eat, and fuck–I broke off the kiss to give her room to operate. Her hazel eyes met mine and she smiled sexy, her hands flittering along my neck and shoulders, the one at my groin twitching. She groaned and the power of it vibrated my crotch.

Then her eyes narrowed, her nose crinkling up. She looked at me like I'd farted, then it hit me.

At the same time, both of us leapt backward. No longer wedged between us, Chattterbox fell to the ground with a dull thud. His sallow face grinned with reckless abandon. "*Thhhhhrrrrrrreeeeeeeeeeeeeeesssssssssssoooooommmmmmme*"

While there aren't a whole lot of lines I wouldn't cross at least once, sometimes you just have to say no. Disgusted shivers buffeted my body as I realized it was Chatterbox who'd been rubbing up against my dick.

Karra giggled and dropped to a seat. "Bad zombie." The words came out stuttered because she couldn't stop laughing.

Feeling dirty in a way I've never felt, I circled way around Chatterbox and went to sit by Karra. I wondered if I had any bleach at home.

Karra scooted over and rested her head on my shoulder. "So, what was it you needed?"

A million things popped into my head at once, but when the filter sorted need from desperate want, only one thing made it through the wash. "I'm planning a little get together and I need help passing on an invitation."

Her hand squirmed into mine and squeezed as she lifted her head to look at me. "Who are you looking to invite?"

"I've got the Nephilim hosting, but I need to make sure the weres crash the party. You think you can get a message to the vamps?"

She nodded. "Easy enough."

As a necromancer, Karra had a special connection to the dead. While I won't pretend I know how the damn thing works, I do know she has an effective means of controlling the lower level undead. Chatterbox's continued existence was proof of that. That's what made me think she could pull this off in the first place.

"Can you make it subtle?" I asked. "They're gonna be suspicious enough as it is, so I really need them to think this is a legitimate tip."

"I can do subtle." She gave me an amused smile and winked.

I could attest to that. She'd led me around by my pe—nose in her quest to resurrect her father. I never once realized she'd been using me to set up Lilith, so I figured this wouldn't be a problem. So thinking, I told her the specifics of what I needed her to pass on.

Time running short, I thought it best that I got going. As much as I wanted to stay, to wrap myself up in Karra and lose myself in her until the world comes crumbling down around us, there were people counting on me.

Fools.

Her hand still in mine, I got to my feet, dragging her up with me. She stepped in and hugged me tight, nuzzling my neck as I returned the hug with fierce enthusiasm. After several minutes, neither of us willing to let go, I leaned into her ear.

"I need another favor. Can you look after Chatterbox."

She loosed a whispery sigh, her warm breath caressing my neck, then leaned back so we were face to face. "Until you come back."

"Yeah, until I come back."

We were both dancing around reality, neither willing to spoil the moment. The truth was, while she didn't know what I had in mind, and I only vaguely knew, we both understood this could very well be our last moment together.

Only recently reunited, it felt as though we'd never been apart. For me, it was a dream come true, but like my uncle, the world conspired to ruin everything. The one thing I wanted most was right here in my arms and yet I had to leave, had to run off to fight a war that had nothing to do with me. It made me sick to think about it.

Karra, realizing I wasn't strong enough to let her go, took the lead. Again. She pulled back and gave me a smile. "You need to go."

She kissed me gentle, her hand grazing my cheek, before she broke off with sigh. "Come by and pick him up when this is all over."

She went over and snatched up the zombie head as I tried to make my tongue work. Inflicted with rigor mortis, I couldn't get it to move. Karra gave me one last smile and held Chatterbox up for a second so he could say his goodbyes, then she turned to disappear into the darkness. Once again, I was alone.

Though I should have been getting ready to hand the key piece over to the Nephilim, I just stood there. My chest felt tight, every breath an effort of will. Karra gone, what little energy I had left flickered and faded away. It had been a rough couple of days and the gauge was dipping below empty.

Lulled into believing I was gone, the nearby crickets started up again. Their quiet chirps flittered in the background, the gentle breeze carrying them to my ears. Bound to fall asleep if I stayed any longer, I forced my feet forward, scooping up my makeshift bag, Black's arm, and the manacles on the way.

As I circled around to the front of the mausoleum, I listened for the night guy and heard him talking to himself as he went around adjusting the sprinklers. Not wanting to run into him, I changed directions and headed toward the back gate. The breeze had picked up some, its gusts helping to keep me moving.

A rumble of thunder sounded overhead and I sighed. A good distance from the closest teleporter, the last thing I needed was rain. I picked up the pace a little, expecting to get soaked, as another boom shook the sky, followed by another. Lightning flashed above and I caught its shimmering reflection in the polished stone of a grave marker. It glistened purple for a split-second, then vanished.

Spurred on by the increasing winds, I did my best to put a little more oomph in my step. I'd made it about ten feet before my sleep-deprived brain processed what I had seen.

My heart stilled in my chest, and I stopped, looking straight up at the mass of white clouds that hung low and thick right above me. Purple lightning cavorted in the sky, its flickering tongues licking at the clouds that encased it. Like a cornered cat, my eyes flitted back and forth trying to find an area of clear sky.

There wasn't any.

The winds slowed and died away as the overpowering stench of death began to fill the air with choking bitterness. The clouds started to lighten, the storm illuminating the sky with an eerie glimmer.

My eyes alighted on the mausoleum, the only shelter in the area close enough to reach. Terror lit fire to my feet and they flew across the grassy field of graves, the bag flapping behind me, the manacles clinking together and slapping my back. I closed the distance fast, my breath whistling in my lungs. As I swung around the far edge of the building, I spied a flashing light a couple of gardens away. Screeching to a stop, my heels digging into the asphalt, I looked out across the cemetery to see Marvin. Flashlight in hand, he stood there casting its beam along the ground, looking for something. Oblivious to the storm, he made no effort to flee.

I looked up at the sky again to see the first flutters of the deadly snow drifting down. The mausoleum just ten easy feet from where I stood, a quick dash away, the voices in my head screamed for me to go inside. That is, all but one.

My mother.

"You better be proud, woman." The things us mama's boys do. Certain I was gonna die playing hero, I beat feet toward Marvin. Caught up in his own world, he didn't notice me until I was huffing and puffing right in front of him.

He shrieked and curled up in a ball as soon as I reached him.

"Damn it, Marvin, get the Hell up!"

He whimpered, muttering something about God and forgiveness, spewing out a list of sins that was impressive. It sounded like a perverse prayer, rattled off in hyper speed.

No time to talk sense into him or congratulate him on a life well-lived, I looped my arm around his and tried to pull him to his feet. No friend of gravity, all three hundred and fifty pounds of him resisted.

"Get up!" I screamed again, damn near yanking his arm out of socket.

He got to his feet only to save his arm. Wide eyed with terror, he just stood there staring, his body rigid in defiance. A quick glance up told me we were fixing to die. The snow was thickening as it fell, ominous in its approach.

No chance of making it back to the mausoleum, not that it would protect us anyway, I surveyed the garden for something to hide under. There was nothing. My heart sank and joined my balls, which were hiding deep inside my ass. Not ready to die, I looked around one last desperate time and noticed a sheet of plywood on the ground just a few feet from us. Suddenly remembering why a board would be there in the middle of the garden, I sunk my hand into the flab of Marvin's arm and dragged him along behind me.

There, I lifted the plywood up and breathed a relieved sigh as I saw the open grave beneath it. No time to worry about kindness, I shoved Marvin into the hole, tossed my luggage in, then jumped in after. Marvin landed with a pained grunt. Whimpers and quiet sobs followed as I straightened the board to make sure it covered the hole completely. Though I knew it wouldn't hold up against the snow for more than a minute, it was something.

A quick look around the grave told me it wouldn't be empty for long; the storm was running a two-for-one sale. Not interested in dying, and even less interested in dying with Marvin, I kicked my brain into high gear. There had to be a way out.

Suddenly, a light came on.

It was Marvin's flashlight, but I had an idea too.

"Is there anyone buried on this side?" I asked the groundskeeper. Still obviously terrified, the bitter stink of urine wafting up inside the confined grave, Marvin didn't answer.

Our lives on the line, I couldn't wait for him to get it together. I ran my hand along the grave wall and the moist dirt crumbled beneath my fingers. It was all the encouragement I needed. Like a dog, I sunk my hands into the dirt about halfway down the wall and started digging. It gave way easily; at first.

Handfuls of dirt flew between my legs as I tore into the wall, but the further I got, the harder it became. Knotted roots ran through the dirt, the tangled mess compressed together by time. The wall came away in solid chunks, each inch giving way slower and slower.

Above us, I could hear the snow sizzling against the board, a quiet creak accompanying it as it settled thick overtop. Desperation setting in, I channeled every ounce of energy I had into my hands, willing my magic into being.

Nothing happened.

Continuing to dig, I pushed harder, wishing I had time to ingest another vial of Lucifer's blood. Too late for that, I scoured the depths of my will and scrounged for every ounce of power I could find. At last, a dull flicker of energy came to life at my fingers.

I nearly soiled myself in relief.

Aided by the wispy strength of my magic, my fingers tore through the wall like a bulldozer. Dirt fell away in massive clumps, crumbling into a pile around my boots. Marvin scrambled to avoid being buried, getting to his feet in a sudden rush of activity.

"Touch that board and I'll kill you, Marvin," I told him without even looking. I heard him thump down behind me, his sobs beginning anew.

There was a sharp crack that sounded above us, just as my hand smacked against the solid wall of a concrete liner. Out of the corner of my eye, I saw a white flake flutter down into the grave; our grave.

Our time was up.

"No!" a voice in my head screamed. More afraid than I'd ever been, I couldn't imagine being eaten away piece by piece, the fall devouring me until I existed no longer. Driven by my terror, I snatched up Black's stiff arm and swung it at the wall of the liner.

It crashed into it with a resounding thud, knocking a fist-sized chunk of old concrete off and splitting the liner to its lid. Marvin screeched behind me and began to thrash about, but I didn't look back. I knew what happened when the smell of seared flesh stung my nose, so I put everything I had left into the next swing. With a solid boom that rang my ears, the arm shattered the liner wall, its rebar reinforcement sagging under the weight of the concrete.

Safety but a second away, the smell of old death rushing out to assail my nose, I dropped the arm and grabbed onto the rebar frame. Pulling with all my weight and strength, remnants of my magic fluttering at my hands, the frame buckled with a loud squeal and collapsed at my feet. The liner's decayed occupant glared at me through cavernous sockets.

No time for the dead, I spun and grabbed Marvin just as another couple of flakes ate through the plywood and fluttered down. One struck my arm, but I ignored it as I hauled Marvin bodily into the liner. He squealed like a stuck pig when he saw the body, but he didn't resist. He'd gotten it at last.

Barely able to fit him in alongside the corpse, I pushed until Marvin was packed in tight, and then crawled in right beside him. I reached out and grabbed my stuff and pulled it close to my chest just as the board gave way above.

A poof of white fell into the hole, disintegrating everything it touched, the light of Marvin's flashlight extinguished permanently. My breath froze in my lungs as the silent flakes fell less than a foot from my face. I didn't dare move for fear of rolling out, my position tenuous at best. I didn't even want to risk breathing, but I could only hold my breath for so long.

Several minutes crept by and the snow continued to fall. I could see the ground on the far side of the grave being devoured by inches and I knew the earth above us was experiencing the same. I could only hope we were deep enough.

Far from religious, for what I imagine are obvious reasons, I said a quiet thanks to no one in particular that the snow fell straight down. Under its assault, the bottom of the grave just outside our hidey hole sank deeper and deeper. Uncomfortably wedged in as I was, I hoped the storm wouldn't last so long that it reached the water table. It'd really suck to survive the storm only to drown as the water filled the void.

Fortunately, that wasn't case. After an excruciating fifteen minutes, every tentative breath feeling like the last, the storm slowed, and then crept to an end. The snow disappeared as though it had never been. Darkness returned to chase away the preternatural light. I waited a few minutes before I thought about moving, just to be sure.

When I finally found the courage, I crawled out of the liner and tumbled into the now deeper grave. It was close to three feet lower than it had been before the storm. The walls on both sides had been chewed down about that much as well.

My stomach lurched as I examined the earth above our sanctuary. There was maybe an inch or two of ground left over the concrete liner that had rested above our heads. Had the storm lasted another five minutes, it would have killed us where we lay. Cold sweat tickled my scalp as I thought about how close we'd come to dying. I couldn't keep the smile off my face.

Then that's when reality sunk in. The clouds had gone on for as far as I could see, in every direction. Nestled in the middle of town, the cemetery was surrounded by houses. As lucky as I had gotten, only because I knew what the storm could do, there would be thousands of people who didn't make it. My exhilaration died with the thought of their end.

Trying not to vomit, I tugged Marvin out of the liner before helping him out of the grave. I gathered my stuff and climbed out behind him, my eyes not believing what they saw. My first choice of hiding places, the mausoleum had vanished, no trace of it left. Had I gone with my initial instincts, there'd be nothing left of me either.

The maintenance garage across the road was missing as well, in fact, so was the road. The ground level lowered by several feet, there was nothing but darkened dirt. There were no trees, no grass, no anything, just a blackened crater in place of what used to be the cemetery. Under the gentle light of the moon, it looked like an alien planet, barren and hostile.

Marvin hadn't moved since we'd climbed out of our hole. He just stood there, a puppy dog look of confusion on his round face.

No words of wisdom to help him cope, I told him the only thing I could think of. "Go home, Marvin."

We both stood there for another few minutes, just taking it all in. What had existed but a half hour before, was now gone forever. Wiped away without mercy, it was just plain not there anymore. In its place was a vast swath of emptiness.

When the nothingness became too much to bear, we both staggered off in different directions. He headed for home, or so I imagined, and I wandered off to find a teleporter to take me back to DRAC.

It was close to a mile from the cemetery that I came to the end of the crater. At its edge, a small group of people gathered and mourned. Shellshocked faces stared at the ruin of what had been their neighborhood just the night before. Their neighbors, friends, and family who had lived there had been erased from existence. In the span of minutes, the course of their lives had been horribly altered.

Ignoring their questions and shouted pleas for answers as they saw me emerge from the crater, I pushed my way past. There was nothing I could do for them. For me to save what was left, I needed to get to Heaven.

Right then, salvation wasn't looking so good.

Chapter Nineteen

As I neared one of DRAC's hidden gates, ready to make my way back to where Scarlett and Katon waited, I heard the crackling static of a telepathic connection open up inside my head.

Abraham's quiet voice drifted into my brain. "Frank. It's Abe. Where are you?"

Never quite able to answer in my head without getting a lot of superfluous thoughts jumbled together into the transmission, I told him aloud where I was. My brain engaged a split-second after that.

He'd called himself Abe.

In all the years I'd known him, he never once referred to himself as Abe. It had always been Abraham. In fact, I was probably the only person who did call him that. My gun was in my hand before I'd even completed the thought. Something was up.

Just a few feet from the back alley door that obscured the gate, a gentle wave of energy washed over me, signaling the portal had been activated. It hadn't been by me.

Paranoia in high gear, I aimed my gun at the door and waited. The energy subsided after a moment and a gruff voice from the other side of the door called out to me.

"I'm coming out, demon. We have the old man, so don't try anything funny or you'll never see him again; at least not in anything resembling one piece." The voice finished with a rough chuckle.

My heart thudded hollow in my chest as I realized how stupid I'd been. Abraham had tried to warn me and I'd figured it out too late. It had to be about the key piece.

Cold sweat tickling my scalp, I tied the end of my pillowcase bag into a sloppy knot and delayed for time.

"Who is it?" I sang.

"No games, demon. Either let me out peacefully, so we can speak face-to-face, or we kill your mentor."

I waited until I heard the grumbled reply start, then tossed the bag onto the nearby roof. It landed with a muffled thump and I hoped, with all my heart, the vials survived.

Timed to cover the sound, I loudly muttered my agreement.

"All right, all right!" It wasn't the best of hiding places, but with humanity hunkered down awaiting the end, I figured the piece was safe enough. It had to better than having it on me.

The door creaked open and a furry snout peeked out from behind it, its muzzle pulled back in a vicious smile. The whitish lightning bolt fur on its forehead told me it was Rampage, the same werewolf who'd been carrying Adam's skull when the weres jumped us; Grawwl's right-pawed flunky.

His reddish-orange eyes locked onto mine. My gun still in my hand, pointed steady at his face, his smile slid away. I knew it was a bluff, but he couldn't be sure. It was a satisfying moment of defiance, however futile.

"Do you really want to be responsible for the old man's death?" he asked. He didn't say anything else. He didn't have to. With those few words, he knew he had me by the short and curlies. The fact he used one of DRAC's gates was more than sufficient evidence to prove he told me the truth.

As much as I wanted to ventilate his smug lupine face, it wouldn't help Abraham. Not that I expected mercy from the bastards. Certain they would kill Abe the second they got what they wanted, I could at least delay and hope to pull something out of my ass. My putting a bullet in Rampage would guarantee Abraham's death, and it would be on my shoulders.

Shit. I hated having a conscience.

The stare down lasted only a second longer before I gave in and lowered my gun. I was only delaying the inevitable.

He crept out from behind the door. "Smart move, demon. Now put it away so we can get going."

A bit surprised he didn't take it from me, I certainly wasn't gonna complain. Though on the other hand, not disarming me meant they didn't think I was a threat. They had to believe they held all the cards or they wouldn't risk leaving me armed. That blew a big hole in my dreamy concept of hope.

"Take me to your leader." My pistol stuffed into my pants, I gestured to the gate. Might as well get it over with.

Rampage chuckled and turned his back on me as he went and stood inside the gate. Nothing to do but follow, I stepped onto the pentagram right after. Uncomfortable standing so close to the werewolf, I inched back as far as I could go, making sure I faced him the whole time. Once we were both situated, the gate throttled to life and zipped us on down the line.

We appeared inside the secure entryway inside the main

DRAC headquarters. My heart skipped a beat as the room came into focus. It wasn't secure anymore.

The array of defensive wards had been scoured from the walls. Their colorful faces were marred, blackened singe marks lay overtop of each, their energies neutralized. The room smelled of sulfur and bitter ash, the taste of it stung my tongue.

My moist eyes drifted upward toward the behemoth roof and I couldn't help but stare. The thirty ton weight was warped and disfigured, twisted so badly it had dug into the walls around it and failed to drop.

The door leading into the main complex had been ripped free of its sunken hinges. It lay on the floor beside us. The outer edge was bent inward, the three foot thick steel mangled and crumpled like paper.

Amazed and horrified all at the same time, I couldn't imagine the kind of power it would take to bypass the security system so casually. Despite the presence of the werewolf, there was no doubt in mind that it hadn't been Grawwl. While powerful in a physical way, he didn't possess the kind of mystical aptitude it took to lay waste to DRAC. I had a pretty good idea who did.

I glanced over at Rampage's smiling face and he just chuckled, waving me down the hall. It took some willpower to get my feet moving, but I managed to follow him after a second or two.

Out in the corridor, I saw several of DRAC's security team scattered about. They lay on the floor motionless, obviously dead, but there were no signs of trauma on any of them. No blood or bruises were visible. Their uniforms were immaculate as though they hadn't even put up a fight. It was if they'd just dropped dead where they stood.

Seeing that made it real clear as to why Rampage hadn't cared whether I kept my gun or not. Compared to the defense array and the firepower the security forces could bring to bear, one measly little pistol wasn't but a drop of spit in the ocean.

It suddenly felt like I was taking my last walk, a condemned man's final journey.

Rampage wound his way through the compound with confidence, his head held high and his arms easy at his side. The lifeless men we passed at every turn only reinforced his seeming invulnerability, a casual swagger seeping into his gait.

I thought about all the people who worked at headquarters and then pictured them all dead. My stomach churned with bile and I could feel my face growing flush, but there was nothing I could do for them. The men already gone, I needed to think about Abraham and the rest of the world. The longer this went on, the more people who were gonna die.

Certain I knew where we were headed, I slipped past Rampage and picked up the pace. He chuckled behind me and matched me stride for stride. After a moment I reached Abraham's office and opened the door. As it always did, the smell of old wisdom met me at the door, but I wasn't there for that. The feedback on my senses told me I'd been right in my assumption.

Once inside, Rampage shut the door behind us and took up a position right in front of it. The werewolf the least of my concerns, my eyes swung toward the desk and saw Abraham uncomfortable in his chair behind it. He met my gaze with a palpable sadness that stole my breath away. I nodded to Abe and looked away to the skeletal figure beside him before his sorrow could infect me.

"Not pulling any punches are you?"

Azrael floated around the desk and drifted closer. "I warned you to stay out of the conflict, Triggaltheron, yet you persisted. You have only yourself to blame for what has happened here." He gestured around him.

"That may well be true, but seeing how all life on Earth is probably gonna be wiped out in a day or two, I can live with my guilt that long." The way things were going, I didn't really think I'd make it through the day.

A rumbling laugh spilled from his blackened lips. "You are so much like your sire, defiant even in the face of overwhelming odds."

"I'm nothing like my father." Incensed at the comparison, the words spewed out like razors.

Azrael broke into a cadaverous grin. "You are, young Triggaltheron, you are. I see him in your face, in the spiteful fury that courses through your veins. Yet unlike him, you have no sense of ambition. You're content to wile away your time amongst the pitiful humans as if they'll ever accept you as one of them. You disgrace the glory of your bloodline."

I spit at him, but Azrael batted it away with but a thought.

"Be grateful I hold your father in such high regard, little demon, otherwise I would have your soul for such impudence."

My eyes flickered to Abraham, hoping I had his attention. We were only gonna get one shot at this. "You can shove that regard up your bony ass."

The words out, I spun, pulling my pistol free, and went for

Rampage. He needed to go if Abraham had any chance of getting away.

Caught off guard, the werewolf's eyes went wide as he suddenly came face to face with the business end of the barrel. No time to aim, I squeezed the trigger like a madman.

An invisible force slapped the gun from my hand right then. The two rounds I'd managed to get off struck the wall just to the left of Rampage's fuzzy head. They weren't even close.

Rampage stood there wide-eyed and stiff-limbed as I was yanked off my feet and spun about. The room a blur, I felt gravity take hold again and I was rag-dolled onto my back, my breath knocked from my lungs.

When my eyes stopped spinning, I saw Azrael's drawn out face just inches above mine. "There is no time for your childish heroics."

A deep, gasping breath supplied me with enough air to answer, my voice hoarse. "What do you want?" It's not as if I didn't know, I just liked being difficult.

Azrael drifted back and I took advantage of the space and got to my feet. Abraham still sat in his chair, his glasses magnifying the sadness in his eyes. Everything happened so fast, he didn't have time to budge, not that it would have done him any good.

"You well know what I want, Triggaltheron. Tell the wolf where to find Eve's key piece and let's be done with this."

"I know what Marmaduke back there gets out of all this, but what's in it for you?"

"My interests don't concern you."

"I'm thinking otherwise, seeing how you went out of your way to bring me here." He obviously didn't want to reveal his role in the bigger picture. Bad villain. He was breaking rule number one: the onus of the monologue is on the antagonist. Fortunately, Abraham was clued in.

"Like his lycanthrope minions, he stands to inherit the world." Azrael shot him a murderous look, but Abraham kept going, undeterred. "His dominion death, Azrael has long since evolved from an angel to something far more closely related to the creatures that live in the shadows between worlds. When the Tree dies, he becomes a god; the only one left."

The flames in Azrael's eyes roared as he flew at Abraham faster than I could follow. He snatched him up by his throat and held him in the air before him. "Silence, mortal."

Abraham's face flushed pink as he tried in vain to breathe. His glasses hung from his ear, flickering under the fluorescent lights.

"Let him go," I shouted as I took a step forward, digging deep to summon my magic, desperation giving me just enough spark to light the fuse. Rampage growled a warning close behind me.

"Had I not promised your father I'd respect his wishes with regards to you, I would eviscerate you where you stand." He dangled Abraham before me. "I made no such promises regarding this pathetic creature. Now tell me where the key piece is or I'll hang his lifeless husk upon the banner of your ill advised resistance."

Even though he couldn't breathe, Abraham's position was clear. His reddened face screwed into a pained scowl, his eyes begged me to defy Azrael.

I thought of Rachelle. How could I tell her I'd let Abraham be killed, doing nothing to stop it? Yet, how could I not? I'd been willing to let Scarlett die on principle, believing the end of all life a greater choice than its submission. Once more my convictions were being tested. Should I stand in defiance and watch everyone I know die, or do I condemn humanity to enslavement, to be bred as cattle, food for the vamps and shifters? Was there even a choice?

My gaze shifted back to Abraham and he strained to shake his head, Azrael's crushing grip limiting his motion. Tears moistened my eyes and threatened to drag them down. I forced them to stay with Abe's and gave him a subtle nod.

"Like I told the bear, you can't have it." The words came out heavy, each syllable a nail hammered into the coffin of the greatest man I'd ever known.

Azrael's mouth settled into a grim line, the fire in his eyes sputtered into blackened coals, which simmered in their sockets. "Impudent dog."

Abraham stiffened and his eyes flew open wide. The purplish tint of his face began to fade, a pallor washing over him like the tide. He reached out for me, his eyes locked on mine, their green fading to white. His hand trembled, the flesh growing paler with each breathless moment.

Every voice inside my head shrieked for me to look away, but my conscience wouldn't allow it. His death was my burden to bear, and I would own every horrific second of it. The image of a marbled Abraham seared itself upon my memory, blackened veins standing out like serpents against his graying flesh. I'd see the terror in his sunken eyes until the day I fell into my own grave.

His hand fell limp, as if weary of waiting for mine, and his arm swung down and then ceased to move. His irises, cleansed of all color, he stared hollow-eyed at me until his head lolled back.

Azrael laughed at his passing, his callous tune the dirge that accompanied Abraham's soul into the abyss. The angel released him and Abe's limp body fell to the floor with the gentle grace of falling leaves.

My heart fell with him, shattering on impact, jagged shards tearing me apart inside. Tears burned my eyes and I looked away at last, the image replaying inside my head. Agony constricted my chest and I panted to draw in air. My knees shuddered, and then gave way. I found myself kneeling on the floor. Bile clogged my throat and I sat there numb. The voices in my head were silent except for one. A small, still voice cried in the depths—

—I killed Abraham.

A shadow at the edges of my vision, Azrael hovered before me. "Save your tears, Triggaltheron, you will need their comfort in the hours to come."

A frigid hand lifted my chin and drew my gaze to his. In his swirling sockets, the flames swayed and danced, their flickering forms becoming the images of Scarlett, then Katon, Michael and Rachelle after that. Each image dissolving, rancid flesh peeled back into a skeletal grimace, his threat needed no words.

He leaned in close. "Your mentor spoke true of my destiny. I *will* live on forever, the new God. Though I have made arrangements to repopulate the Earth, should I fail to obtain the key piece, I would much prefer a verdant kingdom to rule. There is even a place in it for you, should you choose to reconsider the folly of your misguided allegiance and hand the key piece over." His blackened lips pulled back into a smile. "Your father would be pleased to see you embrace your nature at last."

My thoughts a maelstrom, I drew in a deep breath to steady the tremors that rattled through me. Azrael grinned, his arrogance weathering me as though I were a stone. Sickened by what I'd done, I stared deep into the fires of his eyes and made my choice.

I spit in his face.

Too close to swat it away like he had the last, the thick ball of phlegm struck him right between the eyes. His smile wilted and roared into a snarl as spittle oozed down his pale nose and cheek.

I never saw him hit me.

My chest collapsed as if I'd been hit by a car and I was whiplashed backward. The wall, built sturdy in the hopes of withstanding supernatural attack, spider webbed around me as my back sunk into it several inches. My skull snapped back and added its own impression to the mosaic, a carousel of lights spinning playful in my eyes. The rumbling in my chest was a clear sign something was broken.

Azrael was in my face before my vision cleared. "You have sealed your fate, demon, no matter my vow." His words slithered over me. A watery blur of motion, I saw him float back. "Rampage, take him away." He waved a hand, dark tracers swimming in its wake. "Keep him sedate until I return, but keep him alive."

The werewolf growled a reply and I was yanked to my feet, my chest screaming in protest. As the pain washed over me, I became more focused. Able to see a tiny bit better, I saw Azrael glowering at me as he stood over Abraham's body. The old man looked peaceful, if nothing else.

"Soon, the Nephilim will lay dead upon the field and their key piece will be mine. Once they are vanquished, I will return to ask you for yours once more. You'll have one opportunity to defy me for each of their lives, Triggaltheron, then you'll have no more." He grinned feral and gestured to Abraham. "How many bodies shall be piled at your feet before you see reason?"

Afraid my voice would give away just how much his threat bothered me, I kept my mouth shut. Finally able to see worth a damn, I just stared at him. It was the best I could do.

He laughed. "While your courage is commendable, don't let it be the sword your friends and allies fall upon." He waved me away. "I will return soon, Rampage. Treat our guest well."

The werewolf smirked in reply as bubbling clouds of inky blackness rose up from beneath Azrael. The darkness floated upward and swallowed the archangel whole, a moment later he was gone, leaving me and the furball alone in the room.

I'd just started to think of how I could handle Rampage when his fist slammed into my side. Bright light washed out my vision and I hit the floor, gasping for breath. Through the haze, I felt him take my gun. The metallic tinge of blood swirled in the back of my throat and I rolled to my back to relieve the pressure at my side. It was really obvious then that Azrael had busted open something inside me. Rampage's punch had only made it worse.

Vaguely, I realized he had opened the door. Two more werewolves strolled inside, looking down at me with sharpened smirks. They each took an arm and hauled me up, then out into the hallway. Too beat to pretend I was tough, I hung limp and let them drag me.

"You see, demon? This is why us shifters are taking over. One little punch and you're down for the count." His friends sniggered at me, their ringleader electing not to tell them Azrael had already cleaned my clock and saved his furry asshole.

"Is that why you took my gun, brave guy, because I'm no threat?"

My sarcasm earned me another shot to the side. Lucky for me, I didn't have to worry about falling. Unlucky for them, the pain of my internal injuries caused me to throw up.

Black blood and yellow bile spewed from my mouth, a waterfall of pungent nastiness that hit the ground and splattered everywhere. Wolfen paws squished and I could see the vomit squeezing up between their clawed toes. They grumbled in disgust and sped up, the lingering scent keeping pace.

"You're going to pay for that," one of the werewolves threatened and shook me roughly. The other grumbled in agreement, joining in on the fun.

If I could have spoken, I would have told him to put it on my tab. Of course, that would have only made things worse. Given my already precarious position, it was probably a good thing I couldn't dig the hole any deeper.

Or was it?

A dimly lit bulb fluttered to life inside my thick skull. If I weren't around, I wouldn't have to worry about Azrael finding the key piece in time. He also wouldn't need to torture my friends. While I couldn't guarantee he wouldn't do it out of spite, I could hope I wasn't worth his effort.

Thinking along those lines, a plan began to form, no matter how half-baked it might seem to anyone not currently inside my head. While Azrael had told Rampage not to kill me, the message hadn't been passed on to the other two flunkies, as far as I could tell. Besides, even if they had been told, I can be very persuasive. Seriously, who wouldn't want to kill me?

As they dragged me down the hall, I glanced over at the werewolf on the left and did my best to force a smile onto my face. He glared at me.

"What's your problem?"

"I'm just curious about something," I choked out. "Are you neutered, or do werewolves just naturally lack balls?"

He snarled and pulled me to the ground by my arm and delivered a vicious kick to my ribs. The world disappeared in an explosion of white that faded fast to black, a piercing hum bouncing around inside my ears. Another kick brought the world back into focus, and what little was left in my stomach vacated it in search of better climes. My generosity was rewarded by a stomp to the head, my face smashed into the concrete floor, Humpty Dumpty reenacted. My vision tunneled and the darkness closed in. The warm slime against my cheek was so far out I barely registered it. I felt something like a water balloon burst in my chest, a warm, wet sensation tickling me inside. Waves of exhaustion washed over me, everything slowing down.

As my eyes slid closed, I heard Rampage howling at the other werewolf. Too tired to care, I let go. Mission accomplished.

* * * *

A sharp pain against my cheek snapped my eyes open. They came into focus on a furry lightning bolt, reddish-orange eyes glimmering just below.

"You're not getting off that easily, demon."

Damn.

Still laying in my spew, warm and sticky against my fingers, it was obvious I hadn't been out but a few seconds. So much for my master plan. Now I was just beaten up more, and still alive. What's a guy got to do to die?

Rampage leaned over and pulled me up, supporting my weight, but making me stand. The movement just reinforced my wish to die. It hurt—a lot.

The other two werewolves stayed a little ways behind us, their faces looking like beaten dogs; one of them carried my gun. Rampage ignored them as we traveled on a little further until we reached the area of DRAC that housed the holding cells.

"Get the door," he told the other two.

They snapped to and slipped past us, one yanking open the heavy, reinforced steel door while the other stood by.

A blur of black and white whipped through the air behind them. Geysers erupted where the werewolves' heads had been just a split-second before. Warm blood rained over us as their bodies danced in place for a moment, then crumbled to the floor. Their heads landed with moist splats right after.

Rampage's grip loosened and I drooped to the ground across from the spurting corpses. A rumbling, basso growl came from beyond the door and echoed down the hall, vibrating the walls. The werewolf stood there without moving as a monstrous blue-black form appeared in the doorway. Red stained claws led the way as the creature hunkered down and eased through the door, a grinning ursine face coming nose to nose with Rampage.

It was another werebear, but it definitely wasn't Grawwl.

It nudged Rampage with its snout, its muzzle pulling back to show a mouthful of razor sharp teeth. A low growl rolled thunderous from its mouth and Rampage stiffened in response.

A quick slash later, the werewolf stumbled back, an oozing, crimson hole where his throat had been just seconds before. He clutched to the wound, a quiet whistle slipping between his clawed fingers, and stared wide-eyed at the werebear. His eyelids fluttered: once, twice, then closed, never to open again. His arms fell limp at his sides and his legs gave way. He crumbled into a heap and laid there, his life's blood staining the tile floor.

The need for me to die now passed, I looked up at the giant bear and sighed, lowering my face. It was just my luck.

"You look like you could use a hand," the bear told me, its voice deep and smooth, a gentle chuckle rounding out his words.

I recognized its intonation and looked at the creature again. This time, my eyes saw him for who he really was; Rahim.

"Are you serious?" My excitement was tempered by internal bleeding.

He grinned and hunched down lower so we were face to face. "In the fur."

His movement was fluid and graceful. He held out a monstrous paw to me and I grabbed ahold so I could get to my feet. Amazed by his transformation, I couldn't help but stare.

"We thought you were dead."

He nodded. "I know." He motioned behind him. "I had a little angelic help chasing away the weres after Rachelle gated all of you out of there."

Beyond the behemoth, Akrasiel leaned casually in the doorway. In his hand, he held Katon's replacement sword, along with Scarlett's blade, Everto Trucido.

"Hi Akrasiel, or do you prefer Raguel?"

He smiled, the leather of his face seeming to crack. "Names are just names. It's all the same to me."

I gave the angel a grateful nod, then my eyes went back to Rahim. Like Grawwl, he was nearly as big as a house. Though he wasn't standing up straight, he looked to be several feet taller than Grumpy. His fur was a black so deep it shimmered blue when he moved. He had short swords for claws and his body was built for power.

While he didn't look like Rahim—he looked like a bear—there was a definite resemblance in the facial mannerisms and the way he carried himself. His old confidence was back, glistening in the shimmering red of his eyes. Seeing the fluidity of his motion, I had to ask.

"The back?"

A wicked grin spread across his face. "It's perfect. The transformation healed it completely."

Returning the smile, I was glad he was still among us. I just wish I could say the same for Abraham. Reminded of the old psychic, my eyes teared up and I suddenly couldn't look Rahim in the face.

"Abraham's dead." I nearly choked on the words. Just saying them made me feel weak.

Rahim gently set a reassuring paw on my shoulder. "I know."

"It's my faul—"

Rahim cut me off. "I don't believe that, Frank. More so than any of us, he knew the risks associated with what we do."

"But if I had—"

"We don't have time for this." The last word segued into a growl. "You can worry about pointing fingers later. We need to get you fixed up and get to Heaven. Any plans been made?"

I took a second to compose myself before I answered. He was right. No matter what happened, I needed to focus. Abe would come back from the dead to kick my ass if I let him die in vain. "We should still have our key piece and we've agreed on a tentative assault plan. It'll need some tweaking to adjust for Azrael's mucking about, but with you and Akrasiel over there, I think we're better off than we were before."

The old man shook his head, picked up my gun, and came over beside us, his leather face serious. "I've done all I can for now. You'll have to do this without me." He handed the swords to me, and then my pistol.

I accepted them and slipped my gun into my waistline as I thanked him, glad to have them all back. No point in arguing with the angel, we just said our goodbyes. He disappeared in a golden flash.

Once he was gone, I shrugged at Rahim. "I've recruited Alexander Poe to help us, Baalth's mentalist, who just happens to have a little magical aptitude. It's not much of an addition, but since we're looking at a smash and grab, followed by a suicide run,

I think we're as ready as we can be."

Rahim groaned and rolled his eyes. "Sounds charming. Where is the key piece?"

"It's just outside one of the gates." My insides feeling like an overripe tomato, I waved him on and headed for the portal room—or what was left of it. On the way, I laid out our plan of attack. Grim-faced, Rahim listened. As the gate powered up and we were whisked away, the wizard werebear sighed.

"Suicide run it is." He grumbled deep. "Seems a waste of a good disease."

* * * *

Just a minute later, we exited the door into the alley. Well, I exited the door. Rahim kind of had to go through the wall because he wouldn't fit. I could see a bunch of remodeling in DRAC's future, if we made it through the day.

Once the dust cleared, I pointed to the roof where I'd tossed the bag and groaned. Rahim's eyes snapped upward.

"Friends of yours?"

Tired, hurt, sad, and sick and tired of getting my ass kicked, I snarled at Jonas Black and Ethan White. "What the Hell do you guys want?" With Rahim there, I knew we could take these guys easy. It's easy to be confident when you have a bad ass to back up your smack talk.

Black grinned like he was gonna sell me a used car and wiggled his reattached arm for me to see. "You got us good last time, Trigg. Sneaky." He gave a shallow nod. "We still need you to come with us though."

White held my pillowcase up and shook it gently. While it sucked they had the bag, I was glad to see there weren't any stains on it and I hadn't heard the distressing jingle of broken glass. That meant the vials were still intact.

"Seriously, guys, I don't who you are or what you want, but I really don't have time for this."

Rahim growled to reinforce my point, posturing up to his full height, red energy glistening at his paws. Courage warmed my heart as I saw he still had his magic.

"Then I suggest you make time," a cold, steely voice said, its source appearing beside Black, out of nowhere.

My senses shrieked and I nearly fell, emanations of power washing off the figure like a nuclear detonation. Out of the corner of my eye, I saw Rahim flinch and his stance became more defensive. His face drew back in a wary grimace, his eyes narrowing. The courage I had a second ago yipped away like a frightened Chihuahua.

Dressed Jedi-like in a long, flowing black robe with its hood pulled up, the figure stared down at me through mercurial eyes. A black mask covered everything from his nose down, so there wasn't much in the way of identifying features. The only thing I knew was that it was a he, the voice giving that away, and that he was super powerful. My shriveled nut-sack confirmed that.

His point made, the stranger reined in his essence. It felt as though the sun had been ripped from the sky, the sudden release of pressure immediate. I looked to Rahim and his eyes told me we were screwed. Now, here I was without any lube.

So, fighting out of the question, we'd have to reason with the guy. That meant Rahim would have to do it. I nudged him in his furry side. He glared at me, then looked back up, swallowing deep.

"Who are you and what is it you want?" There was the slightest hint of a tremble in his voice.

"This does not concern you, wizard. It is to the demon I wish to speak." The glare of his silver eyes settled on me. "Come, Triggaltheron. I am Xyx. I have been sent to retrieve you and I will not fail my master."

Though I obviously couldn't see my face, I figured it looked a lot like Rahim's; slack-jawed and incredulous mixed with a little bit of *holy shit*. Having felt the guy's power, to hear he answered to someone else, and that someone was looking for me, made my knees weak.

No clue who this guy was, or his master, I couldn't for the life of me think of what I'd done to get their attention. I thought I knew all the major players in the world, but I was drawing a big blank on this one. Unsure of what angle to play to get a rain check, I took a chance on the truth.

"I have no idea what's going on, but if you haven't noticed, we're having a bit of a world crisis here. The longer we're delayed, the worse it's gonna get for all of existence. I'm needed somewhere else right now."

"I care not for your problems."

"Does your master?" It was a long shot, seeing how the guy was coming off as a serious hard ass, but I had to try. I didn't know where cloak boy came from, but for his boss to need me, for whatever reason, he probably had to have some kind of investment in the world I resided in. It made a weird sort of sense.

Xyx's eyes shimmered gold for a second, then returned to silver. He stared at me a moment before speaking.

"My master offers you one opportunity to avail yourself to him of your own free will." Before Xyx, a demonic contract appeared in the air. It fluttered down to me. "Agree to surrender to me three days hence and we will leave you until then to resolve your issue."

The contract in my hand, I looked it over and saw it had been marked by Xyx, not his master. It was your standard demonic contract. Signed in blood it meant a couple of things. The first one was, once I committed to it, I either had to follow its demands to the letter or I forfeited my soul to the contract holder. The second thing was that it confirmed Xyx was a demon, though certainly not one I ever met, or even heard of.

That in itself was quite a surprise.

I glanced at Rahim and there weren't any answers in his expression. He was leaving this one up to me. Great. That never worked out well.

My thoughts on Abraham and how I'd let him down and couldn't do it again, I bit my hand and made my mark in fresh blood. Once I finished, the contract drifted back up to Xyx. He glanced at it for confirmation, then it disappeared.

"You have three days. I will come for you then, regardless." He motioned with his hand and White tossed the bag down to me.

Terrified I'd shatter the vials, I caught it as gentle as I could, grabbing it high and letting its momentum play out a little. Bag safely in hand, I looked back up and all three of them were gone.

"Any idea what that was about," Rahim asked, worry in his voice.

My hand in the bag snatching up a vial, my eyes checking to make sure everything was still there, I shook my head. "No clue, but I guess I'll find out in a few days. Of course, I could be dead by then."

I tried to make light of it, but the truth was I was more than a little worried. There weren't any guarantees of success against Azrael and his fuzzball minions and their undead entourage, not to mention the Nephilim. Even if we did win out and manage to make our way into Heaven, we were only leaping from one deadly conflict to another. With no way to awaken Metatron, we were stuck killing ourselves on the front line or dying when the Tree of Life gave up the ghost.

Bleak didn't begin to describe our chances.

Then, to top it all off, if by some miracle we did win out, I'd be stuck handing my ass over to who-knows-who for who-knows-what. It was like being told you were cured of cancer only to learn the world is gonna end in three days.

Let's face it, life is morbidly cruel.

A couple of sips of Lucifer's blood whizzing its way through my veins, I reminded Rahim that we needed to pick up Poe and we were on our way.

He made me promise I wouldn't tell anyone about Abraham until it was all over, not even Rachelle. While I really didn't think it was right, from a moral standpoint—if you can believe that—I knew it was for the best. That was the kind of news that got a person killed. They didn't need the distraction.

On the mend, but really not feeling any better, we hit the metaphorical road. I had zero expectations that it wouldn't hit back.

Chapter Twenty

"You're doing what?"

"I'm comin' with ya'll," McConnell told me, his hillbilly accent twanging on all the wrong nerves.

My first thought was that he looked like shit. Not a doctor, though I've played one on many a closeted adventure, there wasn't much of a medical legitimacy to my claim, but he didn't look healthy to me.

Normally close to three hundred pounds of solid muscle, McConnell had lost a good twenty to thirty pounds of his bulk. His cheeks looked gaunt, his usual resemblance to Santa Claus now veering dangerously close to homeless veteran chic. His full white beard was scraggly and seemed as lifeless as he did. He stared at me through sunken blue eyes, no hint of the old fire in them.

Nearly eviscerated by Karra in her quest to resurrect her father, he had barely been patched up from that when Lilith stepped in. Like a puppet, she'd used him to spring a trap on me and her daughter, the ex-wife. It didn't work out so well for poor Henry. His wound too much for Lilith's magic to fix up, he popped a stitch or twelve trying to kill Veronica and I. Only a couple of weeks out from that, he couldn't possibly be ready to use his magic, let alone go slugging it out with supernaturals.

Not that I cared about his well being or anything—the damn redneck could go suck a saddle horn—I just plain didn't trust him. Given the opportunity, and there would be plenty of them, McConnell wouldn't hesitate to add me to the body count if he felt he could get away with it. My hands would be full enough without having to worry about not-so-friendly fire.

That aside, even if he wasn't looking for a chance to kill me before the world went boom, he was too beat up to be much of an asset. He couldn't be relied on. Those things combined made him more of a liability than anything.

"Look McConnell, I—"

"Forget it, Trigg. You need me."

Need is a very subjective word. "No one is gonna have time to hold your hand, McConnell."

"This ain't personal 'tween us." He stuck out a pale finger and poked me in the chest. "If this goes south, I wanna know everything possible was done to prevent it. Even beat to shit like I am, I can turn the tide if it's there to be turned."

Rahim leaned over my shoulder and whispered, his grumbled voice vibrating my ear. "He's right, you know. Let him come along."

Desperate for support, I looked to Poe. There wasn't any to be found there. He shrugged and suddenly invested his attention in brushing the invisible lint from his sleeve.

"Fine, cowboy, but you better remember whose side you're on. One wayward fireball singes so much as a single ball hair and I'm crawling up inside your belly and kicking your ass from the inside. We clear?"

He just laughed and I smiled right back, my thoughts on the magic-dampening manacles in my bag. I'd shut him down with them once, and I'd gladly do it again. This time, there wouldn't be a reprieve.

The verbal cock fight over, Rahim zipped us off to meet with Scarlett and Katon.

* * * *

Unannounced, we arrived just a little ways from where Katon and Scarlett were camped out, readying the troops. While I hadn't expected wild cheers of adulation at our return, as much as they would have been appreciated, I certainly hadn't expected a standing ovation.

An angry hum filled the air as everyone jumped to their feet and stared at us through narrow eyes. A merciless symphony of chambered rounds followed. Not fond of McConnell myself, I didn't think he'd warrant that negative a reaction, and then it hit me. It wasn't The Gray they were freaking out about, but my Care Bear companion.

"Whoa there, folks. It's Rahim." I gestured to the wizard turned werebear, stepping in front of him and raising my hands. His giant paws mimicked my motions behind me.

Katon's disbelieving glare lasted until he looked into Rahim's eyes and heard his bellowed voice. The snarl dropped from his lips and he waved the men down as he went to Rahim. The wizard slipped past me and met him halfway. Scarlett wiped at her eyes as Michael looked on in awe.

Rahim lowered his head and smiled broad, a gentle giant.

"Good to see you, my friend."

Katon laughed like a pardoned death row inmate, his voice cracking as he wrapped his arms around Rahim's furry neck. "I—I—"

The wizard wrapped his arms around the enforcer and hefted him up into air like a doll, a rumbling chuckle bubbled from his ursine throat. "I thought so too. It was close, but it all worked out as you can see." He set Katon down and posed, arching up to his full height.

Katon gave him an approving shake of his head. "It suits you." The shadow of a thought passed over his face, obscuring his smile. "Can you change forms or are we going to have to widen all of the doors?"

"I believe I can revert to my old self, though I've yet to test it. Until then, it's probably best for me to stay this way until I have the time to become comfortable with the lycanthropy. It's not a field I've studied, certainly not this closely."

As the two friends chatted, Rachelle slipped from the back ranks of DRAC's forces and sidled up to Rahim. Her smile lit her face. The wizard, bowed low to her and opened his arms. With a giggle, she fell into them, burying her face in his fur.

"I'm so glad you're okay. Abraham was heartbroken when you didn't return, believing his vision had come true. He'll be so pleased to see you."

A pang of guilt wormed its way down my spine at her words. Rahim looked to me, his eyes pleading. It was too much. Never much of an actor, Keanu Reeves a master thespian in comparison, I walked away to keep from breaking down. Scarlett saw me and came over.

"You all right?"

I didn't turn to face her. "Yeah, I'm fine. It's just getting a little mushy round here." My voice quavered and I hoped she didn't notice.

She put her hand on my shoulder and turned me around, her narrowed eyes meeting mine. "What aren't you telling me?"

What indeed. I got on my bullshit bike and started pedaling. "Azrael is working with the weres to tear down the Tree of Life."

The suspicion on her face turned to disgust, shades of disappointment mingled in.

"He's on his way to assault the Nephilim and claim the other key piece. After that, he threatened to come after DRAC; after you and Katon, Rachelle..." I left it at that.

A feral snarl flickered across her lips. "Let him come."

Off the hook, I took a deep breath and let it out slow. "Don't worry, cousin, we're taking the fight to him." Forcing a smile onto my face, I reached into my bag and drew out Everto Trucido. "I've got something that'll help."

Her eyes lit up as she snatched the sword from me. "Thank God. Where did you find it?" Like a kid at Christmas, she spun the blade over and over in her hands, examining every inch of it.

"Golden boy picked it up when he saved Rahim's ass. It seems he's one of the good guys after all." For now, at least.

She grinned as she slid the sword into its sheath, her hand remaining on the pommel. "So, what's the plan?"

"Let's get everyone over here first."

She grumbled but called out for the group to come over. Rahim separated from Rachelle, grateful relief etched into his face. Without a doubt, he felt just as guilty as I was about keeping Abraham's death a secret.

Morbid as it was, I caught myself wishing Azrael would succeed, or maybe even McConnell would man up, and then our betrayal wouldn't matter anymore. How pathetic is that?

No time for self-flagellation, as fun as it is, I laid out the general plan of attack. "Azrael isn't gonna be expecting us, so the idea is to lay low until we have a shot to snatch the key pieces. He's gonna be super pissed when he sees us, so I want everyone to stay out of his way as best you can. I'll draw him off and let you deal with whoever ends up winning the tug-o-war."

"You looking to get yourself killed, Frank?" Rahim asked, more than a hint of accusation in his voice. Scarlett stood behind him glaring. McConnell had a glimmer in his eye.

"Not particularly, no. Azrael has it in his head that butchering me goes against an oath he gave a long time back. While I figure he'll get annoyed with me enough to void that agreement at some point, his possible hesitance might give us the time we need to pull something off." Besides, I had a little surprise in store for old Grim.

"So in essence, the plan really hasn't changed from the last one: grab the key and try to be the first into Heaven?" Katon asked as I nodded, passing him his sword to help soften the lack of a cohesive idea.

"With Rahim, Poe, and Santa Claus, we're packing a little more firepower than we were before. If you guys can hold the gate while Scarlett contacts Uriel to shut it down, we might have a chance.

With a little backup, maybe Uriel or Forcalor can spare a moment to try and rouse Metatron."

Their eyes told me just how little hope they had.

"We all know we're farting in the wind, but it's all we've got. If something better presents itself, don't hesitate to take it, but keep your eyes on the ball. If the bad guys get into Heaven, we're done." I handed Eve to Scarlett, then turned to Michael and Poe. "I want you two to keep an open channel with me, and keep Rachelle in the loop. If things change, I want to be able to redirect on the fly. Any questions?"

Stone-faced, they all looked at each other, then back to me. No one said anything.

"Okay then. Seats in the upright position, we're ready for take-off." I looked to Rachelle and asked her to open a portal.

Once the shimmering blue settled, we were on our way back to Iran, and to the earth-side entrance to Eden. We were headed to war; a ragtag bunch of wizards, mentalists, mystic, vampires, demons and angels, along with a couple hundred humans with minimal powers but lots of guns.

It was like we were the first soldiers to step off the boat at Normandy. My breath held as we filed through the gate, there was a heaviness that pressed down overtop, weighing on me. Despite all the trials I'd been through, despite all the furious battles I'd managed to scrape through, there'd always been a glimmer of hope off in the distant horizon. I couldn't see it now.

A tear ran cold down my cheek.

Chapter Twenty-One

A ways from the gathered Nephilim, Rachelle set us down on one of the foothills of the mountains that ran to the south of Eden's gate. An almost full moon and the height allowed us to see the grassy plain while being far enough away to avoid letting them know we were there. The men and women of DRAC rustled around, nervous energy making the whole group ripple-like waves as they waited to engage.

Rahim magicked a viewer into place so we could watch the Nephilim as if we were right there beside them.

Azrael had yet to attack apparently, the half-breeds still milled about. Though they didn't look like an army, their people scattered all over the place without any obvious discipline, there was no mistaking their ability to do harm. Easily five thousand of them clustered on the plain beneath Eden, each with some kind of weapon. They were ready to fight. Just seeing them gave me chills.

"It looks like we're early." Just as I spoke, the Nephilim broke out in a panic. "Or not."

Through the viewer, we saw the clusters of the Nephilim turning in on themselves, pockets of activity springing up all over. Flashes of gunfire boomed to life as they reacted to the invisible threat, the muted sounds hitting us seconds later. In their frenzy, a number of the half-breeds fell from friendly fire.

Unsure of what had riled them up, it was a few more seconds before we realized what was happening. From the ground, immaterial vampires drifted up in their midst. They solidified and attacked, then sunk back into the bloody earth below as the Nephilim mounted a frantic defense. Bodies crumpled in their wake.

"How come I've never seen you do that?" I asked Katon.

He shook his head. "Because I can't."

He looked a little jealous, so I let it go, my attention back on the battle.

Within just a minute, the vampire sneak attack had sown chaos. The Nephilim ranks began to spread out to better see the vampires as they materialized, the edges of their lines fraying. That only helped the vamps pick them off. Uncertainty spreading like wildfire, the half-breeds began to panic, jittery shots claiming more of their own lives than those of the enemy.

Near the center of the Nephilim a thick cluster of them pulled together and formed a tight circle of bodies. Unlike their brethren, they held their ground and fought smart, working together to minimize their losses. The Nephilim around them slowly drifted further away from the pack, isolating the group more every second.

From where they sat, it was a subtle thrust, but from up high it was very telling. Whoever was leading the attack, Azrael or Grawwl, knew what they were doing.

Katon said aloud what I was thinking. "The vampires are a scouting mission more than they are an attack."

Scarlett and Michael looked at him with wide eyes neither a tactician. Poe just nodded, clearly seeing what we had.

"The Nephilim only worried about their skins are scattering under the assault. Those who have a greater purpose are closing ranks and fighting with passion and discipline," Katon explained.

Rahim cut in. "They're fighting to defend the key piece."

Katon nodded, giving Scarlett a gentle smile as she too caught on.

"Azrael doesn't have the numbers for a direct assault," Poe noted. "That's why he's singling out the piece holder. He'll bring in the lycanthropes once they're isolated."

A hopeful thought popped into my head. "He doesn't think he can beat the Nephilim at full strength or he wouldn't be separating them."

"Who could?" Rahim asked.

The glimmer of hope I couldn't see earlier suddenly winked to life at Rahim's words. "Katon, find me Venai in that clusterfuck down there. She'll probably be a part of the organized group." He started scanning the viewer immediately. "Rahim, once we find her, I need you to port me down there."

"You think popping in to that is a good idea?" He pointed to the manic swirl of ants in the distance.

"No, but if I can get Venai to crack the whip and get the rest of her people organized, it might be worth it." I shrugged, trying not to think about what I was getting myself into. "If Azrael could wipe the Nephilim out himself, he would have done it without a second thought. He wouldn't be hiding behind the vamps and shifters and he certainly wouldn't be fighting a technical battle unless he felt he had to. He's either holding back to save his energy for the battle in Heaven, or he doesn't have it in him to beat five thousand half-breeds. Either scenario works in our favor."

Katon called out that he'd spotted Venai. Rahim raised a furry eyebrow as if to ask if I was sure.

I borrowed a white shirt from one of the security force and scavenged a vial of Lucifer's blood to take with me. Then I handed my bag to Katon and turned back to face Rahim. "Just keep an eye out. Azrael and the weres are bound to be in play soon. I'll stall them when they show, but if the Nephilim can't pull it together, we aren't looking at much time."

Rahim nodded, sharpened teeth showing his disapproval. "Be safe, Frank."

I was gone before I could respond, appearing a short distance from the clustered Nephilim, my head nodding imbecilely. Several of the half-breeds turned to look at me and I waved the shirt, my makeshift flag, before they got it in their head to shoot.

"I need to speak to your leaders and to Venai." I kept the flag going as a number of them trudged toward me. There was some doubt in my mind that they understood the gesture, because they didn't look happy.

"Back off!" Venai's basso voice roared from behind them, my balls dropping a little at the sound. She looked at me, her expression no less fierce than those of the other Nephilim circling me like hungry animals. "I thought we had a deal, demon. Where is your piece?"

Thunder rumbled above us as if in response to her anger, small billows of white appearing to dot the night sky. We glanced up at the same time, our gazes returning to lock on one another's after a solemn moment.

"Well, the Grim Reaper fucked all that up." I pointed upward at the building storm, certain the battle so close to Eden was throwing the Tree into fits. The clock was ticking faster.

Her eyes narrowed as she moved closer. "What are you talking about?"

"The werewolves and vampires work for Azrael. He wants the key too. He's using the vamps to isolate your piece holder." I motioned toward the clustered Nephilim to make it obvious the plan had worked. "He's holding back because he doesn't think he can take all of you at once. You need to martial your troops and—"

"We'll do no such thing, demon." A bronzed behemoth strode toward us, a toothy snarl glistening feral behind his thick and wild beard. Cold gray eyes glared at me from under bushy eyebrows.

While not quite as big as Longinus, or even McConnell for that matter, he packed a busload of muscle onto his six foot frame. "As far as I'm concerned, you're working with the vampires. Kill him." He waved his hands as if dusting me away.

"No!" Venai shouted and stepped in front of me to block her cohorts. They froze, uncertainty oozing from their expressions. "We don't have time for this, Errik." She drew his attention to the storm. "His people still have a key piece, regardless of why he's here. If we kill him now, we'll never get it in time to escape the storms."

The clouds had already thickened, rolling in fast like a tsunami wave. There were still slivers of moonlight peeking through here and there, but not many. Another few minutes and there wouldn't be a sky left. A little while after that and there wouldn't be anything left.

Sense and logic clearly weren't one of Errik's strengths. A monkey with a math problem, all dragging knuckles and grunts, he clenched his fists and dug his heels in. "Don't make me have to kill you too, Venai. This demon is a—"

I didn't get to hear what he thought of me because his sentence ended when a wash of magical energy splashed over us like someone had just done a cannonball in the dimensional pool. We all turned to see a glistening red portal ripped open in the air just twenty feet above the gathered Nephilim. Through it dropped a wave of furry ninja lycanthropes, Grawwl in the lead.

They fell over the packed group who barely had time to look up, blood flying in gallons at impact. Guttural snarls were met by piercing screams, the weres wreaking havoc in the tight formation of startled Nephilim. Body parts were tossed into the air, pieces of shredded meat flung in all directions.

Unable to resist, I looked at Errik as he stood there with his mouth hanging open. "I told you."

Venai gave me a dirty look and raced toward the attacking weres, shrieking for the scattered Nephilim to come back to the main group. Errik and his men stood there a moment longer, dumbfounded, before it finally sunk in. At last, they bolted off to join the fight.

The Nephilim around me oblivious to my presence, one mutt pretty much the same as any other, I looked to see if Azrael had arrived without me noticing. He was still nowhere to be found. That worried me, but it also confirmed my earlier suspicions. He was holding back for some reason. I just didn't know what that reason was, and that worried me.

I watched for a moment longer as Grawwl and his buddies tore through the Nephilim ranks, the half-breed discipline and grace fading fast under the sharpened claws of the lycanthropes. Hesitant to give the okay to attack, Azrael likely lurking about for exactly that scenario, I knew we were running out of time.

The clouds had completely obscured the moon, their bright white a roiling blanket that covered the entire sky, casting an eerie white glow over the land. The wind picked up in gusts and the tangy stench of ashes stung my eyes and nose. The longer the battle went on, the deeper the shit we were gonna be in.

Yet another moment passed and I dug deep, but I just couldn't find it in myself to give the order that could condemn my friends. In the back of my mind, my mother applauded the gesture, but now really wasn't the time for her sentimentality.

A deep breath of decision burning my lungs, I sent a telepathic message through to Rahim, telling them to stay put for a little longer.

I'm such a mama's boy.

My gun out, I sidled around the abattoir of moaning Nephilim and took aim at Grawwl. I might as well have been chopping my dick off for all the pain I was opening myself up to, but sometimes the smart move isn't always the right one. Before I could think about it further, I pulled the trigger.

The first shot hit him in his neck, his head snapping sideways in irritation. The second and third thumped into his massive shoulder as though it was made of steel. He didn't even wince as his red-orange gaze swung about and honed in on me. When our eyes met, he loosed a savage roar and dropped down on all fours, barreling through were and Nephilim alike to get to me.

"They told me you were out of the fight, mutt. Obviously I'm going to have to do the job myself."

Puckered up so tight I could shit diamonds, I looked around to make sure no one was sneaking up on me, and got ready to face down Grumpy.

"There's nothing but air and opportunity between us, furball. Come get some." I'd probably regret antagonizing him, but it wasn't like he was gonna kill me any deader than he already planned to.

He came at me fast, but his retinue stayed busy at the dog pile. Sometimes you get lucky.

More room to move this time and having a better estimate of

his speed, I waited until he dove at me before I leapt out of the way. I slipped past his flashing claws and tucked into a ball, rolling to my feet a few yards away untouched.

"*Olé*!" I waved the white shirt at him and smiled.

Momentum and size working against him, Grawwl spun and fell into a tumble as he tried to adjust. The two bullets I put in his ass probably didn't help his balance any.

After a moment, he got to his feet and came at me again, his breath huffing like an overloaded freight train. He muttered something but all I caught was the word *dead*. Me thinks he was a little ticked off.

Once more I waited until he was close, then feinted right, waving the shirt in his face before diving left. Again, his claws whistled past without hitting me and he struggled to slow down and turn around.

I emptied the clip in his back and slapped another one into place as he spun around. A solid hunk of muscle, my bullets weren't doing anything to stop him, barely penetrating his hide, but at least he wasn't near the key piece.

He stood his ground for a second, as if wondering how to handle me, then apparently decided he wasn't quite finished with the charging approach. He tucked his head and sped toward me again. The look in his eyes told me he thought he had it figured out.

A quick glance at the Nephilim told me they were starting to bite back. Their numbers, slowly being rallied by Venai's call, began to sway the tide against the leaderless lycanthropes. Surprised and a bit annoyed that Azrael had yet to show his face, I couldn't imagine we were gonna get a better opportunity than now to make a play for the key piece, trap or not.

Concentrating to keep from saying it aloud, I sent a message to Rahim to go when he thought best just as the skies rumbled overhead and the wind started to sputter, the gusts petering out. Lightning flashed above and cast a purple shadow over the ground. It was an ominous warning of the fall to come.

My attention jumped back to Grawwl before he tore me a new one. He came at me and swung both of his claws out to his side, expecting me to leap away. Instead, I threw the shirt at him and ducked and rolled between his legs—doing my damndest not to look up—and popped out behind him. He earned a couple more bullets for his effort.

Just as he got himself turned around, I suddenly felt the oozing presence of Azrael. It rolled over me like fresh tar, a moist and sickening creep of energy that enveloped me as though I had slid into a pool of quicksand. A flutter at my neck told me he had appeared right behind me.

Then the pain came.

Struck in the upper back, the blow slammed me into the ground face first. A crash test dummy, I bounced a couple of times before coming to rest in the grass, my ears ringing. Through the whistling, I heard Grawwl's gravelly roar of triumph, the sound growing closer.

"Enough!" The power of Azrael's voice rattled my skull. "You fool."

Not sure who he was talking to, I rolled over to see sparks of fury flying from Azrael's eyes. He was looking past me, his bony finger crooked toward the battle.

"The demon's friends are going after Lilith's rib."

Grawwl and I both turned our heads to see Katon and Rahim tearing into the weres with abandon. Aided by his magic, the wizard was a force to be reckoned with. Were-bits were exploding all around him and his blackened body was soaked with blood, wet red trailers following in the wake of his claws. He had a vicious grin on his face, pieces of fur and flesh caught up in his teeth.

Katon flittered around Rahim, his sword lashing out at anything that moved. Silver sweeps left dead or rigid werewolves falling left and right. Playing wingman, anything that even dared go for Rahim met its end at the furious tip of Katon's sword.

"Get them!" Azrael screamed to Grawwl, who stood there indecisive.

Finally, Grumpy saddled up and stormed off to join the fight. Azrael growled and turned his attention back to me.

"I had hoped you would be repentant when I returned, but I see stubborn has won out as the dominant trait." He floated toward me, the flames in his eyes throwing up black smoke.

Not looking to antagonize him, I stayed down, inching back along the ground slowly. Through my peripheral vision, I saw Grawwl entering the fray, his bellows rallying handfuls of weres and vamps to his side. Rahim and Katon met him head on.

"Just like my father, right?"

He laughed, the fire easing back. "So, now you wish to speak of your sire here as you prepare to die?" The whirling obsidian cloud beneath him melted away, black tendrils fading out of sight, and he stood before me with a skeletal grin. "I'll entertain your sudden curiosity, not because your ploy to delay me worked, but because it suits me." He glanced over at the fight, and seeming satisfied for some strange reason, he looked back to me. "Your father was a murderer and a rapist, and quite masterful at both. In fact, that was how you came to be."

My face warmed as his implication hit me. I'd engaged him to allow DRAC time to operate, but I was beginning to regret it.

Azrael's grin grew wider, obviously feeding off my discomfort. "Does it bother you to think of your mother being raped, grunting into the sod like a common whore being rowed?"

Without even realizing I'd done it, I fired on him, the gun barking fury in my white-knuckled grip.

Azrael batted my bullets away as though they were nothing, closing the distance in an instant. My gun flew from my hand and he struck me in the chest, the blow reverberating all the way through to my back.

Lightning bolts of white pain exploded in my torso and radiated out, searing a path along my extremities, ending at my fingers and toes. A tingling numbness followed in the aftershock. My body twitched and flopped as my nerves reacted, then relaxed, dropping me flat. My eyes whirled and my vision tunneled for a moment, before widening and returning to focus.

Azrael stood over me, his toothy smile splitting his face wide, a macabre Jack-o'-lantern.

"The best part of it was she liked every moment of it; the moist dirt of the field pressed cool against her face, the smell of her sex as it mingled with the morning air. Her scent was an aphrodisiac, Triggaltheron, sweet and tempting like a ripened fruit plucked straight from the tree."

Numb, I did my best to ignore his words and get to my feet. Azrael laughed and pinned me down by holding my arms, his cadaverous face moving in closer. "I know all this because I was there, demon. I watched as your mother squirmed beneath your father's strident ministrations, her hands clawing at the dirt. She screamed and thrashed about like a banshee, yet ever pushed back to meet his every thrust like the wanton little cunt she truly was."

Napalm tore through my veins and I fought against his hold. His bony fingers cut into my arms as I struggled to rise. My clutching hands sought his heart, falling just short.

"She cried when he released his seed, but they were tears of joy, Triggaltheron. They were tears for you, little demon. She knew right then she was special, that she'd been honored by the rutting she'd received; that she would soon be with child."

"I'll fucking kill you," I screamed, frothy spittle flying. Everything was hazy, my fury screaming inside me, shrieking to be released.

"Will you? Is that what you'd like to do to me? Carve me up over the course of days and feed my remains to the fire?"

I screamed again, feeling something pop in my back as I strained against his grip. Thrashing about, I flailed and struck at him, but Azrael just laughed as my pitiful blows.

"Let me tell you another secret, Triggaltheron." He leaned in close and pressed his clammy lips against my ear, his grip tightening. "Long have you lived a lie, an illusion fed to you to keep you docile, to keep you in your place. Lies perpetuated to steer you from your rightful rewards." His words wormed inside my head, slithering cold and harsh. "Your friends lie to you because they fear you. They use you to go against your own, to defy the wishes of your father."

"My father is dead." Thunder rumbled overhead as if in sympathy.

A cold, bitter laugh tickled my ear. "Of all the lies you've swallowed like the lonely whore desperate to find love in a mouthful of bitter seed, that's the greatest of them."

The words sunk into my mind like hammered railroad spikes. My anger bled away through the holes and I went still to hear what he had to say.

Azrael kept his grip tight, but his smile warmed at my sullen compliance. "Aah, you're listening with our mind at last. Well then, listen close. The man you killed with such passion, with such glorious brutality, for which you paid Baalth so dearly for the pleasure, was not your father. He wasn't even the man who murdered your mother."

My stomach clenched into a solid knot and I stared into his flickering eyes, into his soul, desperate to see the lie there, to know his words were false. The truth stared back at me. It wasn't what I wanted to see.

Bile roiled inside me, flicking serpent-like at the back of my throat. Azrael nodded as the sickening reality sunk in. The man I'd killed for murdering my mother was not who I had been led to believe. I'd been deceived.

My heart sank and I went limp, the truth draining everything from me. I'd traded my innocence for the power to kill the man I thought was my father, the man who murdered my mother. It was *all* a lie. My soul mortgaged to Baalth for years, the cost of my freedom something that still haunts my dreams, had been for nothing. Though I knew the man I'd killed was no innocent, he was of the crime I'd so horribly torn him to pieces over. The image of his dying face came to life in my mind's eye, his horror so clear.

Guilt boiled over with my vomit. Azrael released his hold and stepped back as I rolled to my side, retching.

"You should have run to Hell and waited this out, Triggaltheron. It would have spared your heart such brutal revelation. Now you must live without knowing your father's true face or that of your mother's killer."

I puked again, sick with myself and all I'd done. Questions swirled inside my head like my vomit did in the grass, running into itself and going nowhere. There was no exorcising guilt.

"I thank you for bringing Eve to me. I'll reward your servitude by slaying your friends quickly; both those who challenge my minions and those who still hide upon the hill." He held up Eve and winked. The bone in his hand was sickening proof of his boast.

My heart slowed. Spittle dripped warm down my chin as I lifted my head to look toward the fight. Rahim and Katon had done well it seemed, bodies were piled thick at their feet, but the tide had turned against them. Grawwl still stood, an army of vampires shielding him as he closed on Rahim and Katon.

To make things worse, the Nephilim had pulled together, their numbers apparently the confidence they needed to engage the weres, as well as DRAC. They were lashing out indiscriminately, anyone not one of them was an enemy. Surrounded, Rahim and Katon looked battered, defending attacks from all quarters. It wouldn't be long until they fell, Azrael's addition guaranteeing it.

I concentrated as best I could, and reached out for help, for Michael. There was only silence.

Thunder rumbled, shaking the ground as if in triumph as I rolled over to look up at Azrael. He stood a few feet away, his black lips peeled back in a fearsome grin.

"Enjoy what's left of your immortality, Triggaltheron, for its moments are numbered. Perhaps if you are appropriately humble, I might one day tell you who your father is." He stood over me and laughed, gesturing toward the battle where Rahim and Katon were desperately fighting to stay alive. "Now, I must put an end to this nonsense."

Everything crumbling down around me, I dug deep for one last sliver of hope and reached out for Poe.

A whispered voice answered back. “How nice of you to call, Mister Trigg.”

Despite the sarcasm, my heart leapt at hearing Poe’s crisp monotone. “Glad you guys are okay.”

“That’s not the word I’d use, but Mister McConnell and I managed to win a few of us free from Azrael’s vampires.”

My sliver faded. “Is Rachelle with you?”

There was only silence from the other end, its agonizing nothingness driving defeat into my heart, one pounding beat after another.

“I’m here, Frank,” Rachelle’s voice echoed inside my head like the voice of an angel.

Still on the ground, Azrael having only walked a few paces, I called out to him. “Tell me something, Azrael.”

He looked back to me, his arrogance framing his face with smug confidence. “Be quick, little demon, I’ve a world to conquer.”

I got to my feet and met his fiery gaze. “You’re a fan of rape, right?”

He looked at me, his eyes narrowing. “What are going on about?”

“That’s what you said, isn’t it? You got off watching my mother being raped, right?” I couldn’t keep the venom out of my voice, his words careening through my head, Abraham’s dead eyes staring at me.

Azrael grinned. “Don’t make this your last stand, boy. Either quiet down or die, the choice a simple one.”

I grinned back. “I’ve got another idea.” In my head, I passed on a message to Rachelle making damn sure I didn’t say it aloud.

The words sent at the speed of thought, a shimmering blue portal the size of a house appeared just inches from where Azrael stood. His eyes flew open wide as he looked into it and stumbled back.

“Sic him, boys.” A horde of dread fiends burst from the portal, crashing into Azrael with fearless tenacity. “Welcome to our own private gang-rape, Azrael.”

The archangel shrieked as he was dragged under a pile of snapping jaws and sharpened claws. Eve fell beside him, being kicked about as Azrael fought back against the fiends.

“One of you, bring me that bone.” I pointed at Eve, then turned to face the still flowing line that spilled from the portal. “The rest of you, kill the Nephilim and *only* the Nephilim.” Over a hundred fiends laying into Azrael, the remaining couple thousand stormed from the gateway toward the wide-eyed half-breeds who scattered before them. Poe still on the line, I had him convey a message to our guys not to worry about the fiends; they were the cavalry, as unlikely as it seemed.

Still unsure of my control over the dread fiends, I didn't want them confusing a certain friendly werebear and vampire for the rest of the rabble, so I kept the commands simple. At least with the Nephilim out of the way, Rahim and Katon could handle the rest. I sent another quick message to Poe to have Rachelle close by and to get McConnell ready to join us once the gates were open. Scarlett apparently out of the picture, details unknown, I was gonna have to improvise.

A dread fiend panted up to me, holding Eve in a bloody claw. Giving it a pat on the head as thanks, I snatched the bone and sent the fiend back after Azrael. It did so with morbid glee, its dripping tongue lolling out of his mouth.

You gotta love the enthusiasm.

The last key piece in hand, I made a mad dash toward the remnants of the fight. Rahim and Katon had turned their opponents toward the fiends, and though the dreads weren't attacking the weres, they were distracting them. There's nothing like a couple thousand sub-demons storming past to get the heart rate up to a nice, brisk pace.

The Nephilim who had been swarming them were now scattered across the field, many of them in fleshy chunks and bloody pieces. The tight organization had crumbled under the wave of dread fiends, and the few who still stood nearby were falling fast.

Grawwl had organized his men and was flinging them at Rahim as though they were chess pieces. He hung back as the werewolves threw their lives away, trying to give him a clear shot at the wizard.

The tactic sound, it was a good idea not to take on Rahim head-to-head, but he'd forgotten about me. His back exposed, I stashed Eve and raced toward the oblivious werebear. Knowing full well Grawwl could shrug off my shots as though they were bee stings, it didn't make any sense just to start firing away. Since I was too exhausted to draw upon my magic, it was time to be creative.

Staying behind him, I ran at him full tilt. As soon as I got close, I leapt onto his back and sunk my left hand into his fur and latched on tight. He roared in surprise and defiance as I jammed the barrel of my pistol against his open eye that turned to glare at me.

"Sweet dreams, Grumpy."

As fast as I could, I pulled the trigger, keeping the gun as steady as possible as he bucked against me. Black blood and milky fluid exploded from the socket like a geyser, my hand and gun soaked with it. His razor-throated growl ceased in mid-course and he went rigid. The paw that had reached up to swat me stopped cold and hung in the air for a second before swinging lifeless to his side.

Grawwl twitched, a waterfall of thick blood spilling through his daggered teeth, and then collapsed beneath me. I rode him down with a whoop.

"You're gonna make one Hell of a rug." I slid off his rigid back.

Rahim tore through another werewolf and ran over to me. "We lost the Nephilim piece holder," he shouted over the battle sounds. "We need to find him."

My emotions a roller coaster, I plunged cursing the whole way down. My eyes flitting to find him, Katon saved me the trouble.

"I don't think it matters anymore." He drew our attention upward.

Amidst the gathered white clouds of the storm, illuminated by the purple flashes exploding around it, a brilliant white portal was tearing open the sky. Bright light filtered down as the gates to Eden eased into existence.

"Look," Rahim cried out, pointing to a pile of broken Nephilim not quite ten feet from us.

A glow similar to that of the gate glimmered in the pile of bodies, its source hidden under ravaged flesh, its rays piercing the ruin that lay over it.

"Over there too," Katon added, gesturing to another similar glow obviously emanating from Adam's skull.

I yanked Eve out and saw that she too was glowing and everything clicked. The mystery of how the pieces went together was answered; they didn't. They just needed to be close enough to each other, their presence enough to trigger the gate. "Get those other bones and bring them closer to keep the gate open." Rahim and Katon responded immediately and ran off after them. In my head, I called out for Poe.

"McConnell is already on his way, but he isn't the only one," the mentalist's even voice reported.

My eyes snapped to the sky. Like a flock of birds shooed from the bushes, the air was full of darting shadows that raced toward the opening gate. Vampires led the way but the Nephilim who could fly—and there were a whole bunch of them—were close behind, and gaining.

In the race to reach Heaven, the two groups stopped fighting, concentrating only on being the first to cross the finish line. The clouds surrounding the gate roiled, flashes of lightning blurring the sky in defiance of their presence.

Without Scarlett to race ahead to Uriel, we were gonna have to do it ourselves. "Change of plans," I shouted to Rahim and Katon as they returned. "You guys try to hold the gate. I'm gonna go for Forcalor." Our odds still slim to none, I thought it best to seek out my old mentor rather than risk Uriel killing me in the heat of battle. That would suck.

"No one is going anywhere!"

An explosion of force followed the words and the world around me whipped into frenzy. Like a nuclear blast, a wall of kinetic energy trampled over us, leveling everything in its path. I slammed into the ground hard as if I'd been hit by a giant flyswatter. My skull felt as though it was gonna leak out my eyes, my body tingling with pinpricks of shock. I couldn't get my arms or legs to respond. They lay there trembling as though not connected.

Through the haze of my wobbled mind, I saw Azrael as he came to stand before us. The fiends had done him no favors.

Claw marks ravaged the left side of his narrow face, flesh hanging from his cheek and forehead. His skull was visible beneath the wounds, soft white amidst the oozing black seep. His body was no better off. His robes were shredded, their tattered remnants wet with growing stains of blood. He held a crippled hand out before him, the last two fingers little more than dripping stumps, teeth marks visible in the remaining flesh of his palm.

"You are dead, demon." He spoke through clenched teeth. The swelling at his jaw pretty much confirming it was broken.

I cast a quick glance to where Katon and Rahim lay and neither seemed to be able to get up either. They floundered about trying desperately to stand, their legs in rebellion.

Azrael stepped over me and glared down, infernos in his eyes. His uninjured hand shimmered with obsidian energy that threw sparks in every direction, and he raised it to strike.

"Not so fast, Azrael," a thready voice warned from behind the archangel.

Old Grim spun about and glared. Akrasiel—Raguel— stood there bold in his golden armor, his intricate sword pointed toward Azrael.

Azrael just laughed, the sound muted by his injured jaw.

"You're too late to balance the scales, Raguel." He gestured to the dark forms that flew toward the gate to Eden. "The Tree is in its final throes and will soon die along with your pitiful dream of Heaven."

"It's not dead yet," Akrasiel countered while casting a sideways glance at me.

"You think the little demon prodigy has it in him to save the Kingdom?" Azrael shook his head. "You're as big a fool as Lucifer for believing this runt could be the Anti-Christ. Worse yet, Raguel, you're an incorporeal fool whose time has passed." He waved his hand at the archangel. A tendril of energy snapped out and passed harmlessly through Raguel as though he weren't there. "Without God and Satan in the world, you're nothing but a ghost." His laugh whistled between his teeth.

"I might not have the power to stop you, but sometimes all it takes is a distraction to turn the tide." He winked, a satisfied smile springing to life on his lips.

Azrael looked to me then up toward the gate. Silent explosions, like cascading fireworks, were highlighted against the cloudy backdrop. Vampires and Nephilim alike fell burning from the sky. A fetid rain of flesh and blood followed. I didn't need to see him to know it was McConnell, the gray tracers a sure sign.

While it thrilled my heart to see the cowboy doing a good deed, I knew he couldn't hold out for long. Surprise working in his favor for the moment, it wouldn't be long before he succumbed to his wounds, his magic tearing them open wide. If that didn't kill him, the surging wall of vampires and half-breeds who slipped past his defenses would.

Azrael shrieked and looked back at me as if weighing his options. I must not have made the cut as far as his priorities went. He turned and loosed a burst of energy at Raquel, the sparking bolt of blackness scouring the archangel's presence away, its power dispersing the angel's ethereal image.

Without another word, Azrael leapt into the air and streaked toward McConnell, an obsidian trail of shadows swirling in his wake.

Azrael gone, I crawled my way to my feet, finally able to function somewhat. Rahim and Katon did the same. We staggered toward one another, all of us stumbling as though we were drunk. I could only wish.

Despite the head start of everyone else, I was confident we could still get to the gate first, with Rachelle's help. I just wasn't sure what we could do when we got there. Looking into Rahim's eyes, I saw he was running on empty, Katon only slightly less weary. I knew where I stood and it wasn't good.

"You ready for this?"

Both nodded without hesitation despite knowing we had no chance. Talk about balls.

As I sent a message to Poe, I glanced up and saw Azrael plowing his way toward the gate, bowling over vampire and Nephilim alike in his rush. McConnell's energy had begun to slip, the wall of explosions I'd first seen now little more than the flicker of candles. He was running out of power, his body defying him.

The storm around the gate had grown worse, the first signs of its deadly fall beginning to manifest. Lightning flickered through the clouds with such tenacity that the entire sky seemed purple. Azrael was right, the Tree was on its deathbed, thunder its death rattle.

Rachelle's voice sang inside my head and I started to give her our locations when a thought sparked to life, cutting through the murky gloom of my defeatism. I told her to wait a second and looked to Rahim and Katon.

"I've an idea."

Rahim shook his head. "We don't have time to get laid, Frank." He glared at me impatient.

"Though that's a great idea, it wasn't what I had in mind."

McConnell's explosions now gone from the sky, the first in the wedge of Nephilim and vampires reaching the gate, there was no time to explain. I gave Rachelle coordinates and hoped dearly I hadn't just helped to screw the pooch.

As a shimmering blue portal appeared before me, way too small for any of us to fit through, Rahim snarled, his eyes flickering red as he realized I'd gone ahead with my plan. Katon just stared as I dug in my pocket and yanked out the vial of my uncle's blood.

I popped the stopper and stared at the shifting blood inside for just a second. A frustrated sigh slipped out and I growled, then made up my mind to hurl the open vial through the portal. It spun and zipped through the passage, a scarlet arc whipping about behind it as it flew out the other side of the portal and careened into Heaven.

"What are you thinking, Frank?" Rahim asked with a graveled stutter, his ursine face just inches from mine. Katon stood behind him, his sword wavering in my direction, fury and confusion engraved upon his dark face with equal measure. He'd always thought I'd betray them one day, believing I still owed a debt to Baalth. He might be right about the betrayal, but in my defense, I'd never do it on purpose.

By accident or incompetence was an entirely different matter.

Watching as Azrael and thousands of violent intruders disappeared into Eden's gate, I felt my chest tighten as the stress of the last few days caught up to me all at once. My legs going limp beneath me, I fell to my knees staring up at the ashen flakes that drifted down toward us. Thunder rumbled so loud it shook the ground, but the gates stayed open, enemies pouring into its gaping maw.

"I'm thinking I just fucked us all," I answered in all honesty. "How was it?"

Though the original plan never really had any realistic chance of a happy ending—at least not for us—had I stuck to it we could have gone out with some semblance of honor, dying in battle, however futile. Instead, I went with a stray thought that popped into my head after days of sleep deprivation, drunkenness, and plain old fashioned physical abuse. It wasn't one of my most rational moves.

After a moment of screaming at me, Katon and Rahim stumbled off and I barely noticed. My eyes were frozen on Eden. Not only had I condemned us all, but I'd pushed Uriel and Forcalor under the bus while I was at it. I'm nothing if not generous.

My stomach a boiling pit of guilt and acid, I heard a high pitched whine scream to life. It sliced through my skull. Above us, flickers of light, like a million matches being lit at once, appeared before the gate.

I looked to Rahim as he readied his magic to take him and Katon up to Eden, apparently oblivious to the sound. "Wait!" I screamed at them as the whine grew inside my head. Pointing to Heaven, they glanced up to see the flickers.

Right then, the world exploded.

Chapter Twenty-Two

A wave of energy erupted from Eden, a searing light burning away everything in the sky in a whitewash of brilliance. The piercing whine a physical agony that threatened to shatter my skull, I covered my head and curled up in a ball as the sky rained down on top of us. Hurricane winds buffeted my back and its sharpened tongues licked at any exposed flesh, searing lines of agony appearing red across my arms and scalp, a patchwork of razor cuts.

After a moment of slicing torment, the wind subsided and I braved a quick glance through shredded fingers. The energy disbursed, I could see again, though tiny flashes of pop-lights plagued my vision, flickering in and out to the frantic rhythm of my heartbeat.

From above, pieces of flesh and bone, scraps of clothing, and a wet red rain fell all around us, the ground pooling moist beneath it.

The gates of Eden were charred an ashy gray, wisps of smoke drifting out in great tendrils. The skies around them were blotted out by an oily blackness, the clouds and deadly snow gone. The world was silent, though I wasn't sure if it actually was or if my eardrums had just burst. I touched my hand to my ears and came away with spots of blood. Both were an option apparently.

Nearby, Rahim and Katon got to their feet, appearing just as disheveled and battered as I felt. There was no doubt we all looked like twice-warmed shit. They glanced at me with questions in their eyes, and I shrugged, all of our gazes swinging upwards as the world suddenly became brighter.

The obsidian dark was squeegeed from the sky in thick swaths revealing shining stars and glimmers of moonlight as the unnatural blackness was washed away. Quiet thunder sounded in the distance and I began to be able to hear the muffled splashes of the morbid rain that fell around us. Guess I wasn't deaf after all.

Then suddenly, a whispered song fluttered into my head, a melodic chant that seemed to float around us as though it had substance. After a moment, the song rose in volume and a shimmering light appeared in the darkness of Eden's gate.

Roughly spherical, the light drifted from the gate and hovered in the sky above us. Tiny wisps of dimmer lights circled about the sphere like moons in orbit around a planet. Its light so bright, that after a minute, I had to look away, flickering dots searing on my eyeballs.

A gasp drew my eyes back up, the light having dimmed. At its center floated what appeared to be an old man, a long white beard flowing down his narrow chest. His bald head glistened in the light and golden eyes stared down at the battlefield from under thick white eyebrows. He held out his hands, his light brown robes fluttering despite there being no breeze.

Though I'd never seen him before, it didn't take a genius to realize that this was Metatron. His power butted against my senses like hurricane force winds, and I was kind of glad I hadn't chosen to stand, the feeling humbling.

"Begone! Heaven is not yours to defile." His voice roared through the air and his words slapped against my face as though they were a solid object.

Already in retreat mode, the Nephilim needed no further encouragement to hit the road running. Cockroaches scrambling for cover under the lights, they scattered in every direction but up. There was nothing to see but half-breed assholes and elbows for miles.

I caught sight of Venai as she summoned an escape portal, Jorn's massive bulk alongside her. She cast a furious glance my direction and slid her thumb across her throat before diving through her gate. Jorn trundled after and the portal disappeared.

The vampires were long gone by then, and what remained of the weres imitated the Nephilim and hightailed it out of sight. After just a few minutes, the battlefield was clear of the living, only the dead and us still in attendance. If I'd had any energy left, I'd have been right there with them.

Metatron watched the retreat for a moment, then turned his focus on us. He looked from Rahim to Katon and then his golden gaze settled on me. It took everything I had not to look away. His power still battered my senses, but it had been tempered to a manageable level.

He drifted down and settled before me, his sandaled feet floating inches above the ground. He shook his head as he appraised me. Still on my knees, I felt a bit awkward so I got back to my feet. Weariness helped keep my fear in check.

"Duke Forcalor told me you were a fool, Triggaltheron, but I would never have imagined it was to such an extent." He stuck his hand out and there was an empty vial in his wrinkled palm. His face was expressionless, but there was a sense of dire seriousness wafting off his words. Not sure what he wanted me to do with the empty vial, I left it sitting in his hand.

When I had imagined the blood of my uncle rousing Metatron, I hadn't thought it would actually work. I also hadn't thought about the consequences of Satan's essence returning to Heaven after all these years. While I'd hoped it would be enough of a shock to Metatron that it would rile him up and get him to react, I really hadn't given any thought to what would happen after he woke up and finished dealing with the angelic rebellion. That's me: one step ahead, two thoughts behind.

Rahim and Katon took a few steps back, leaving me alone before the archangel. I could feel the love, though I couldn't blame them. I'd have done the same thing.

Metatron cast the vial aside and stared at me a moment longer before a soft chuckle spilled from his mouth, the sharp lines of his eyes softening.

"It seems, however, that we were in need of a fool." Once more he stuck out his hand, but this time I didn't shy away, his smile encouraging. I took his hand and gripped it tight. "Long have I mourned the loss of God, blinded in his absence by my self-pity. When I felt Lucifer's essence, I was startled into awareness with hope that He, too, had returned." I tried to look apologetic, but I really suck at it. "Alas, though it was not to be, I am grateful to be awoken to world where I once again have a purpose."

He nodded to me and reclaimed his hand, casting thankful smiles to Rahim and Katon.

My adrenaline dumping and my mind shifting gears to think of all the things I'd overlooked, I asked, "What about Scarlett?" Ambushed by Azrael's vampires, I didn't have much hope Metatron's answer would be a positive one.

His smile faded some, but didn't disappear entirely. "She is gravely wounded, but she will heal in time. She is in Heaven, with her family." He rested his hand on my shoulder to soften the blow of his words.

I barely noticed, glad she had made it through the other side. Abraham dead, and possibly Michael as well, I couldn't imagine losing Scarlett too. That would be too much for me to handle.

"Azrael?" I had to ask.

"I have taken his powers and given them to Raguel for safekeeping. I cannot find it in my heart to condemn him for he was nothing if not true to his nature, but he will be banished to Limbo until such time I believe he can be trusted again." He gestured to Heaven. "As for Gabriel and his followers, Uriel and Forcalor have seized them, and they await punishment." He sighed slow and long. "They will suffer greatly for their misdeeds against Heaven and humanity alike."

Gabriel had been nothing but trouble since God's hiatus and it was high time he paid for all the chaos he'd sown. As spiteful as it was, I hoped Metatron was true to word. If he weren't, I'd do everything in my power to ensure Gabriel paid for what he'd done. Abraham's death was on his head, as well as my own. The remnants of my heart cracked brittle in my chest.

A gust of wind drew my vexed attention skyward, a handful of angels flying down toward us, a silver bier balanced between them. My heart drummed a blast beat in my chest imagining who lay upon it. I only had a moment to wonder before they were upon us.

The angels settled, placing the bier reverently upon the ground. Having expected Michael, I was surprised to see McConnell—and strangely not relieved.

His arms crossed over his chest, his eyes were closed in peace despite the myriad burns and wounds that covered his face and body. Though I hated the man, always believing him to be a coward and a betrayer, he had gone out on his sword to save the world. He may well have done it for selfish reasons, but he'd still done it. Alone, his promised backup never showing up, he stood before the gates of Heaven and fought an army of invaders.

No matter my personal feelings for the man, I couldn't help but respect that. He'd died with honor and courage of the sort I could only imagine. As weird as it was to think, his death was tragic.

Don't quote me on that because I'll deny it.

Rahim stepped up beside me to get Metatron's attention. "What of Earth?"

The archangel's expression turned sad, his gold eyes narrowing. "There is little I can do for its people, the dead beyond my ability to help with no God to gather their souls." Rahim sighed and I knew it was reserved for Abraham. "As for the Earth itself; as the Tree of Life heals, so shall the wounds it caused. All life connected to its heart, its recovery will bleed out into the world... in time."

At least there was some good news. Sickened by all that had happened I wanted to make sure it didn't happen again. I dug Eve out of my pants—and you'll notice there are no boner jokes—and passed her over to Metatron. "I don't think we need her down here anymore."

Metatron smiled as Rahim and Katon handed over their pieces as well. He looked the bones over and smiled, cradling Adam and Eve in the crook of his arm, while he held Lilith in his free hand, apart from the other two.

"I remember these three when they were first created. God was so proud. Despite it all, I believe he would be happy to see them returned to Heaven...even Lilith." Once more he graced us with his smile. "Thank you all. You have earned a friend this day."

He bowed and leapt into the air, the angels who'd carried the bier following him up. In a flash of gold, he streaked toward Eden. A moment later he disappeared inside and the gate shimmered and shifted, closing behind in silence.

Distracted by the sight above, we didn't notice Rachelle had gated in. Our eyes at last free of the glory of Heaven's light, we looked back to Earth to find her there, along with Poe and a bruised and battered, but very much alive Michael. It was great to see him there.

My heart caught in my throat as Rachelle smiled and gave me a gentle hug. "The angels took Scarlett. They said she'll be okay."

Unbidden, tears welled up in my eyes, but not for my cousin. I pulled Rachelle in tight and fought back a sob. She clung to me and whispered everything was okay, though I'm sure she thought I was upset about Scarlett. She had no idea how wrong she was. Things would never be okay again.

I glanced over at Rahim. His head was bowed, but his eyes locked onto mine. We agreed in silence. It would only be cruel to hold back the truth any longer.

I drew in a deep breath and gently separated from Rachelle. She caught my eyes and latched on as she realized there was more to my grief.

"I need to tell you something."

Chapter Twenty-Three

It had been almost three days since we'd averted the end of life, but for me, things really hadn't gotten any better.

Pissed and hurt and feeling betrayed, Rachelle had exploded with grief when I told her about Abraham; and for good reason. It was wrong to mislead her, but we'd needed her to be there in spirit, mind, and body. Often in her own little world under the best of circumstances, we couldn't risk her retreating to it when we needed her the most. We couldn't have succeeded without her.

Deep down I think she understood that, but that didn't make her feelings any less valid. She was mad that I had no faith in her, and she had every right to be. It hadn't been my intention, but not telling her only made things worse between us.

Rahim tried to tell her it was his idea, but I warned him off. Rachelle needed a pillar of strength she trusted, one who wouldn't let her down. I'd burned that bridge and there was no point in making them suffer more than they already were. He fought me on it, but in the end he gave in. This wasn't about the truth. Maybe it would be one day and we'd clear the air, but until then, Rachelle needed Rahim more than she needed to know the truth; certainly more than she needed me.

Katon was mad too, but more than anyone, he understood. A warrior to his marrow, he knew why we hadn't said anything. He'd get over it faster than Rachelle would, but he'd been quiet since we'd let the truth out, a little cold.

Though hurt, Michael could rationalize our choice and agree with it. He knew how delicate Rachelle was, and though it pained him to see her suffering, he was just glad she was alive to feel anything at all.

On a more global scale, Metatron had been right. Shortly after he sealed the gate to Eden, storms sprang to life across the world. Gratefully, these weren't the same kind of storms that devastated the planet. These brought wind and rain, to spread the seeds and nurture them.

Humanity on edge, they panicked and scrambled to escape the weather, but it was all in vain. Rain fell over the barren patches of earth that had been scoured away. In defiance of all the laws of nature man has come to know, the planet began to repair itself. Blades of grass sprung up in the wake of the storms, tiny trees and shrubs sprouting to life within hours to start the process.

No less miraculous than the storms that had wiped it all away, humanity found a reason that reinforced their belief in something beyond their senses, their faith renewed. Most simply attributed it to God, whatever their flavor might be; in anger he'd cleansed the earth, in forgiveness he'd begun to heal it. It was easier to let them believe that than call attention to the supernatural beings who lived amongst them here on Earth. However, the door had been cracked open for some and could never be closed again.

The world governments leapt to action in the aftermath, promising to seek out the truth in the wake of their failure to protect their lands and people. The war in Heaven brought consequences to our plane of existence. The world was different now, and people were starting to realize it. As always, there would be repercussions that followed knowledge. The blinders still in place, though slipping, humanity was still largely oblivious. They likely wouldn't be for long.

For us who knew different, today was a bitter reminder that God was gone. His departure left ripples that washed over us daily, stirring up the supernatural. Its consequences were laid out before us in the silver coffin that held the earthly remains of Abraham Solano.

The service held at the slowly rebuilding, Rest Land cemetery, it was a somber, private affair. Not famous or in the public eye, his funeral flew under the radar amidst the masses of burials taking place in the wake of the destruction. Humanity buried their dead with a collective sigh of bitter relief that they were still alive to do so.

To those who knew who Abraham truly was, it was as if the world *had* ended. The skies bowed their head at his passing, thick clouds turning out to witness his burial. Gentle thunder rumbled overhead, a mournful dirge for a man who had done so much to defend humanity, though they would never know his sacrifice. Soft cold tears tumbled from Heaven at his loss, mirroring those in attendance.

I stood away from the gathering, conscious of Rachelle's feelings. As much as I wanted to go to her and beg her forgiveness, I couldn't bring myself to intrude upon her sorrow. Katon sat with her, as did Scarlett who held her hand cradled in her lap.

Even as beaten up as my cousin was, her bruised and battered face barely hidden behind her large black sunglasses, she came for Rachelle. It hurt to know I couldn't be a part of it, that I couldn't offer my own sympathy to her for a man who was more than my father, but that's life. Cruel and painful, you roll the dice with every choice and hope in the end you've done what's best.

Karra stood beside me, her hand entangled in mine. Pressed warm against me, there was no solace to be found in her embrace. That hurt too. No matter what there was between us, what we could become, it was fleeting, the clock pitting time against us.

Rahim came up behind me to show solidarity, his human hand on my shoulder. He'd learned to shift back in time for the funeral so that he could attend. He gave a tight squeeze and slipped me a smile as he passed, on his way to Rachelle.

Michael nodded as I glanced his way, the preacher just finishing up the last rites. Though we all knew them to be hollow, tradition carried its own comforts. In the bushes, my cemetery buddies sat quietly waiting to lower Abraham to his final resting place. Obligated to be elsewhere, I wouldn't get to watch them lower him into the ground.

The thought triggered my tears and I turned and headed for my car, Karra attached to me the whole way. Like a condemned man taking his final walk, I drove away slow finding no reason to hurry.

At home at last, Karra and I trundled into the house. Chatterbox at her place, the house was eerily silent, only the quiet hum of the refrigerator there to greet us. Like zombies ourselves, we trudged over to the couch and dropped down limp.

"You sure about this?" she asked me, turning my face to look at her.

"No, but I don't have a choice. I signed a contract. Besides, I don't have the energy to fight."

Karra's face drooped and she kissed me quick to try and hide it. "I could ask my father to intervene."

"No." I shook my head, then looked away. "I don't know what these guys want, but I don't think they intend to hurt me. They've already had the chance and let me go. I'm sure everything will be all right."

While I didn't really feel that way, I didn't want Karra to worry more than she already was. I didn't have the slightest clue what Xyx and his master needed from me, and I was worried. More than I wanted to let on. There's no rationalizing the supernatural world, so assuming just because they hadn't killed me meant they wouldn't was a fool's bet.

"You know, for a demon, you really don't lie very well."

Her words brought a smile to my lips. "Yeah, I know. That's why I pretend to be the strong, silent type. It's easier to get away with shit when you keep your mouth shut."

With a quiet chuckle, she leaned into me and rested her head on my shoulder. Her breath was warm on my neck, tickling me. She felt great wedged in against me and I could resist leaning in to kiss her.

Just as I did, I felt the nauseating ripples of Xyx's presence. Karra had as well as she pulled away and jumped to her feet, anger and frustration seared in deep lines across her face. I didn't bother to get up, knowing full well the demon stood in my house, just a few feet away.

"You're the only demon I know who understands the concept of punctuality, Xyx. That's unfortunate." I turned my head to stare at his silver eyes. Jonas and Ethan were at his sides, both standing there quietly watching Karra.

"It's time to go, Triggaltheron."

Nodding, I sighed deep and pulled Karra to me. She resisted a little, ready to throw down, but she gave in reluctantly. I turned her face to mine and adjusted so she couldn't see the idiots behind me. My stomach in knots, I kissed her deep and hard.

If it was gonna be my last kiss, I wanted it to convey just how much I cared. After a moment, I broke away to take a breath. Her hazel eyes moist, I wiped away a tear and said my goodbyes.

Leaving behind everything I cared for, everyt*hing I loved, I walked over to Xyx.*

"Let's get this over with."

He nodded and I felt his magic amping up. I turned and took one last look at Karra, blowing her a kiss.

"I'll be back."

She did her best to smile, and then I was gone.

About the Author:

Raised on a diet of Heavy Metal and bad intentions, Tim Marquitz has always been interested in writing, but it wasn't until about 1995 the urge became a compulsion. However, it would be many years later before the ability matched the interest. Fortunately, the two have reconciled...mostly.

Writing a mix of the dark perverse, the horrific, and the tragic, tinged with sarcasm and biting humor, he looks to leave a gaping wound in the minds of his readers like his inspirations: Clive Barker, Jim Butcher, and Stephen King.

A former grave digger, bouncer, and dedicated metalhead, Tim is a huge fan of Mixed Martial Arts, and fighting in general. Involved in the Live Action Role Playing organization, Amtgard, since he was fifteen, he derives great pleasure from bashing people into submission.

He lives in Texas with his beautiful wife and daughter, a neurotic dog and their finger-crippling cat.

Other books by Tim Marquitz from Damnation Books:

Demon Squad: Armageddon Bound
Demon Squad: Resurrection
Sepulchral Earth: The Long Road
Sepulchral Earth: The Temple of the Dead
Skulls

Also from Tim Marquitz:

Sepulchral Earth
by Tim Marquitz

eBook ISBN: 9781615720767
Print ISBN: 9781615720750

Horror Dark Fantasy
Novella of 12,645 words

Two years after the furious dead rose up to murder the living, the remnants of mankind face a brutal extinction. Wretched and broken, trading humanity for life, the survivors suffer under the inevitable shadow of death.

Aided by friendly spirits, the necromancer Harlan Cole wages war against the merciless forces of the undead. Driven to bring peace to the souls of his wife and daughter, Harlan vows to return the dead to their graves, or join them trying.

Also from Damnation Books:

Into the Red
by Sandy DeLuca

eBook ISBN: 9781615724901
Print ISBN: 9781615724918

Horror Dark Fantasy
Novella of 20,694 words

Love is a bloody triangle.

Danie only wanted to be loved. She found pain, suffering and mourning instead. Two lovers changed her life. They conjured her darkest hours. One taught her the art of pain. The other deceived her, and then committed a heinous act against her. Death found both men. Onc returned to her. Will he save her or will he cast her into eternal night?

CPSIA information can be obtained at www.ICGtesting.com
Printed in the USA
LVOW041538261211

261107LV00001B/11/P

9 781615 725557